When the corpse of a young girl arrives on the steps of a Catholic Church in New Orleans, it falls to detective Jo Crowder to unravel the hidden connections and find the killer—all with her superiors, and the prickly local clergy, dogging every step. *The Easter Murders* does everything a reader could want: Jo Crowder is a plucky hero with plenty of grit, navigating a world where competing personal agendas often threaten the execution of justice. Zappa's *The Easter Murders* keeps readers entertained with solid police procedural work, tense courtroom drama, and insidious backroom dealing.—*Indie Readers*

An unconventional detective hunts for a killer among the churches of New Orleans in Zappa's latest police procedural. Detective Crowder can be short-tempered and doesn't suffer fools gladly, resembling the older-and-wiser version of FBI agent Clarice Starling in Thomas Harris' 1999 thriller sequel, Hannibal. Religious elements play a key role in the narrative, and Crowder's suspicions quickly fall on a respected clergyman. The fact that she's an agnostic working a religiously charged case makes the situation even more delicate. Zappa beautifully captures these multifaceted tensions in a way that keeps the story moving at an easy clip. The book's climax is a marvel of suspenseful precision, and the key confrontation at the story's conclusion will have readers holding their breath.—*Kirkus Reviews*

A young teenager's nude body is discovered in front of a church. Unfortunately, she is not the last girl who will be slain—a serial killer is on the loose. *The Easter Murders* is a thrilling crime drama/mystery with some romance thrown in for good measure. The author is a retired trial lawyer, so he is qualified to produce this book, much of which takes place in the courtroom. Engrossing and difficult to put down 4/4 stars.— *Online Book Club*

The Easter Murders

AIA PUBLISHING

Richard Zappa

The Easter Murders
Richard Zappa
Copyright © 2020
Published by AIA Publishing, Australia
ABN: 32736122056
http://www.aiapublishing.com

Paperback ISBN: 978-1-922329-14-1
Hardcover ISBN: 978-1-922329-15-8
Cover design by K. Rose Kreative
Author's photo by Scott Ellis

For Katie, a kindred spirit

Introduction

I met Jo Crowder for the first time quite by accident. While Veronica Westbrook was gallivanting around two continents, scheming, lying, and murdering her way in and out of families in *Identical Misfortune*, Newton's third law flashed in neon lights in my unbridled imagination—the novelist's playground—that for every action there is an equal and opposite reaction. The reaction to Veronica Westbrook's crimes was the actions of the irrepressible, unflappable, no-nonsense, tough-as-nails homicide detective, Jo Crowder. They proved to be Westbrook's undoing. Or did they?

Every good murder mystery that showcases a complex plot needs a sleuth who's up to the task of solving the most well-planned, perfectly executed crimes. Moriarty had his Holmes; Lector, his Starling. The faint of heart need not apply for the job. Enter Jo Crowder, armed with modern-day forensics skills, and, more importantly, a keen intuitive sense and an uncanny knack for thinking like the calculated, cunning, cold-hearted murderers she pursues. She doesn't just get under the skin of a suspect, she wears it like a cloak.

Jo Crowder isn't that once-in-a-lifetime, squeaky-clean

hero who follows rules, plays fair and square, and expects to be rewarded for her efforts in the end. Far from it. She disdains bureaucratic red tape and flouts the rules, even breaking a law or two along the way for the greater good. She's impatient and can be intolerant and headstrong.

Crowder's world isn't black and white; it's shades of gray. Everyone has a dark side. Everyone is capable of killing another human being. "People kill for a lot of reasons," she reminds us, "and for no particular reason at all." She knows what it's like to kill. She has angst over the perpetrators she's killed in the line of duty. Yet she's never been hesitant to pull the trigger. So far, at least.

In *The Easter Murders*, Jo Crowder once again faces a dilemma—what to do when she believes that someone accused of heinous crimes may be innocent when the evidence she uncovered cries otherwise. In this second novel, Crowder shows us how far she's willing to go in the search of truth and the pursuit of justice.

Enjoy the ride.

Many thanks to my publisher and editor, Tahlia Newland, who has been by my side since the start of my incredible journey as a novelist. Kudos to Rose Newland for another stunning book cover, and to my daughter and transcriptionist, Katie Zappa, for whom this novel is dedicated. Lastly, my humble thanks to all of you who read my novels. It is for you, too, that I dedicate this novel and the many more I hope to write.

Prologue

Friday before Palm Sunday,
St. Stephan's Cathedral,
New Orleans, Louisiana.

Her deep sobbing interrupted her speech and caused her to stammer. "Bless me Father for I, I have sinned ... I'm a-afraid to go home," the young girl said to the priest seated behind the mesh-covered lattice opening of the confessional.

The dim lighting of the priest's chamber was barely enough for the girl's tear-filled eyes to see the cleric's hand pressed tightly against his left temple, blocking her view of his face, and his of hers.

An eighth grader at St. Vincent's parochial school, the thirteen-year-old girl had been the last one to leave her pew and wait in line for the priest to hear her confession and absolve her of an adolescent's sins. Heavy-footed, she'd dragged her way to the penitent's crypt-like cell, entering through a windowless oak door, which, once closed, illuminated a low-wattage bulb that allowed just enough light for her to see the cushioned kneeler inside.

The priest leaned forward to hear better. "No wrongdoing, my child, should keep you from a mother's comfort and a father's counsel. What makes your fear so great?"

The girl's sobbing subsided when she heard the mellow tone of the cleric's voice. "I'm going to have a baby, and I don't know what to do," she whimpered, wiping her tears and runny nose on the sleeve of her hoodie.

"Are you afraid to tell your parents who the father is?"

"It's my stepdad," she blurted out. "He makes me do things to him and … and he does things to me … when my mom's at work. She cleans office buildings at night. He comes into my room after she leaves the house."

The priest paused a moment before answering. "To be the victim of another's sin is not a sin in the eyes of the Lord. You need not worry about that. Have you told your mother?"

"My mom can't help me." Her tone sounded desperate. "He hits her. Makes her cry. She's afraid of him. He … he told me he'd kill my mom and me if … if I tell her what he does to me."

"Is there anyone you can go to? A relative? A friend?"

"No, Father. My real dad died when I was six. It's only me and my mom. My stepdad wants me to have an abortion. He has someone who'll do it."

"Have you seen a doctor?"

"No."

"Does anyone else know?"

"No."

"How long has he been abusing you?"

"Since last September," she whispered. "It started on the day I turned thirteen, after my mom left for work."

"What your stepfather wants you to do, this abortion, is not only a sin in the eyes of God, but unlawful. You did the right thing to confide in me about it."

2

"I have no place to go," she lamented, fighting back another downpour of tears. She took a moment to regain her composure, and then she continued, "I was gonna take a bus to Baton Rouge. I have an aunt who lives there. But I didn't have enough money for the bus ticket."

"How much money do you have on you?"

"After I put some clothes and pocket change in my backpack, I took a twenty from my stepdad's wallet while he was sleeping."

"Here's what I want you to do," the priest said firmly. "Take a taxi to the convent of the Sisters of St. Mary. It's part of St. Joseph's Parish at Jefferson and Thirty-second. There's a taxi stand at the Berkshire Hotel a block away from St. Stephan's. When you get to the convent ask for Sister Agnes and Sister Ann. They will help you. Can you remember what I'm telling you to do?"

"Yes. The convent at St. Joseph's Parish at Jefferson and ..."

"Thirty-second."

"Yes, Thirty-second. I'm to ask for Sister Agnes and Sister Ann."

"Now go with God's grace, my child. You've committed no sin in the eyes of the Lord."

PART ONE

The Murders

Chapter 1

Palm Sunday

"Sister Theresa, fill the fonts and basins while I turn on the lights in the church and unlock the doors," Father Julian told the nun as he switched on the lights in the sacristy, the room adjacent to the main altar where the priest's vestments were kept. It was six-thirty in the morning but still dark outside. There was much to do before the congregants gathered for mass at eight o'clock to celebrate Palm Sunday and begin Easter week.

"Yes, Father," she said obediently. The nun, a rail-thin, diminutive woman twice the priest's age, placed the basket of palm cuttings she was carrying next to the two baskets she'd brought in the day before.

The priest's garments—his alb, cincture stole and chasuble—lay on a table next to a cabinet where the altar linens and vestments not being used that Sunday were stored. The holy water and sacramental wines used during services were kept elsewhere—in a locked cabinet that the priest opened with a key from the pocket of his cassock.

Moving to the priest's side, the nun reached in and removed

a decanter of holy water.

The priest went to a panel of six light switches and turned them on. Each one illuminated a section of the nave, the heart of the church where the Catholic faithful sat on hardwood pews and knelt on thinly cushioned kneelers to satisfy their weekly holy day of obligation. The altar lighting was controlled from a different panel of switches as was the peripheral lighting that illuminated the statues of Jesus, Mary, Joseph and six other saints strategically placed to provide a line of vision for congregants who had a favorite one to address in prayer. The priest switched them on.

The nun filled the basins and fonts of the main altar in time for her to join Father Julian at the center aisle. In perfect unison, they genuflected and made the sign of the cross before turning and walking side by side down the aisle to the vestibule at the rear of the church, like a bride and groom departing after having exchanged vows. The nun used the holy water she carried to fill fonts at each of four arched passageways into the nave where it would moisten the fingertips of worshippers who felt the need to cross themselves as the symbolic price of admission.

The priest carried two baskets of palm cuttings that had been interwoven into small crosses for congregants to take with them as mementos of the special occasion. He placed them on a table in the center of the vestibule, then unlatched and opened the front doors—two ten-feet high by five-feet wide solid oak slabs with religious symbols etched into them. The doors swung inward.

Similarly shaped exterior iron-slatted gates that opened outward remained across the entrance. The priest unlocked them using a latchkey. In the twilight of dawn, the cleric's eyes caught sight of a shopping cart blocking the gates. It was parked on the half-moon shaped slab of granite parishioners traversed before entering the cathedral after ascending fifteen steps from the sidewalk.

"Someone's put a cart, a shopping cart, directly in front of the gates," the priest groaned, his words within earshot of the nun.

"Something's in the cart, Father," she said, joining him at the entrance. "Do you wish for me to go to the front and move it."

"No, Sister Theresa. I'll open the gates slowly and push it forward until I can slip through and move it out of the way."

The cart, a white sheet covering its contents, straddled both gates. The priest gave the gate on his left a nudge, and the cart rolled forward a few inches. Another nudge. It rolled a few inches more. The third time he pushed on the gate, the cart moved forward but didn't stop.

When it no longer blocked the opening of the gates, the priest moved quickly to reach for the shopping cart but, as his fingertips touched the plastic covering on the handle, the front wheels rolled over the uppermost step. The nun had followed Father Julian out and stood by his side as the cart bounced its way down each step, rocking sideways and shaking whatever lay beneath the sheet.

The first rays of sunlight beamed across the Mississippi River and erased the shadows of early morning twilight just as the cart reached the sidewalk and upended.

The sheet remained with the cart; its contents did not.

The naked body of a young girl catapulted out of the cart to the sidewalk. She lay there on her back, arms outstretched, legs together and bent slightly at the knees, head turned down and to the side. Her unblinking eyes and vacant stare fixed on a similarly configured stone body of a dead man nailed to a twelve-foot crucifix that rose above the cathedral's dome.

The nun's piercing shriek shattered the tranquility of early morn like a clap of thunder. The soft chirping of the meadowlarks and starlings in the trees of the park across the street evaporated into the still quiet of a windless day. Only the sound of the decanter of holy water crashing on granite could be heard above the din of an old woman's wailings.

~

The call came to his cell phone while he was in his bedroom dressing for mass at St. Stephan's. "O'Malley," he answered in his usual no-nonsense manner.

Frank O'Malley was head of the Violent Crime and Homicide Division of the New Orleans Police Department. The promotion came when he made captain ten years ago. Since then, he'd had to answer to the police superintendent and the mayor for crimes of violence in New Orleans.

No small or easy task … in the Big Easy.

Famously heralded for the uniqueness of its French Creole architecture, cuisine and multilingual, multicultural heritage, New Orleans also laid claim to having one of the highest urban murder rates in the country. The massive investment of resources to rehabilitate the metropolitan area in the aftermath of Hurricane Katrina did little to improve on its ranking as the fourth most dangerous city in which to live and visit.

The call came from O'Malley's boss, police superintendent Russell Sullivan. "Frank, I hate to interrupt you at home on Palm Sunday, but I just got off the phone with Monsignor Rossi. He was calling on behalf of Archbishop Santini."

Antonio Santini was the Archbishop of New Orleans, and the head of an archdiocese that included the entire state of Louisiana and the three-quarter-of-a-million Catholics who resided in New Orleans. Thomas Aquinas Rossi was the archbishop's personal assistant and believed by many to be his likely successor.

Irish Roman Catholics, Sullivan and O'Malley were longtime parishioners of St. Stephan's Cathedral.

"What? Someone's been stealing from the collection baskets?" O'Malley quipped.

"If it were only that simple," Sullivan replied.

"So what's so important that it can't wait until after Sunday services? After all, it is Palm Sunday."

"That's just it, Frank. Sunday services have been canceled at St. Stephan's."

"Oh. And why is that?"

"It's hard for parishioners to get around the crime-scene tape and naked body of the young girl who's sprawled on the sidewalk in front of the cathedral."

"What in God's name happened?"

"Someone decided to put the body of a dead girl in a shopping cart and park it in front of the gates at the entrance to the cathedral. This morning, while Father Julian was trying to open the gates, the cart rolled down the steps and upended on the sidewalk."

"Who's responded?"

"A couple of black and whites. Forensics. Jones is on his way with a thermometer and a body bag."

Travis Jones was the chief medical examiner's autopsy assistant. He also drove the meat wagon—slang for the van that transported dead people from crime scenes to the parish morgue.

"So let me guess. His Grace wants the investigation to be resolved quickly and with the utmost discretion."

"According to the monsignor, His Grace's earnest desire is that we assign our very best detectives to the investigation and ..." Sullivan paused long enough to prompt a query from O'Malley.

"And what?"

"... and that the detectives be Catholic."

"Did you tell the monsignor to tell the archbishop that he can have the best detectives or the best Catholics, but not necessarily both?"

"You want Crowder on the case."

"Right. Crowder and Steele."

"Are they Catholic?"

"Crowder's an agnostic. Steele's a bass-guitar player and singer."

"Tell Crowder to keep a low profile on this. You know how she is when she gets her teeth into something."

"She steps on toes. She ruffles feathers. But that's why she's solved eighty percent of her homicide cases. No one in the department comes close."

"Still, I want you to keep a tight leash on her. The press will be all over this one."

"I'll do my best. But it'll be like putting a harness and muzzle on a pit bull in heat."

"Use a choke chain if necessary," Sullivan said, his voice a decibel higher. He paused a moment. O'Malley heard his boss sigh before continuing. "Father Julian has posted a notice for parishioners to attend services at St. Vincent's or St. Mary's. Helen and I are heading over to St. Mary's. See you and Ellen there?"

"St. Mary's it is ... Russ?"

"What Frank?"

"It's a hell of a way to begin Easter week."

Chapter 2

"So what do we have, Jo?" Detective Sergeant Sid Steele asked Detective Lieutenant Jo Crowder, his partner for the past three years, when she jumped into the front seat of Bugsy, Steele's pride and joy, a restored '68 VW Beetle.

Crowder, the youngest Louisiana patrol officer to earn a detective's gold shield, was not your typical cop: a bachelor's degree in criminal justice with honors; a master's degree in forensic science with honors; a crack shot with a pistol and rifle; and the lowest number of cold-case files in the department since she became a homicide detective eight years ago. Yet she'd never boasted to the press or her peers; instead, she let the collars—arrests—convictions, and occasional body bags do her talking.

Crowder learned early to fend for herself. She helped her father raise her three younger brothers after her mother died in a car crash when Crowder was thirteen. Her father, twenty-five years with the Louisiana State Police and the twice-elected sheriff of St. James Parish, taught her to shoot when she was twelve. She hunted buck and bear. She rock-climbed, kick-boxed, even fought in the octagon a few times. When she got knocked out, she took martial arts seriously, earning black belts in karate and judo. She cross trained four days a week to keep her 125 pound, five-foot-five-inch frame lean and muscular.

A tomboy growing up, Crowder excelled at sports, choosing to try out at high school for the boys' basketball and baseball teams, but having to settle for All-State honors on the girls' teams. Growing up in Breaux Bridge, population 8,223, she knew that looking and acting like a girl wouldn't get her picked when the boys teamed up to play on the sandlots of her hometown. And the boys always chose Crowder—sometimes first, and never last—because she played hard every minute on the field of play.

Crowder played being a homicide detective the same way. Police work was her life. She ate it, drank it, and lived it day and night. It made her irrepressible, confident and bold.

And to some who locked horns with her—she could be stubborn as a mule and a royal pain in the ass.

"Dead girl," she said matter-of-factly. "Early teens. Naked. Spread-eagled on the sidewalk in front of St. Stephan's. Cap said the archbishop wanted Catholic detectives assigned to the case."

Cap was the detectives' name for O'Malley, who was known as a stand-up guy to most of the cops in the department, including Crowder and Steele.

"So why us?" Steele asked. "You're an ex-Methodist, and I only show up in church for weddings and funerals—the last to arrive and first to leave."

"He wants the case to go away as quickly and tactfully as possible."

"The *quickly* I can understand when he assigns you a homicide case," Steele said, a smile on his face. "But *tactfully?* The toes you step on investigating a case make people want to wear steel-toed boots."

Crowder chuckled at the remark, but knew it was true. The complaints filed from suspects and targets of her investigations about her brazen behavior in uncovering evidence were overflowing. "The fact that the body shows up at one of the oldest, most historical cathedrals in the country may have nothing to do with the Catholic Church," she said. "Or it may have everything to do with it. It is what it is."

"Has the girl been identified?"

"Not yet. We'll want to get her prints and photos over to missing persons. But for now, let's take a look at the scene and the body, and talk to the priest who found her."

Overlooking a park on the Mississippi River, St. Stephan's Cathedral occupied a full city block. Steele parked in front of the cathedral behind the meat wagon. Police tape stretched across the entire facade of the building, then all the way down to the sidewalk. Two patrol vehicles flanked the crime scene, flashers going like lighthouse beacons.

Rubbernecking motorists slowed early morning traffic. A crowd of crack-of-dawn joggers and dog walkers gathered behind the tape, jockeying for positions with the best views of the sheet-covered body on the sidewalk. Local news stations had their reporters and camera operators broadcasting live from the scene, occasionally interviewing spectators who complained about the rampant crime in the city and the need for more police.

The detectives got out of their vehicle and went immediately to the body. Travis Jones and a patrol officer stood beside it. Crowder recognized Jake Tolliver, the patrol officer. "Were you the first responder, Jake?"

"Dispatched just before seven, arrived just after," he replied. "Father Julian, the pastor, was standing by the body when I got here. He said the girl was in that grocery cart with a sheet covering her, and it was blocking the front entrance." As he spoke, he nodded in the direction of the cart sitting upside down on the sidewalk. "He accidentally pushed it down the steps trying to

15

open the gates. She fell out when it hit the sidewalk. Not a stitch on her, just a religious medal hanging from her neck."

"Did he touch anything?"

"The sheet. He used it to cover her body."

"The cart?"

"Barely. He tried to grab the handle before it rolled down the steps."

"Jake, have forensics dust the handle for prints and look for blood and fibers on the cart, sheet and medal after we get the girl in the van."

"Will do, Jo."

"And make sure someone gets the priest's prints before he leaves the scene. We don't want his prints confused with any others. Has a CSI tech done a sketch?"

"Yep. After she chalked the body."

"Photos?"

"The girl, the cart and the scene."

"Let's take a look at the girl, Travis."

Jones knelt down beside the covered body; Crowder knelt on the other side across from him. Steele and Tolliver took standing positions at the girl's head and feet, providing her a modicum of privacy, much to the dismay of the press and thrill-seeking public. Jones handed Crowder a pair of clear latex gloves, identical to the ones he wore. He pulled down one end of the sheet, stopping at her waist just above the navel; the other end he folded up from her feet stopping just below her private area.

"Has anyone touched the body?"

"Not according to the priest," Tolliver said.

"Travis?"

"Only to check for a pulse and get a rectal temperature."

"What was her temperature?"

"86.2 degrees Fahrenheit."

"So an approximate time of death around midnight," Crowder said. Her training in forensic sciences qualified her as a specialist in crime-scene evidence detection. She also had a keen intuitive sense.

"Looks that way," Jones said. "Dr. Sessions will be able to give us a more precise estimate of the time after he looks at her and does the autopsy." Jones was referring to his boss, Dr. William Sessions, the chief medical examiner and elected coroner of Orleans Parish.

"Be sure that a forensic team is involved before Sessions opens her up. Hair combed out—all of it. Any visible evidence of penetration—vaginal, anal, oral. Fluids—semen and saliva. Scrape the fingernails and toenails for blood, hair and fibers, anything that might provide some DNA evidence. Don't forget the nasal passages and between the toes—might find something environmental."

"Jo, you need to see something," Tolliver said. "The priest saw it when he put the sheet over her."

"I saw it too when I took her temperature," said Jones, who raised the folded sheet just enough for Crowder and Steele to see the young girl's private area.

"Jesus! What in God's name did he do to her?" Steele exclaimed as the four of them glared at an incision across her lower abdomen—a ten-centimeter slit across the girl's stomach just below her belly button jaggedly stitched closed with clear nylon sutures.

"Someone removed something from inside her," Crowder said.

"A botched abortion," Steele suggested.

"Unlikely," Jones said. "Even the back-alley abortions are done vaginally. You know, insert a coat hanger and perforate the fetal sac."

"The girl can't be older than fourteen or fifteen," Steele said, shaking his head.

"Younger, judging from how undeveloped she is," Crowder said as she reached for the medal and inspected it without removing it from the girl's neck. "It takes a very sick mind to do something like this."

"Let's hope this is a one and done," Steele said.

"Something like this; I don't know," Crowder mused aloud. "Whoever did this planned every step very carefully. He, if it is a he, took his time. He had the needle and suture material to stitch her up after he took what he wanted from inside her. He could've dumped her in the river to float away or in the swamps for the gators to feed on. Instead, he leaves her to be found in plain sight … at the steps of a church so the congregation will know what he's done? No, whoever did this, isn't finished, not by a long shot."

Chapter 3

"It is on a matter of great importance that I wish to see you," Father Julian said to Monsignor Rossi in his office located at the archbishop's New Orleans residence.

"Is it about the girl?"

"Yes. She came to confession on Friday. I counseled her and she made her way to the convent where Sister Ann received the girl into her care. I received a call from Sister Ann Saturday night that the girl was not in her room and could not be found. Then, this morning, the body of a young girl shows up at St. Stephan's."

Rossi leaned forward in the chair behind his desk to close the distance between them. "I know. Sister Ann called me right after she came to the convent. The girl was sobbing so deeply that all she could do was feed her and put her to bed. On Saturday, I learned the girl was thirteen and pregnant, afraid to go home, and wouldn't reveal the father.

"Sister Ann brought her to the clinic. Dr. Latham confirmed her pregnancy and gave her a sedative. She told him her name was Amy, but refused to give her last name. She returned to the convent. I spoke to the girl by phone early Saturday evening and arranged to counsel her. While I was on my way over to the convent, Sister Ann called and told me she was gone."

"I never saw the girl's face, of course, when she confessed to me," Julian said. "So I couldn't identify the dead girl as her. When I spoke to the police this morning, I told them I'd never seen her before. But after I called Sister Ann and she described the girl, I was certain it was her. I told her to call the police and tell them that she might be able to identify the girl."

"Well, the matter, as tragic as it was, is now a police matter, Father Julian. You have done all you could for the girl and have assisted the police in identifying her."

"But, Monsignor, the matter for which I see you is something that weighs heavy on my mind."

"And what is that?"

"I think I know who murdered the girl."

Rossi tensed up and moved uneasily in his chair. "Have you told the police?"

"What I learned about the girl … about who the father is … about who probably killed her … I learned during her confession."

"I see," the monsignor said, relaxing a bit. "Your vows absolutely forbid you from revealing what you learned during her confession."

"The sacramental seal of secrecy is absolute even under threat of my death or the death of others," the priest acknowledged with a heavy sigh.

"And, if violated, would lead to your excommunication," Rossi announced emphatically. "Even when the penitent gives permission—something not possible now — it is always limited in scope and without revealing the penitent's identity."

The clergymen sat back in their chairs and neither spoke for a full minute. Rossi broke the silence. "Well, our hands are tied. We can only hope that the police investigation will uncover what you know and lead to an arrest and justice for the girl."

~

"What did you think of Father Julian?" Steele asked Crowder when they left the rectory of St. Stephan's where the priest lived and had been interviewed. It was Sunday morning, shortly after eleven, when the detectives had concluded their questioning of the priest and nun who found the girl.

By then, the body was in the meat wagon on its way to the morgue. The news people were headed back to their offices and studios to report, mostly speculate, how and why a naked dead girl ended up in front of St. Stephan's Cathedral on one of the most important holy days of the Catholic Church. The bystanders dispersed as soon as the girl was in a body bag and the rear door of the coroner's van slammed shut. Remnants of police tape on the steps and chalk marks on the sidewalk were all that remained.

"He seemed uneasy and hesitant about whether he knew the girl," Crowder said in response to Steele's question. "I don't know. Maybe I'm reading too much into his facial expressions and body language. I think he suspects something about the girl that he's not sharing with us."

Crowder's cell phone rang. It was from Jack Gardner, another detective, calling from district headquarters. "Crowder, you'll probably want to put something extra in the collection basket at church service today because your prayers have been answered."

"What, Jack? You decided to take early retirement."

"Very funny, girl detective. But I just solved your rape case involving the McNair girl."

"So you decided to confess?"

"Close. I'm holding the signed confession of one Desmond Sanders, who says he kidnapped the girl and had some fun with her before hosing her down and dropping her body behind a dumpster."

"How did you collar him?"

"I was like a magnet to metal. He came into headquarters a couple of hours ago and insisted on giving me a confession. No lawyer. Told me you don't need one when you intend to plead guilty. Waived his Miranda rights and spilled his guts. Must have something to do with coming clean during the religious holidays. The guilt must have been too much for him."

Crowder was the detective in charge of the case—the rape of the eight-year-old daughter of a prominent local businessman who was found naked behind a dumpster on River Road, just outside city limits. The girl's back had multiple lacerations from having been whipped. According to the ER physician who examined the girl, the perpetrator had bathed her in laundry detergent and douched her before leaving her for dead. Forensics came up empty. No semen. Nothing to extract DNA.

The girl was catatonic for two months. When she returned to earth, she didn't speak for another two. After that, the rape counselor got only no-one's-home stares when she asked her about the ordeal.

Crowder and Steele had pounded the pavement interviewing neighbors, teachers, the girl's friends and their parents. Not a single lead surfaced. The psychological profile predictably described a depraved, sadistic pedophile with a penchant for cleanliness.

The case had cold file written all over it.

"What do you know about Sanders?" Crowder asked.

"Must have been a one and done. Not much there. An arrest for indecent exposure. He dropped his pants in front of some old lady a couple years back. Another for peeping into the window of his neighbor six months ago. He watched as she nursed her infant, one hand on the windowsill, the other on his dick. The postman caught him and called it in."

"Jail time?"

"No. Just psych evaluations and some court-ordered therapy. But he does have a couple of voluntary commitments. Once he checked himself in, claiming he was being pursued by extraterrestrials. Another time, he said he was a Soviet defector seeking asylum."

"Did it ever occur to you, Jack, that the guy is just a nutcase?"

"No. He gave too many details only the perp would know."

"Okay. We're on our way. I'd like to see his statement and talk to him before they move him to the Hole." The Hole was what cops, criminal defense lawyers and prison reformists called the Orleans Parish Prison, noteworthy for being in the top-ten worst prisons in the country. "I don't want him traumatized before I have a chance to talk to him."

"Knock yourself out," Gardner said. "So long as I get credit for the collar."

~

"The statement is pretty sketchy," Crowder said after she and Steele had a chance to read it. She sat behind her desk back at headquarters. Steele, in a chair in front of Crowder's desk, held a coffee in his hand and a stirrer in his mouth. "Most of the facts he gives were in the newspaper accounts," she continued. "When the girl went missing, there were newscasts with a photo of the girl describing when and where she was last seen. Her photograph was everywhere but on a billboard and milk carton. Later, when she was found, it was front page news for a week."

23

"If he did the crimes, Jo, he'd know those facts. Maybe he's just telling it the way it happened."

"But the things he added to his story that we didn't know about are things we have no way of substantiating from independent sources. He knows the girl wasn't able to describe her attacker because we never gave a description of him or provided the press with a composite drawing. So he knows the girl can't say it wasn't him. He knows we don't have prints because they would've been matched to his in our database from his previous arrests. Same goes for DNA evidence. He says he leased a car but can't remember from whom, and rented a cabin at the Apalachee campgrounds out on Route 7 that's a known haven for drugs and prostitution, a place where DNA evidence would be impossible to retrieve. He checked in with an alias he can't remember, stayed three days, and paid cash."

"Playing devil's advocate," Steele interjected, "isn't that exactly how the creep would do it so he doesn't get caught?"

"That's exactly my point. It makes no sense that he'd go to such lengths to keep from being caught and suddenly decide to walk into district headquarters and turn himself in. Another thing: Gardner asked Sanders to describe how he injured and raped the girl, and he answers vaguely, saying only, 'I hurt her bad' and 'I had my way with her.' He said it was too painful for him to give the details. And on the most important facts that were known only by us, Gardner brings it up, not Sanders. Listen to this."

Crowder flipped to the page of the statement and read from it. "Gardner asks, 'So why did you wash her body with laundry detergent and douche her before leaving her behind the dumpster?' He answers, 'I don't know. Maybe I felt bad about what I'd done and thought it would wipe clean what I did to her.' Gardner's giving him the facts. That way, Sanders can

24

conveniently include those facts in his narrative later. He didn't even ask him why he suddenly decided to come forward and confess."

"Why is that important?" Steele asked.

"I'll let you know after I hear his answer."

The detectives proceeded to the holding cells located in the basement of district headquarters. Sanders, a short, thin, balding man in his mid-thirties with delicate features, sat alone on a bench in one of them. When they entered his cell, he was staring at a wall through thick prescription eyeglasses. He said he didn't want a lawyer, and he answered Crowder's questions in a calm, emotionless, non-threatening monotone. Most answers were along the lines of, "I answered that question before and have nothing else to say."

Finally, Crowder got to the questions she wanted answered. "Were you in Baton Rouge in September of last year?"

"No ... not that I remember," he said haltingly.

"Did you know that another young girl was abducted and raped in Baton Rouge? That case is very similar to the McNair case in all the important details."

Sanders' expression became a blank stare of surprise. Finally, he said, "Oh," lowering his head, like he'd been caught in a lie.

"Have you ever done anything like this before or after you say you abducted the McNair girl?"

"I-I don't think so," he stammered.

"Mr. Sanders, why did you come forward to confess to these crimes?"

Sanders remained silent for a full minute before answering. When he spoke, he looked at the ceiling and said, "It's God's will that I be punished for my sins."

Crowder looked at Steele and saw him roll his eyes. The guy was certifiable. But was he capable of kidnapping, beating and raping an eight-year-old girl?

They huddled up at Crowder's desk after the interview. "I don't know, Sid," she said. "My instincts tell me the guy needs a psychiatrist more than a lawyer. A public defender will be appointed even if he doesn't want one. Hopefully, he or she will convince him to be evaluated before he enters a plea."

Steele nodded. "Gardner wants credit for the arrest even though Sanders came into headquarters asking to see you. I learned through the grapevine that Gardner told him you were no longer in charge of the investigation, then he put him in a room and told him to speak up or get out."

"I don't blame him. It's a high-profile, unsolved case," Crowder said. "The D.A. will want to move for an early arraignment and, if he pleads not guilty, for a trial as soon as possible. The confession, unless recanted, will be enough for a conviction unless Sanders couldn't have been involved because he was someplace else."

A portly, middle-aged man in a wrinkled polyester suit showed up at Crowder's desk wearing the proverbial shit-eating grin on his face. "Well, did you get anything from him I should know about when you got sloppy seconds?" Gardner asked smugly.

"Just that he was on a mission from God when he came in to confess," Crowder said. "Did you check his whereabouts when the girl was abducted?"

"Crowder, you're not the only detective with a brain around here. I just got off the phone with his landlady. He's been living alone in a basement apartment at her rooming house out on Harrison Avenue for the last two years. I'm getting a warrant to search his place. I know it's your investigation and I need to go through you, but it's the logical next step."

"You're right, Jack. It is. We'll meet you there."

"I'll let you know when the judge signs the warrant."

Gardner took off with a noticeable pep in his step.

"Schmuck," Steele said. "I've never liked the arrogant son-of-a-bitch. He pulls rank on his partner whenever they're assigned a stakeout. Makes him do it alone. He hasn't booked an arrest in months. Has him do that, too."

"I guess I don't blame him for moving in on our case. But he doesn't know what we know, and it could be the undoing of the slam-dunk case he thinks he has against Sanders."

"You mean the Baton Rouge rape case?"

"Right. Same MO. A kid about the same age abducted at a private school. Kept for three days—whipped, raped, washed and douched, then dumped naked on a side street. I gave him the chance to confess to the incident. He had no idea what I was talking about."

The phone rang on Crowder's desk. It was O'Malley. He did most of the talking, his comments and directives only interrupted by an occasional, "Right," and, "Will do," from Crowder. When the call ended, she briefed Steele.

"Cap says Sessions will meet us tomorrow at noon to go over the autopsy findings. He also said he received a call from a Sister Ann at the convent over at St. Joseph's Parish; she thinks she can identify the girl. Cap wants someone over there with the photos for a positive ID. Looks like we'll need to split up."

"You want me to go with Gardner when we search Sanders' place?"

"You do that. I'll speak to the nun. Something's not right about her knowing the dead girl."

"Why's that?"

"Father Julian and the nun who was with him this morning

claimed they didn't know the girl. And nothing's been released to the press. We have the only photos of the girl. How could this Sister Ann possibly know who the dead girl is?"

Chapter 4

Across the street from St. Joseph's Catholic Church sat the convent of the Sisters of St. Mary, a hundred-year-old, three-story brick building with small leaded-glass windows on half a city block. A sculpture of Mary, holding out her hands in a welcoming gesture, rested atop an otherwise unassuming entrance. In its heyday, the convent housed twenty nuns, but no more than six have lived there the past ten years. Two years ago, the diocese of New Orleans dedicated the unused rooms as a temporary shelter for homeless women, abused spouses, teenage runaways, sex-slave castoffs, and the occasional prostitute strung out on drugs.

The St. Joseph's Clinic, a rundown, two-story shingled building with the best days of its half-century existence behind it, sat across the street. The clinic provided healthcare services to the uninsured from the poor neighborhoods of the district. Hurricane Katrina did much to worsen the signs of poverty that hung over the ghetto like an unending plague. FEMA aid found its way elsewhere. The local politicians' promises of help were as unfulfilled as the dreams of those who occupied the shabby looking homes that barely outnumbered the vacant houses and closed businesses—a place very few residents liked to call home.

Crowder arrived late afternoon on Sunday, and an aged nun in a traditional black habit, who took baby steps without raising her shoes off the carpeting, led them to a small office. Mother Superior in faded gold leaf lettering was barely visible on the open door. A middle-aged woman in a corduroy skirt and paisley blouse got up from the chair behind her desk and walked over to Crowder with her hand extended. Crowder shook the woman's hand.

"Detective Crowder, I'm Sister Ann. Please sit down."

"Thank you for seeing me so soon," Crowder said, taking one of the two chairs in front of the desk. The slender, gray-haired nun with a mother's smile took the other. "I brought the photos of the girl you thought you might be able to identify. There are two of her face."

Crowder reached into her folder and handed them to her. Sister Ann looked at them one at a time and handed them back to Crowder. As she did, she closed her eyes and moved her lips without speaking while making the sign of the cross. Only afterwards did she speak.

"Her name is Amy. She came to the convent Friday evening around seven-thirty. Through her sobbing she told me she'd run away from home and needed a place to stay. Naturally, we took her in. She had a meal and I encouraged her to go to bed early and that we'd talk in the morning. I gave her a cotton nightgown and checked in on her an hour later. She was sleeping soundly. When I went to her the next morning, she told me she was thirteen and pregnant. She didn't want to tell me who the father was. I didn't press her and figured she'd be more forthcoming if Monsignor Rossi counseled her."

"And did the monsignor see her?"

"When I spoke to him on the phone Saturday morning

and told him about Amy, he said he'd see her that evening after dinner. He phoned around six-thirty and spoke to her, I assumed about their meeting. When I discovered the girl had left, I called the monsignor and told him she was gone."

Crowder showed the nun the photo of the medal. "Recognize this?"

"Of course. It's a religious medal, one of several sold at Catholic bookstores here in the city."

"Who's the person on the medal?"

"St. Mary."

"As in Mary, the mother of Jesus?"

"No. As in St. Mary Magdalene."

"The one who was a … " Crowder hesitated, not wanting to say prostitute.

Sister Ann picked up from there. "Who some believe was a repentant prostitute, others, Jesus' lover or his secret wife. The theories are mostly debunked by biblical scholars. The modern view of the Catholic Church is that she was a faithful disciple of Jesus who witnessed his sermons, crucifixion, death and resurrection."

"Did you notice whether Amy was wearing it?"

"No. But Sister Agnes, who's a nurse practitioner and works with Dr. Latham at the clinic, would know. She was with Amy when she was examined there."

"What did Amy do during the day here?"

"When I spoke to the monsignor about her, he suggested she see Dr. Latham to confirm she was pregnant. He felt she might need medication if she was experiencing anxiety over her circumstances. After she was examined, I brought her back to the convent. She stayed mostly in the community room with the other residents, watching television."

"Did she leave anything behind when she left the convent?"

"No. Her knapsack was gone. The nightgown was folded neatly on her bed, which she'd made before leaving."

"A note. Did she leave one?"

"No."

"When was she last seen here at the convent?"

"I last saw her when I told her Monsignor Rossi was on the phone and wanted to speak to her. I showed her to my office and closed the door when I left so they could speak in private. I came back ten minutes later and she was gone. I assumed she'd gone back to her room."

"Were you the last to see her?"

"Yes. I checked with the other sisters and residents. No one saw her after dinner but me."

"How many exits out of the convent?"

"There are three. The front door and two doors in the back. One exits into a small parking lot, the other into a walled garden. All doors are locked at nine in the evening."

"What do you know about where the girl lives? Her parents?"

"Nothing. When she told me she was afraid to go home, I thought it best not to pursue the matter with her. Perhaps she confided more to the monsignor."

"I'm curious about something, Sister Ann. How did the girl know to seek shelter here?"

"Many of the women who come here are referrals from parish priests. Then, when the clinic opened, the convent became a logical transitional residence for the homeless women who were treated there."

"Who operates the clinic?"

"The clinic was the monsignor's idea—the first thing he did when he returned from Rome to be the archbishop's personal assistant. He recruited Dr. Latham, who was formerly a priest, and together they convinced other physicians and nurses to help staff it."

"Is Dr. Latham paid?

Dr. Latham and the other physicians have private practices elsewhere. Very few patients who are seen at the clinic have private insurance. Unless they have Medicare or Medicaid, we receive no payment. With the exception of Sister Agnes, the diocese pays stipends to the nurses who work there, and it funds the clinic's other expenses."

"And Sister Agnes?"

"She's a nun of our order who lives here at the convent. Her needs are met by a stipend from our order."

"Who currently lives at the convent?"

"Right now, in addition to the five nuns who live here, we currently have six residents, all with various problems brought on by poor lifestyle choices or plain bad luck. Sadly, the pregnant ones we get are too often like Amy—scared young girls, abused or abducted, with no place to go, no one to help them. Amy was sent here by Father Julian, pastor of St. Stephan's Cathedral where the poor girl was found. He told her to see me and Sister Agnes and we would help her."

Crowder remembered Father Julian's hesitation when asked if he knew the girl. Why didn't he admit he knew her? What was he hiding?

She intended to find out.

Crowder drove her Dodge Ram pickup over to her brother's rehabbed, two-bedroom brick townhome located in the fashionable Uptown District of New Orleans. Tom Crowder was a rising prosecutor in the criminal division of the Orleans Parish district attorney's office—LSU undergraduate with honors;

Tulane Law School, also with honors; managing editor of *The Law Review;* ten years with the D.A.'s office, the last two as chief prosecutor; thirty-eight felony prosecutions, including eight murder trials; thirty-five convictions—the other three copped pleas mid-trial to avoid the needle or get a small break on their sentence.

He loved his job, his new home, and Claire, his fiancé.

He loved his life.

He hated his boss.

Max Hellman was a real asshole. He had an unspectacular ten-year career as chief prosecutor before being elected the district attorney of Orleans Parish three years ago. He pled out ninety-five percent of his cases, gobbled up the high-profile ones, and only went to trial when the case was ironclad—confession, DNA evidence, eyewitnesses.

The hard work in preparing a case was beneath him. He had subordinates do that. They'd present the case to the grand jury, handle preliminary hearings, file and defend motions in court, and prepare witnesses and exhibits. He'd then make his grand entrance at trial, sitting first chair. He alone handled the press conferences, always speaking of justice and his tireless efforts to put the lawless scum of the earth behind bars for the rest of their unnatural lives.

Hellman lambasted the death penalty, not because he opposed capital punishment, but because it was too humane to kill someone by lethal injection. He favored legislation that brought back death by public hanging and electrocution, and that the choice be given to the victim's family.

To get elected, he ran a dirty campaign against his opponent, an experienced prosecutor who opposed the death penalty and supported prison reform. He called the man "gutless," "weak-minded," and "in bed with the liberals" who wanted to handcuff police—not criminals—make the prisons into country clubs, and offer counseling services and educational opportunities to undeserving inmates at the taxpayers' expense. His mantra at campaign rallies was, "You do the crime; you'll suffer for a long, long time." The first order of business when he took office was to fire his opponent.

In short, the district attorney was an arrogant, self-centered, showboat opportunist without an ounce of human kindness in his body.

"I thought you might cancel," Tom said when he answered the door. "I heard O'Malley gave you the murder case. I know how you like to dive right into your investigations."

"It's bizarre, Tom," she said as she walked into the house. "The girl, thirteen years old and pregnant, sought help from the nuns at the convent at St. Joseph's Parish, is taken in, and then leaves without a word to anyone last night." She looked around. "Where's Claire?"

"She's spending the weekend with her grandparents in Lake Charles. So it's just us. I picked up dinner at that new restaurant down the street from the office. Jambalaya and crawfish etouffee."

Jo Crowder was thirty-six years old, single, and with no immediate prospects for a permanent relationship. Married to her job, she had little time or inclination to hook up with a significant other. Not that she hadn't been in relationships. Department policies prohibited sexual relationships between cops. She'd dated prosecutors and criminal defense attorneys from time to time. A two-year relationship with a public defender was her second longest relationship. The longest to date was her present one—three years with Fred, a dog of unknown age and breed. He'd showed up one night. No place to stay. Hungry. Down on his luck. She took him in. They'd been roommates ever since.

Crowder went into the den where the food sat in cartons on a coffee table. Her brother grabbed a couple of Budweisers out of the refrigerator, popped the caps, and sat beside her on the sofa, his feet propped up on the coffee table next to hers.

"Hellman's personally handling the Sanders case," he said, changing the subject. "He's holding a press conference tomorrow morning to announce he'll be moving the case to trial in record time. The confession Gardner got from Sanders makes it an open-and-shut case. The search of his apartment uncovered a collection of news articles on the McNair abduction and rape. He had her photos, you know, the ones of her in her school uniform that were posted the day after she went missing. It was almost like he was following the case from day one."

"Tom, the guy's a pervert and a nutcase. But he's not someone capable of kidnapping, beating, and raping a child. The statement Gardner got from him has details that were all reported by the press or on the television newscasts. The collection of articles in his apartment could have been his way of memorizing facts that ended up in his confession. Sid was with Gardner during the search. He told me that important details in the articles were highlighted and underlined."

"It won't matter if you're right," he said. "Hellman doesn't care about the truth, only in whether the evidence guarantees him a conviction, and the confession and stuff in the apartment are more than enough to get him there. And, one other thing…"

"What's that?"

"When Sanders went before the magistrate this afternoon to be formally charged, he objected to his court-appointed public defender speaking for him. He announced in court that he committed the crimes and wanted to plead guilty to all of the charges. Naturally, the magistrate told him that it wasn't the time or the place to enter a plea."

"Hellman will most certainly use his statements to the magistrate against him at trial."

"He's already requested the transcript."

"When's the arraignment?"

"Wednesday before Judge Allen."

"Sanders needs a psychiatric evaluation. He's been in and out of mental-health clinics and psychiatric hospitals. He's made up things about who he is and what he's done. And something else, Tom ..." She hesitated long enough to take a long, slow swallow of beer.

"What else?"

"Sanders had no knowledge of another abduction and rape that occurred in Baton Rouge before the McNair girl was snatched. Nearly identical MO. I believe the two were committed by the same person. Why Sanders would admit to one and not the other makes no sense."

"You're saying there's a serial rapist out there?"

"It wouldn't surprise me. The crimes combine a unique set of circumstances: how the children were taken; what he did to them—the ligatures around their necks, wrists and ankles when he tied them up, exactly twelve lacerations on their backs when he whipped them; and both vaginal and anal penetration. There are too many similarities."

"Might be a copycat?"

"Not if Sanders is the copycat. He'd have no reason to lie about the Baton Rouge case. He'd want to take credit for it. Add it to his resume."

Crowder finished her dinner and left her brother's apartment ambivalent about the sudden turn of events in the McNair rape case ... and about the absence of leads in the death of a thirteen-year-old pregnant girl named Amy.

Two hours later Crowder rested in bed at home with Fred asleep beside her. She lay there awake, reflecting on the events of the past two days. She had no suspects in the Amy Stillman murder case, only suspicions and unanswered questions.

Father Julian.

Why didn't he admit he knew the girl? What was he hiding?

Monsignor Rossi.

Why did the girl suddenly pick up and leave the convent shortly after he called? Why didn't she wait and meet with him at the convent?

A return visit to Father Julian was at the top of her to-do list. Then a face to face with the monsignor.

Her thoughts shifted back to the McNair rape case. The Sanders confession, the more she thought about it, was a joke. It was what he didn't know and admit to that made Crowder uneasy and made her believe that Sanders was mentally unbalanced—and innocent.

And Max Hellman couldn't care less.

She opened the book she'd been reading the past two weeks. Barely a third of the way through it. Going to sleep was becoming increasingly more difficult; her mind was a speedway of unresolved matters racing around—her unsolved cases. It bothered her to no end that the rape of the McNair girl went unsolved for so long. And now that it was solved, she felt thoroughly unsatisfied.

It wasn't closing a criminal investigation with an arrest and conviction that mattered; it was whether the right person was caught and brought to justice.

Chapter 5

Crowder and Father Julian sat in the same chairs in the same room of the rectory at St. Stephan's where she'd questioned the priest on Sunday. "Thank you for seeing me, Father Julian. I need to clarify a few things in the statement you gave us yesterday."

"Of course. I'll do my best to answer your questions."

"Sister Ann called district headquarters yesterday because she thought she might know the dead girl. She was able to identify the girl from the crime-scene photos we showed her. Her name is Amy. She was thirteen and pregnant. Sister Ann said that on Friday you told the girl to go see her."

"Yes. That's correct."

"But you told Detective Steele and me yesterday that you didn't know the girl. You said you'd never seen her before."

"That's also correct."

"Wait a minute. If you told the girl to go see Sister Ann, you had to have some contact with her. You had to know her ... that she was pregnant ... had run away from home."

"I'm afraid I can't answer that question, Detective Crowder. My vows as a diocesan priest prohibit me from saying anything further."

"I'm sorry. I'm not following you. How can your vows prohibit you from cooperating with a police investigation into the death of a girl you knew and interacted with the day before she was murdered?"

"I can only answer your question by describing the vows we take to become a diocesan priest. When we are ordained, we take vows of obedience and celibacy. Celibacy is, of course, to remain chaste and not marry. Obedience requires us to follow the dogma of the church and to faithfully adhere to the rules our superiors, the bishops of our dioceses, impose on us. One of the rules is the duty of a priest not to disclose anything they learn from a penitent during the course of the Sacrament of Reconciliation."

"So you're telling me you heard the girl's confession?"

"I'm not even allowed to tell you if I did. The sacramental seal of confidentiality is absolute, even as to the identity of the penitent. To violate it would lead to my excommunication."

"Father Julian, if she told you who the father of her child was, you might be shielding her murderer by not telling me. If the person was an adult, he raped the girl even if she consented. That's sufficient motive for someone to want to get rid of her … and the evidence."

"I wish I could help you, but I can say nothing further about the girl," the priest said contritely.

Crowder was far from satisfied with the priest's refusal to cooperate when she left the rectory. She headed over to the coroner's office to meet up with Steele and discuss with Dr. Sessions his autopsy findings.

~

In the heart of the Central District, the Orleans Parish morgue occupied an unassuming, square cement structure—a single-story building with a sub-level area of cinder block construction that had the comfortable look and cozy feel of a bomb shelter. Entry was through a receptionist area barely large enough to fit a desk for an administrative assistant, and two armless, blue-fiberglass chairs for visitors. Down the corridor on one side were two identical small offices for the part-time pathologists who served as assistant coroners. A slightly larger one on the other side had a connecting conference room for the duly elected coroner of Orleans Parish.

The coroner's work was performed below ground—in a large room—on a stainless steel autopsy table with a built-in sink, hose and sprayer, and an attached scale to weigh the heart, lungs, brain and other internal organs dissected from a cadaver. Scalpels, bone saws, rib cutters, skull chisels, and various other tools of the trade lay on a tray table, and a portable X-ray machine stood nearby to document the location of broken bones, skull fractures and embedded bullets.

The detectives arrived shortly before noon. The medical examiner's long-time administrative assistant sat at the reception desk, grumpy as ever. Crowder knew the woman felt overworked and underappreciated, having complained to her on more than one occasion that, "I wear too many bonnets—receptionist, secretary, file clerk, lunch orderer, pencil sharpener … the list goes on and on."

She spoke with her usual sarcasm as soon as Crowder and Steele entered the building. "Batgirl and Robin—keeping the streets of the murder capital of the nation safe for its citizens?" she asked rhetorically. "He's expecting you."

"Is he in his office?" Crowder asked.

"No. He's in the cellar working on number two. A twenty-year-old college student who was found hanging in his closet between his shirts and trousers. They wheeled him in when he was finishing up with number one. He's keeping the girl out so you can see what was done to her."

The detectives walked down the corridor to the elevator, a Great Depression era Empire Elevator Company original, a necessary amenity to move the gurneys—with the bodies—to the autopsy room a floor below.

They chose a safer passageway—the stairwell.

When they entered the autopsy room, Dr. Sessions was doing an external examination of the naked body of a male cadaver with a clothesline noose around the neck. He stopped what he was doing when he heard the detectives enter.

Crowder was used to the malodorous scent of formaldehyde and the pungent smell of body decomposition, tolerable to her when the corpses were reasonably fresh; Steele, who went to a cabinet for some VapoRub to dab under his nostrils, less so.

"Scarpetta and Quincy, come here," Sessions said, calling Crowder and Steele by the names of the fictional pathologists. "You want to play coroner? Take a look at this one. Male. A college junior. Found naked in his dorm room, hanging in his closet, feet on the ground and knees buckled. On his desk was a letter from the dean informing him that he'd flunked out. His wall space was typical for a college man. Pinups of scantily clad models on one wall; posters of two great NFL quarterbacks, Drew Brees and Tom Brady, on the other. Assuming the heart and lungs show no gross morbidity, what's the likely cause and manner of death?"

"Suicide. He hung himself," Steele said confidently. "He was depressed over flunking out. Goodbye, cruel world. No disappointed parents. No flunky labels. No college loans to pay back."

Sessions' eyes shifted to Steele's partner. "Crowder?"

"Three questions. Any history of depression or self-destructive actions in his past?"

"No. The parents say he was well adjusted and, even though he struggled academically, optimistic about eventually getting through college."

"Was he facing in or out of the closet?"

"Out."

"Which wall was he directly facing—the one with the football posters or the pinups?"

"Pinups."

Crowder didn't hesitate in giving her opinion. "The boy's death was most likely accidental."

"How's that possible?" Steele asked.

"Classic case of autoerotic asphyxiation," she answered. "He was suffocating himself for sexual arousal. He fits the stereotype. Male. In his twenties. Fixated on something pornographic—like the pinups he was looking at. Feet in proximity to the ground at all times. And he ends up in a reclining position."

"Very good, Crowder," Sessions said. "A thousand men die each year strangling themselves to induce an erection and enhance an orgasm. Once euphoria is achieved, the unlucky ones pass out before they can stop the inevitable reduction of blood flow to their hearts. They go into cardiac arrest. No one is there to administer CPR. They're dead in five to eight minutes."

"His parents might challenge the finding," Crowder said.

"Why?" Steele asked.

"Some parents feel it's better to conceal the real cause rather than to admit to an accident associated with a form of sexual perversion."

"The best I can offer the parents," Sessions interjected, "is accidental asphyxiation. They can tell everyone he had food stuck in his throat and choked to death."

Crowder nodded her head in the direction of the sheet-covered cadaver on the table closest to her. "So what's the girl's story?"

Sessions picked up his chart and read from it. "Mid-adolescent Caucasian female, fifty-nine-and-a-half inches tall, ninety-three-point-seven pounds. Estimated age: twelve to fifteen. External: ten-centimeter horizontal abdominal sutured incision just above the pubic bone; one-centimeter puncture mark on interior left thigh. No other visible external wounds or injuries. Internal: recent lacerations of the upper vagina by laparoscopy consistent with sexual animate and/or inanimate penetration; microscopic anal abrasions. Abdominal cavity explored; uterus, cervix, ovaries, fallopian tubes absent."

"Could you determine whether she was pregnant?" Crowder asked.

"The bloodwork confirmed she was pregnant. There was no evidence of a fetus. So I can't determine the stage of her pregnancy."

Sessions removed the sheet covering the girl's body. The customary autopsy Y incision extended from below the girl's navel with the branches of the Y going under and around her small breasts all the way to her armpits. Crowder saw her partner grimace, then look away, when the skin flap was pulled up revealing an absent breast plate, and a void created by the removal of the heart, lungs and liver, and a nearly empty abdominal cavity. Crowder had seen several autopsies performed in her forensic science training and was unfazed by what she saw.

"Here, take a look," Sessions said, his eyes diverting to the girl's pelvic area. "I extended the incision to include the lower abdomen." He took a hooked-tipped instrument from a tray and used it to pull back the skin just above the girl's pubic bone.

"See. The reproductive organs. All gone."

"Does it look like something done by a trained medical professional—a doctor or an obstetrical nurse?" Crowder asked.

"The person had a basic knowledge of anatomy. He was able to identify the organs, but their removal is not what you'd expect from a surgeon. Too much surrounding tissue was cut out. The girl essentially had a C-section delivery of her baby and a crudely performed hysterectomy afterwards."

"Did you determine the cause of death?"

"Exsanguination—the girl bled to death."

Steele's gaze bounced from the girl's abdominal cavity to Sessions. "So she bled out while these procedures were being performed?"

"No. The procedures were done postmortem. There would have been minimal blood loss from the incision and the removal of her baby and reproductive organs."

Steele frowned. "I don't understand. Then how did she bleed out?"

Sessions looked at Crowder, who'd aced the college class he'd taught her in medical forensics. "Crowder?"

"He drained her blood from a major artery, probably the femoral in her thigh if the puncture mark matches up."

"Look here …" Sessions took a pencil light from the pocket of his autopsy apron and beamed it on a small puncture mark on the front of the girl's thigh. "Someone inserted a needle," he continued, "probably twenty-one gauge, into her femoral artery. The needle was attached to a piece of tubing and out flowed the blood."

"How long before she died?" Steele asked.

Crowder answered for her former teacher. "Not long. The femoral artery is highly pressurized."

Sessions picked up on her statement. "She'd have suffered a

class-four hemorrhage—the loss of more than forty percent of her blood. Her blood pressure would have dropped to zero in a matter of minutes."

"He wanted to avoid a bloody mess," Steele surmised.

"Precisely. The ovarian arteries supply blood to the reproductive organs; the uterine vein, blood to the fetus."

Crowder resumed her back and forth with Sessions. "When the incision was made and the procedures were performed, there would have been no blood pressure—her remaining blood would have hardened to the consistency of gelatin and be less likely to ooze."

"Right. The blood began coagulating in a matter of minutes."

Steele asked, "Is bleeding to death painful?"

"Only if the blood loss is from an injury. In her case, probably no physical pain. She'd have experienced light-headedness, dizziness, increasing fatigue, and have quickly lapsed into unconsciousness. But if she understood what was happening to her, she'd be terrified."

"Did you find anything that might tell us how she was abducted?" Crowder asked. "There were no contusions on her head, so we know she wasn't knocked out. The absence of abrasions on her wrists and ankles makes it unlikely she was bound."

"She might have been tased," Steele speculated. "Tasers are widely available."

"Possibly," Crowder said. "But that would've incapacitated her for only five, six minutes. It would've taken him much longer to transport her to a place that would serve as his operating room and where he could drain her blood. Did you find anything in the lab work, Dr. Sessions? Any drugs?"

"I had the same thought process as you," he replied. "He needed to sedate her so she wouldn't put up a fight or escape, so I extended the usual drug screens to include sedative drugs."

"And?"

"There was trace evidence of propofol."

Steele looked at Sessions, his forehead wrinkled. "Propofol?"

"A strong sedative commonly used as an anesthetic during surgery."

"Makes sense," Crowder said. "He simply sticks a needle in a vein and empties the syringe. She's out in a matter of seconds."

"The half-life of the drug is two to twenty-four hours. We were lucky there was still evidence of it in her blood."

"Were there any other puncture marks on her body?"

"The addendum will be in the final report. Travis surveyed her neck with a magnifying glass. He found a pinprick-size puncture on the left side where her external jugular vein is located."

Crowder probed further. "Did forensics come up with anything?"

"Nothing. No fibers or strands of hair. No prints on the cart. Not even on the medal that was around her neck."

"Then it couldn't have been the girl's medal. Otherwise, her prints would have been on it. It was probably put around her neck afterwards while he was still wearing gloves. Some kind of symbolic reference."

"We may have a link between the dead girl and the father of her baby," Sessions said.

"What kind of link?"

"The blood work was positive for STD. The girl had syphilis. If she had it, the rapist would have it, too."

"How common is syphilis these days?" Steele asked.

"Roughly ten cases per 100,000. So not widespread. Most cases are among gay and bisexual men. The chances of rape victims getting syphilis are very low—half a percent to three percent. So when a child victim gets it, it's a solid circumstantial link to the rapist if the suspect also has an active infection."

Crowder got what they needed from Sessions. The detectives left the autopsy room and headed back to district headquarters. On their way back, a call from the desk sergeant came in on the radio of their unmarked police vehicle. He advised them that a woman who wanted to report her teenage daughter missing was waiting.

A dull ache formed in the pit of Crowder's stomach.

Chapter 6

"Mrs. Lillian Attwell is waiting to see you," the desk sergeant told the detectives when they arrived at district headquarters. "Her daughter's been missing since last Friday. I figured you'd want to talk to her. She's in room three."

"We're on it," Crowder said, heading toward the hallway that led to the interview rooms. "Sid, I'll be with Mrs. Attwell. We'll need the photos of the girl and the medal, and bring a recorder."

Steele took off down the corridor towards the detectives' offices.

A thin, pale-faced, middle-aged woman with streaky gray hair sat at the conference-room table with an empty glass and unopened bottle of water in front of her. Her saggy cheeks and baggy eyes told Crowder the dead girl's mother had been found. She sat opposite her.

"Mrs. Attwell, my name is Jo Crowder. I'm a detective with the New Orleans Police Department. I understand your daughter has been missing since last Friday; is that right?"

The woman answered in a monotone. "I didn't know she was gone until yesterday. I work nights and slept until noon on

Saturday. I figured Amy was out with her friends." Crowder's eyes widened at the mention of the missing girl's name—the final puzzle piece to the dead girl's identity. "My husband, Amy's stepfather, was away from the house all day."

Steele entered the room with a recorder in one hand and a folder in the other. He took a seat next to Crowder.

"This is my partner, Detective Steele," Crowder announced.

Steele acknowledged the introduction by a head nod and obtained the woman's permission to record her interview. After he recorded the usual, preliminary statements, Crowder took over the questioning.

"When did you first realize Amy was missing?"

"I'm ashamed to say that it wasn't until Sunday. I was on the four-to-twelve shift for the cleaning service I work for. I made dinner, a stew, on Saturday. It was in a slow cooker when I left at three-thirty. When I got home, Amy's door was closed. I thought she was asleep, so I went right to bed. When I got up the next morning and went to Amy's room, she was gone."

"Did your husband tell you if he'd seen her on Saturday?"

"No. We had very little contact on Saturday. I heard the television on when I got home and figured he was watching it. He must have fallen asleep in his chair, because I didn't see him until the next morning. He was having coffee in the kitchen. When I asked about Amy, he said he hadn't seen her since Friday."

"Why didn't you report her missing yesterday?"

The woman moved uneasily in her chair, staring into her folded hands on the table when she spoke. "My husband told me to wait because she might be spending the night at her girlfriend's house."

"Did she have a cell phone?"

"No. Only my husband has one. The cost was just too much

for us."

"Ma'am, how old is your daughter?"

"Thirteen."

Crowder didn't want to be judgmental; inwardly, she was outraged by the woman's neglect. She toned down her criticism. "Isn't that a little young to wait another day to find out where she was?"

The woman's breathing became noticeably uneven, hiccuping to stave off an all-out crying spell. "I called two of her friends who told me they hadn't seen her since school on Friday. I talked to their mothers just to be sure they were telling me the truth."

"Why did you need to do that?"

"Because Amy has left the house before without telling me. She'd stay at a girlfriend's house, telling the mother I'd given my permission for her to stay over, but I hadn't."

"And why would she not tell you?"

Tearing up, the woman pulled a hanky from her purse and dabbed her cheeks. When she calmed down, she spoke unemotionally as though reading from a science textbook. "Amy's father, Paul Stillman, died when she was six. We struggled to make ends meet. I remarried two years ago. My husband, George, was a non-union pipe fitter for a company at the time. He lost his job a year later and has been unemployed ever since. He began to drink a lot and could be very hard on Amy and me. He cursed at us like we were responsible for him getting fired. I learned later that he'd been fired because he came to work drunk. He was denied unemployment compensation. We've been living on my income and Amy's Social Security checks ever since."

"Was Amy afraid of your husband?"

She paused for a long time, as though it was difficult for her to come up with the right words. Finally, she spoke: "It seemed like Amy was becoming more and more uncomfortable around him. She wanted a lock on her bedroom door. My husband refused to put one on. He said it was unsafe for a child to lock herself in her room."

"Has your husband ever hit you or been violent toward Amy? It's important for you to be forthcoming with us, Mrs. Attwell, now that Amy is … missing." Crowder almost said dead but caught herself.

Again, a moment of silence. The woman fidgeted in her chair. "He sometimes slaps me, usually when he's drunk and is mad at me for disturbing him. I've never seen him hit Amy, but I've told her to call the police on him if he ever does and I'm not home. I don't know if he hit her and that's why she ran away. When I asked him about it last night, he got very angry with me. He said some terrible things about Amy. When I defended her, he got physical with me."

"Ma'am, how was he physical with you?"

The woman sobbed deeply into a wet hanky. Her eyes were closed so tight her lids smothered her lashes. It was a full minute before her breathing normalized.

"Did he hurt you?" Crowder asked softly.

The woman got up from her chair, unbuttoned her long-sleeve blouse, and slowly removed it one sleeve at a time, uncovering dark bruises on her forearms—a sure sign of defensive wounds from her husband's attempts to beat her about the head and face with a belt. The full scope of the flogging was revealed when she turned around to show the multiple welts on her back, some still glistening red.

Steele winced empathetically.

"Ma'am, you've been courageous showing us what he did to you," Crowder said. "What he did was a terrible thing. You need to protect yourself or he'll continue to abuse you. We can end it … today. You make a formal complaint, and your husband will be arrested. He'll go before a judge who will enter a restraining order keeping him out of your house and away from you. And he will be punished."

"I don't know if I can do that," the woman said, grimacing in pain as she put her blouse back on. "Can't someone just talk to him? Scare some sense into him?"

Crowder had no choice but to be blunt. "It's more complicated than that, Mrs. Attwell. We think Amy may have been the girl who was found at St. Stephan's Cathedral yesterday morning."

"What do you mean?" she asked, worried.

"It was in the newspapers and on the newscasts yesterday and today."

"I don't have time for newspapers and television."

Crowder nodded at Steele, and he handed over the file he was holding. She pulled out three photos: two of the dead girl, and one of the medal found around her neck. She showed Mrs. Attwell the photo of the medal first. "Do you recognize this medal? It was around the neck of a young girl found in front of St. Stephan's yesterday."

The woman studied the photo through bloodshot eyes. "No. I-I've never seen it before," she stammered.

Crowder placed the two photos of the dead girl's face on the table, the same ones shown to Sister Ann.

The woman said nothing.

The photos were enough.

Mrs. Attwell sat paralyzed, her eyes fixed on the last photos of her daughter ever to be taken, shifting from one to the other between watery blinks. She picked them up, one in each hand, held them tightly against her chest, squeezed her eyes shut, and then, for a very long time—she wept.

Crowder had arrest and search warrants by four o'clock Monday afternoon. Lillian Attwell's statement and the police photos of her injuries were sufficient probable cause to arrest her husband for domestic abuse battery. Amy's identification as the murder victim and her mother's consent were sufficient grounds for a warrant to search the home and her husband's truck.

Two forensic crime-scene technicians and a patrol officer followed Crowder to the shabby two-bedroom, one-story home with uneven vinyl siding where Amy had lived. Attwell's breath had the smell of binge drinking when Crowder arrested him. When she told him the charge, he simply responded, "Fucking bitch." She wasn't sure if he was referring to his wife or to her.

Probably both.

She didn't give a damn.

As soon as Attwell was cuffed and in the patrol car on his way to district headquarters, the crime scene investigators went to work. One scoured the house for evidence of Amy's blood—in the tub, sinks and toilet. If the girl's blood was drained, they were the likely depositories. No amount of cleaning and bleaching would remove trace evidence of blood ... or the cleaning solvents used to get rid of it.

Evidence of semen was central to a rape charge. Using a high intensity ultraviolet light, a technician scanned Amy's room for it—the bed linens, pillowcase, bedspread, carpet, the clothes in her closet and the undergarments in the drawer of her dresser.

Crowder searched for other evidence—in Amy's desk drawers, the pockets of her jeans, her school book bag. Nothing of importance surfaced.

And then she found it: a shoebox in Amy's closet on the top shelf just above her clothes and school uniforms.

Crowder took it into the bedroom, placed it on Amy's desk, and removed the lid. It was stuffed with birthday and holiday cards, a valentine from Kenny, Amy's sixth-grade and seventh-grade report cards, and photographs of Amy, her mother and several girls her age.

It was the last item—in the shoebox under everything else—that caught her interest.

A book.

With a lock on it.

A single word on the cover.

Diary.

Crowder tried opening the book. It was locked. She went through Amy's desk again, this time with a single purpose in mind.

Find the key.

Not finding it, she bagged the book, photos and Kenny's valentine card as possible evidence.

The search took Crowder and her team into the other rooms, through the dressers and closets, under the beds and mattresses, into the waste cans and laundry basket. The kitchen cutlery was examined for traces of blood and the walls for blood splatter.

There was no basement or garage to inspect, only Attwell's decade-old pickup truck.

Crowder had a final stop.

She found the dented metal trash can with the number of the house painted on the lid in the back of the house. She used her cellphone to photograph the lid before opening it. Trash pickup wasn't that day; it was still full—two thirteen-gallon plastic kitchen bags filled with food scraps, paper trash, cans, and empty beer and whiskey bottles. A quick glance into each bag was sufficient to convince her nothing important was there.

But after removing the two trash bags, another bag—a

plastic grocery store bag—remained at the bottom of the can. The handles were tied together in a knot. She untied it and removed what was inside—a piece of clothing folded tightly in a square. She unraveled it.

A girl's nightgown.

A second item fell to the ground when the garment unfolded.

A girl's panties.

Crowder placed the garments back in the bag and returned to the house to be briefed by the forensics team.

"Not a drop of blood anywhere—house or truck," said the blood detection technician. "No evidence of bleach or any cleaning agent either."

Crowder turned to the other technician. "Semen?"

"Trace evidence on the bedroom carpet within a few inches of the bed. The problem will be whether there's sufficient concentration of DNA to extract and match with a suspect. The carpet is pretty worn. Not much fiber there to absorb the semen. Lots of grit to degenerate the sample."

"Hair?"

"Some strands on the carpet, in the bed, and on the pillow."

"What about these?" Crowder handed the plastic bag with the clothing items to the technician. "Probably the girl's nightie and panties."

The tech looked inside. "The material's cotton. DNA concentrates best in cotton. We'll send it off to the lab with the hair and the piece of carpeting we cut out."

"I want this expedited."

"We'll need a known DNA sample that's Attwell's."

"You can get it off the glass of whiskey he was holding when he answered the door."

Crowder was satisfied that all possible evidence had been uncovered during the search. It was time to head back to district headquarters.

It was time to brief O'Malley.

~

Crowder sat in the chair in front of O'Malley's desk. Steele stood with his back to the wall, chewing on a stirrer.

"Short version," O'Malley said, looking over his reading glasses at Crowder.

"Semen in the girl's bedroom, maybe on her bed clothes. No blood anywhere."

"Attwell?"

Steele, who'd handled Attwell's booking and charging, answered: "The magistrate gave his lawyer a choice—either his client bunks at the Hole, or he consents to a restraining order and moves in with a friend. Looks like he'll be buddying up for a while."

"If there's a DNA match, what are the likely charges?" O'Malley asked.

"Aggravated rape, carnal knowledge of a juvenile, sexual battery," Crowder answered.

"That's a hell of a motive to have killed the girl."

Steele took the stirrer from his mouth. "And he had lots of opportunity to take her somewhere, bleed and gut her, and drop her off at the church. The mother worked Saturday night and didn't get home until after one. She didn't see him until the next morning."

O'Malley's gaze redirected to Crowder. "Is he the prime suspect?"

"Right now he's our only suspect. But ... could the wife-beating, pedophile drunk commit a murder that required such planning and attention to detail? I'm not seeing it."

"Where do we go from here?"

"I want to meet with the people at the clinic who saw Amy Saturday morning … and the monsignor who was the last one to speak to her before she was abducted."

O'Malley held up a hand. "Stop there. Let's hold off on contacting the monsignor. I don't want to piss off the archbishop who wants to avoid involving the church in this mess. Just because the girl was Catholic and dumped at St. Stephan's doesn't mean the church or the diocese is being targeted. This could be the only murder we need to solve."

Crowder wasn't so sure, but she said nothing.

At least, for now.

She continued on with her plan of action. "We'll check with the neighbors, her teacher, and her best friends about creeps who might've been stalking her."

"So we have a plan," O'Malley said, shuffling papers on his desk—a sure sign to Crowder the meeting was over. "Let's hope something develops."

We'll need a lot more than hope, she thought but didn't say, as she followed Steele out of O'Malley's office.

We need a murder suspect.

Chapter 7

Steele was dispatched to speak to Amy's best friends and their mothers. The girls, from Amy's eighth-grade class, and Amy's teacher didn't know Amy was pregnant. Nor did they consider her behavior in recent days unusual or suspect that anyone was stalking her.

Same with the Attwell's neighbors.

He discovered that Kenny, one of her classmates—a shy, gangly, nerdy looking boy with braces and pimples—had a crush on Amy.

Dead ends.

When Steele returned to district headquarters, he found Crowder sitting at her desk wearing latex gloves with a book in one hand and a paper clip in the other. The book's cover had the word *Diary* in calligraphy font superimposed on a rainbow.

"What? Breaking and entering a young girl's diary?" he quipped.

"I thought these locks were decorative," she grumbled. "I

can pick a door lock easy enough. I'm losing my touch."

"This could be the break we need," Steele said, looking over Crowder's shoulder as she fiddled with the latch.

"You bet. Amy's way of telling us what happened to her."

The latch finally released. Crowder opened the cover. The first page had *MY DIARY* printed at the top. The remaining page was completed in the carefully scripted handwriting of an adolescent parochial school student.

Name: Amy Stillman

Birthdate: October 20

Zodiac Sign: Libra

Birthstone: Opal

Hometown: New Orleans

"Why the gloves?"

"Just to be safe. It's been dusted for prints but not on the pages inside. I found it in a shoebox in her closet. Locked. No key."

Crowder carefully turned the page.

Blank.

Turned another.

Blank.

She flipped through the remaining pages like a blackjack dealer shuffling cards.

All blank.

"Another dead end," Steele groaned.

Crowder took out a pencil light from her pocket and shone it on the book's spine. "Looks like she removed some pages." She studied the opening in the spine from the side with the book closed. "Judging from the size of the gap, I'd say a good quarter of the pages are missing. Neatly pulled away from the spine. Must have thrown them away or taken them with her."

"Either way," Steele said, "we'll never know what she wrote."

Crowder continued to study the book, looking closely at the first blank page. "I need a pencil. A lead pencil with a blunt point."

Steele walked over to Jack Gardner's desk—the man liked to use pencils—and picked one from a mug full of dull-tipped pencils with ground-down erasers. He gave it to Crowder. She rubbed the side of the pencil tip against the top line of the page about a third of the way through the line, then beamed her light on the shaded area. Partially formed letters of incomplete words appeared on the first line.

Steele leaned forward to get a closer look. "Nancy ... fucking ... Drew."

Crowder sat back in her chair. "Writing indentations from the last page of Amy's diary. People tend to be heavy-handed when writing under stress."

"Can you read it?"

"Not well enough to make sense of it, but Ballentine will."

Harry Ballentine was the department's handwriting specialist and document examiner.

Crowder called him.

"Ballentine," he answered.

"I'm sending down a diary, Harry. There are writing indentations I need you to decipher.

"I'll need a sample of the writing."

"No problem."

After the call ended, Crowder called Lillian Attwell who agreed to locate Amy's school notebooks. Crowder remembered seeing them in a school bag hanging on a hook in her room. Her next call was to the police dispatcher for him to notify a patrol officer in the vicinity of the Attwell's home to pick them up.

An hour later Crowder's phone rang. It was the department's chief of forensics. He got right to the point. "No go on the carpet stain. Too little DNA. Too much degradation."

"Hair?"

"The girl's."

"Zero for two."

"Don't worry. You've got a lock on the batting title. You're batting two for four."

"The nightie?"

"Attwell's semen."

"The panties?"

"Also Attwell's. The semen stains were absorbed in the cotton fabric. Pretty recent too. No older than a week."

"Report?"

"You'll have it with the lab findings in ten minutes."

When the report arrived, Steele wasn't at his desk. She read it and waited for him to return. He showed up a few minutes later with two coffees and handed one to her.

She briefed him. "We have Attwell's semen on the nightie and panties." She handed the two-page report to him and waited for him to read it.

"As long as the mother identifies the clothing as Amy's, we've got him on a statutory rape charge," he said when he finished.

"Not necessarily."

"Why not?"

"The absence of semen in the bedroom raises the possibility that Attwell simply took the items and masturbated on them," Crowder explained. "It's a common fetish among pedophiles."

"If he has syphilis, we'll have enough. Can we get a warrant for a blood sample with what we have?"

"Not without repealing the Fifth Amendment. Something about his right against self-incrimination. He'd need to consent."

Steele sighed. "So we're left with the diary entry?"

"Looks that way, unless Sessions can pull some fetal blood

and test it for paternity."

"That's impossible without a fetus, Jo."

"Not anymore. Private labs are now able to extract fragments of the fetus's DNA from the mother's blood as early as five weeks after conception and test it to determine paternity. Rape victims can now know if their baby's father was the rapist."

An hour later Crowder got a text from Ballentine: *I'm done. Come on up.*

A wave of the hand to Steele was enough to get him to join her. They walked up a flight of steps to the forensics lab where Ballentine was sitting on a stool with equipment on the desk in front of him.

"It came out better than I expected," he said when the detectives joined him.

Crowder, trained in criminal forensics, was familiar with the equipment. "ESDA," she said, pronouncing the acronym as a single word while staring at a piece of machinery that looked like a portable copy machine. "An electrostatic detection apparatus."

What's it do?" Steele asked.

"It helps Harry uncover indented writing a page or two below the missing page."

Ballentine explained: "I place the page from the diary with the indentations on the panel at the top of the apparatus. Cover it with a piece of Mylar, which is like a piece of clear plastic kitchen wrap. I use this electronic wand"—he stopped to pick up a device that looked like an eighteen-inch-long fluorescent light—"and pass it over the document twice. This produces static electricity that's greatest in the indentations. I spread black toner, similar to what's used in photocopiers, which lodges in the indentations. Then I photograph it."

"And the photograph?" Crowder asked.

"I scanned it on the lab's computer. That way I can enhance

the color and enlarge the size of the writing." Ballentine moved to the desktop computer on a table in the middle of the lab and brought the photographed page up on the screen. The detectives looked over his shoulders as he brought the writing into focus.

They read the page in silence: *was drunk again. It hurt a lot more this time. He says mom and me both die if I tell on him. I can't stay here. Aunt Marian will help me. I need money for a bus ticket. I'll take some from his wallet and leave tonight. I know one thing for sure. I don't want to have my stepdad's baby.*

"Are you sure the writing's Amy's?" Crowder asked.

"A perfect match with the handwriting in her school notebooks."

"I'll need a formal report."

"It'll be on your desk tomorrow morning."

Chapter 8

It was after 3 p.m. when Crowder returned to her desk. Gardner was sitting back in Crowder's chair chomping on what remained of a Snickers bar, chocolate smudge marks visible on his tie.

"What? Learning police work through the seat of your pants? I'm flattered you've chosen my chair to sit in and learn," she quipped.

"Funny girl," Gardner said with a smirk. "Thought I'd let you know that you won't be needed at Sanders' arraignment tomorrow afternoon. He's pleading guilty. It's been worked out between Hellman and his court-appointed public defender."

"No psychiatric evaluation before he pleads?"

"Sanders threatened to fire his lawyer for even suggesting one."

"His lawyer could petition the court for a competency evaluation."

"Hellman won't agree to it. He told him he'll insist on a life sentence at hard labor without parole eligibility if Sanders doesn't plead guilty tomorrow."

Crowder stuck out her thumb and yanked it back—signaling

for Gardner to get out of her chair. Gardner lifted himself out of the chair, straining to get his bulky frame to a standing position.

"Knowing Hellman," Crowder said, "he'll insist on the maximum sentence even if Sanders cooperates and pleads out."

"Probably right." Gardner crumpled the candy wrapper into a ball and tossed it toward the waste basket next to Crowder's desk, missing it by a foot. "He's holding a press conference after the arraignment to brag about his latest conviction. He asked me and the girl's parents to attend the show."

"A dog and pony show," Crowder mumbled to Steele as Gardner walked away snickering and leaving the wrapper on the floor.

~

A call from O'Malley came ten minutes later. "I want you and Steele over to the Brighton School on Ashton and Vine. The principal and the parents of a second grader are waiting for you. Someone pulled the fire alarm at the school around one o'clock. The kids were evacuated. They were outside for a half hour while police and fire combed the building. It wasn't until the kids got back to their classrooms that the teacher discovered a girl was missing."

"We're on our way," Crowder said, getting up from her chair and grabbing her jacket from the back of it, the phone still at her ear.

"Crowder."

"Sir?

"We need to move fast on this."

"I know. We don't want another McNair."

Crowder and Steele arrived at the school around three-thirty. The officers waiting in the two patrol cars parked at the front entrance got out when the detectives arrived. The more senior of the two briefed them on what had been done to locate the missing girl—the school had been thoroughly checked, as had the grounds around the building, but to no avail.

The private school's two-story brick building sat on its own block with an open playground in the rear and a park across the street. The neighborhood was upper-middle class with single-family homes and two-car garages on half-acre lots. An APB— All Points Bulletin—had gone out to patrol vehicles in the district to comb the nearby neighborhoods for an eight-year-old, four-foot-two-inch, sixty-pound Caucasian girl with brown eyes and brown hair, wearing a blue-and-gold plaid school uniform answering to the name of Jessica Young.

They'd searched for an hour.

Not a trace of the girl.

The patrol officer showed the detectives to the principal's office where she waited with Jessica's parents and her second-grade teacher. After the introductions Crowder took over.

"When was Jessica last seen?"

The teacher, a single woman in her mid-twenties, answered: "Just after the alarm sounded ... around one o'clock. Protocols for fire drills require that the students leave the room in single file and move to one of four exits that lead out of the front, rear and sides of the building. The gathering points are on the sidewalks in the front of the school and at the playground in the back. The teacher is the last one to leave the classroom to be sure no one is left behind."

"And which exit did your class take?"

"The side-door emergency exit. It's closest to our classroom."

"Did you see Jessica leave the building?"

"No. As soon as the children gathered in the hallway, they stayed in line while I opened the door and watched them leave the building. About half the students were out when a loud pop, like a firecracker, scared the children. They may have thought it was a gunshot. A couple of the girls screamed, and those already out of the building started running around the corner to the front of the school. One fell down. I went to her immediately to help her while some of the children were still in the school. The child had scraped her knee badly and was crying hysterically. It was all I could do to get her on her feet and walk her to the front of the school. I assumed all of the children had left the school and followed the ones who were running."

"Did you see Jessica with the other children when you got to the front of the school?"

"The classes were commingled by then. I still needed to tend to the injured child. It wasn't until the children were back in the classroom that I realized Jessica was missing." The teacher's eyes had become glossy, and it appeared she might cry.

Crowder waited for her to collect herself. "Ma'am, how long have you been teaching here?"

"It's my first year," she said, a quiver in her voice.

"Do you seat the children in any particular order?"

"What do you mean?"

"Do you seat them alphabetically by last name?"

"Well, yes. I do.

"You said the children leave the classroom in single file. How do they leave?"

"They leave in rows. First through the fourth."

"And where was Jessica's seat in the classroom?"

"She would have been in the fourth row, fifth seat back."

"So the last one out of the classroom?"

"Yes."

"And the last one to leave the building?"

"Yes, the last child out."

"Does Jessica have a cell phone?"

Jessica's father spoke up. "Yes, she does."

"Was it with her?"

"Not on her," he replied. "It was in her school bag when we got her things from the classroom."

Crowder's gaze turned to the principal. "Security cameras?"

"In the front and back, but not the side exits. They record weekly and recycle."

"We'll need to see them."

"Of course, I'll get the discs."

The principal left with Steele to collect the recordings. Crowder asked the teacher to leave so she could speak privately to Jessica's parents. Once alone with them, she explained that what had happened was probably an abduction, possibly a kidnapping for ransom, and how important it was for them to stay home in case they were contacted by Jessica or her abductor.

Mrs. Young, wide-eyed and ashen, stared at Crowder in disbelief. "It-it's just ... just like that other girl," she stammered, holding back tears.

Mr. Young put his arm around his wife, who was holding Jessica's sweater tight to her chest, her body visibly shaking. "What are our chances of getting Jessica back unharmed?" he asked.

"The first day is very important. I'll need a current photo of Jessica. It will be posted as an Amber Alert on social media and local television today, and in the newspapers tomorrow. Someone may have seen her or something suspicious."

Crowder finished up. It was time to return to district headquarters and look at the recordings.

"It's him," Crowder announced to Steele in the car on their way back. "The McNair and Baton Rouge abductions were both from private elementary schools and involved seven- or eight-year-old girls. There was always a reason to evacuate the school. With McNair, it was a bomb scare; the Baton Rouge abduction, a power outage; and now, a fire alarm."

"If it's him, we have at most a day or two," Steele said. "He dumps them on the third day."

"And by then, she'll be like the other two. Tortured. Repeatedly raped."

"There's nothing we can do other than to wait it out?"

"Maybe not. Do we still have a copy of the security tape from the Baton Rouge abduction?"

"Yes. But when we looked at it, nothing surfaced."

"But we didn't have another tape to compare it to. The school McNair attended didn't have security cameras at the time. This time we can compare the vehicles that are seen on the tapes in the minutes before and after the last two abductions. His safest way to get the girl in a vehicle unseen is to have a large vehicle, preferably with a large sliding side door."

"A panel truck."

"Or a passenger or cargo van."

Chapter 9

It was after five by the time the detectives were seated at Crowder's desk with their laptops loaded with the security tapes. They watched them simultaneously, beginning thirty minutes before each abduction. Two sets of eyes scanned the screens, watching cars, vans and an occasional truck pass by the front of the schools, looking for a match. From time to time, one of them said, "Stop," and they paused the recordings while comparing similar-looking vehicles. But none looked like a match.

The streets in front of the schools were school zones with crosswalks. So the vehicles passing by moved slowly, allowing the time to study them.

About fifteen minutes before the abductions, a similar-looking white cargo van crossed the front of both schools. The detectives adjusted the recordings so the two vehicles were displayed at the same time.

"The vehicles look the same," Steele said. "Recognize the make and model?"

"A Ford cargo van. Sliding side doors. Used a lot commercially."

"A tradesman's vehicle," Steele offered.

"The girls were taken about fifteen minutes later," Crowder said. "Let's advance the film ten minutes and watch in real time."

About six minutes after the estimated time of abduction, the same vehicle passed by the front of one of the schools, this time traveling in the opposite direction. Two minutes after seeing the vehicle on the Baton Rouge video, the same vehicle appeared again on the street in front of The Brighton School, also heading in the opposite direction.

"It's time we get Cap involved," Crowder announced.

Crowder told O'Malley they had a lead and needed a forensic technician to identify the vehicle on the recordings and its owner. She explained the need to move quickly. They had hours, not days.

By the time the technician had been selected and briefed on the assignment, it was after eight. Another long day. Crowder was beat. She returned home, ate leftovers from her refrigerator, and settled back in bed with a glass of Chardonnay, reviewing her report in another case. Her mind soon ranged elsewhere—to Sanders pleading guilty tomorrow to a crime he didn't commit.

She knew what she needed to do.

And she had to do it alone.

~

Crowder checked her gun with courthouse security and made her way to Judge Allen's courtroom. It was just after nine. The arraignment had already begun.

She sat among the spectators—an assortment of suited lawyers and disheveled family members of defendants being arraigned that day. Today, the local beat reporters showed up, notepads and laptops at the ready.

State v. Sanders was on the docket.

Judge Allen, his thick mane of white hair in stark contrast to his black robe, sat behind the bench, his temper less under control as each year passed of his quarter century of service. Sitting as a judge on the busiest criminal court in the state left him with a short, easily lit fuse.

He looked at Max Hellman, who sat at the prosecutor's table. "Proceed, Mr. Hellman," he said in a tone suggesting he was already annoyed.

"Good morning, Your Honor," Hellman said as he scurried to the lectern with a file in his hand.

Before he could say anything further, the judge expressed his concern. "Isn't this a little early for a defendant to be pleading guilty? The charges against Mr. Sanders carry a potential sentence of life imprisonment without parole."

Allen was both a former prosecutor and public defender. His diverse background made him electable. He seldom faced a formidable challenger when seeking re-election. "The defendant doesn't object," Hellman responded.

"Is that true, Mr. Turner?" the judge asked Sanders' court-appointed public defender.

"That's correct, Your Honor."

"I remember this case, Mr. Turner. Very serious charges. What led to your client's apprehension?"

Hellman answered for Turner. "He turned himself in and confessed, Your Honor."

The reporters in the courtroom stirred at these first newsworthy facts.

"I see here that the defendant initially refused counsel. He wanted to represent himself." The judge looked over his bifocals at Sanders. "Is that correct, Mr. Sanders?"

Defense counsel nudged Sanders and whispered for him to

stand.

He stood and answered the judge: "It's God's will that I be punished."

"No, Mr. Sanders, it's my decision whether and how you will be punished. What I'm asking is whether Mr. Turner is authorized to speak for you … as your legal counsel."

"If it's God's will, Your Honor."

His fuse smoldering, Allen pursed his lips and spoke sternly, "I'll take that response as a, 'Yes,' unless you …" he paused to clear his throat, "or God tells me otherwise."

"Proceed, Mr. Hellman."

Hellman read off the criminal charges against Sanders: kidnapping, rape in the first degree, carnal knowledge with a juvenile, and sexual battery.

Crowder sat silently in the back of the courtroom until she was sure Sanders intended to plead guilty.

"Is your client intending to plead guilty to one or more of these charges?" the judge asked Turner.

Turner stood and answered: "Yes, Your Honor. All of them."

A voice interrupted from the back of the courtroom. "Your Honor, may I be heard?" Crowder stood, her voice loud enough to startle those in front of her who turned to look. "I have some information I'd like to share with the court that has a bearing on this case."

The judge knew Crowder from criminal trials in which she was the arresting officer or chief investigator.

"Detective Crowder, are you the detective in charge of this case? The case file has Detective Gardner as the one heading the investigation."

"Judge, as far as I'm concerned, I'm still in charge."

Hellman, his fists clenched, shot an icy glance at Crowder. "This is most irregular, Your Honor. This detective has no current involvement in the charges against the defendant. Detective Gardner arrested the defendant. He obtained his confession."

In the courtroom, all eyes shifted to Crowder. "That's true," she said. "But I have information that has a bearing on the defendant's guilt or innocence."

"This is absurd," protested Hellman.

Turner stood, his mouth agape, but found that words were not forthcoming.

Sanders stood to add to the chaos and said, "It's God's will that I plead guilty."

"See. He wants to plead guilty," Hellman said, his voice a few decibels higher.

The spectators began to speak among themselves. The reporters rustled about in their seats, typing feverishly on their laptops.

"Order … order in my court," barked the judge, banging his gavel to make his point. "We're recessed. I'll see the lawyers in chambers … and you, too, Detective Crowder," he yelled over his shoulder as he walked quickly from behind the bench to a side door and returned to his office a floor above.

"I'll have you up on departmental charges, Crowder," Hellman vowed when they'd all gathered in Allen's office. Sanders had been taken to a holding cell. Turner, Crowder and a court reporter occupied the other chairs. "Interfering with a criminal investigation, disrupting court proceedings," he squawked.

"I'm not going to sit back and let a man plead guilty to a rape he didn't commit," Crowder said, her tone argumentative.

"Detective Crowder," the judge interrupted, "do you have a suspect in custody who has also confessed?"

"No."

"Then how can you possibly know that Sanders, who confessed to these crimes, is innocent?"

"Crowder, you've lost your mind," Hellman cried out.

"No, but I think Sanders ... and *you* have," Crowder shouted back—outwardly appearing unfazed by Hellman's bullying while, inwardly, her intestines were twisting.

"All right. That's enough from both of you," the judge said, like a proctor at a kindergarten playground arbitrating who got the ball that ended up in his hands. "Detective Crowder, what evidence do you have that suggests Sanders is innocent?"

Crowder moved forward in her chair and methodically summarized her case—Sanders' questionable confession, the comparable Baton Rouge rape that Sanders knew nothing about, the unique similarities of the rapes—the flogging and cleansing of the victims—and Sanders' mental health issues.

Hellman interrupted the detective. "Doesn't matter. The other rapist could be a copycat. '60 Minutes' did a segment on the McNair case, for God's sake."

"Impossible," Crowder said.

"Why so?" the judge asked.

"The Baton Rouge rape occurred before McNair."

Hellman tried to respond but was flustered by Crowder's response. Finally, he spoke: "Then Sanders could be the copycat. He learned of the Baton Rouge incident and tried to replicate it."

"Not likely," Crowder rebutted. "He had no knowledge of it when I questioned him about it on the day of his arrest. But there's another reason he can't be guilty."

"What?" the judge asked.

"We had another abduction yesterday."

A stony silence replaced their bickering.

Crowder then reviewed the similarities of the abductions and the presence of the same vehicle at two of the abductions. She paused a moment so her revelations could be fully absorbed.

"If the girl ends up like the other two," she continued, "we're dealing with a serial rapist who can't be Sanders."

Hellman was the first to speak. "Who cares what you think. We deal in facts, not hunches. And the facts are all in the confession Sanders voluntarily gave us."

The judge shifted his stare from Hellman to Turner. "Detective Crowder says the defendant has mental health issues, been committed twice, made things up in the past. Why haven't you requested a psychiatric evaluation?"

Hellman answered for Turner. "Because, Your Honor, he doesn't want one, and neither do I, the duly elected district attorney for this parish."

"Watch your tone with me, *Mr. District Attorney*. If Sanders isn't mentally fit to make that decision, he shouldn't be making it."

The judge removed his bifocals, folded them and placed them on his desk. He squeezed the ridge of his nose and squinted before resuming. "I can't order the defendant to undergo a psychiatric evaluation if he or his lawyer doesn't want one, and there's insufficient evidence that he was mentally incompetent when he confessed. He was living independently, working part time, and his obsession with God's will isn't enough, unless every born-again Christian is incompetent to admit to a crime." He turned and stared at Crowder. "So far, detective, what you've uncovered is circumstantial and coincidental. There's no direct connection between the two rapes and the three abductions to a *single* person. It's all speculation on your part. So far, at least. So here's what we're going to do. I'm postponing the arraignment for one week. If someone else isn't in custody for the abduction and rape of the McNair girl by then, I'll take the defendant's guilty pleas."

Hellman smiled for the first time since Crowder stood up in

the courtroom.

Crowder was the last to leave the judge's chambers. As she was leaving, the judge said, "You've got a week, Crowder—a week to solve the McNair case. Godspeed."

~

Steele was sitting in the chair in front of Crowder's desk with his feet on it when she returned from court. He was strumming a make-believe guitar and humming a tune.

"I hear you put on quite a show this morning in Allen's courtroom. Hellman was fuming when he got back to his office. Called Cap and lit into him for twenty minutes. He asked me if I knew what you were up to. Naturally, I said I did. So it looks like what happens to you, happens to me, partner."

"Sid, stay clear of the mess I've created for myself … but thanks for the support. We have a week to solve the McNair case, otherwise the judge is accepting Sanders' guilty pleas."

"A week? And so far, the only suspect is a guy in jail who's confessed."

"What bothers me is the timing of the last abduction."

Steele frowned. "What do you mean?"

"Why now? Sanders gives himself up on Sunday. The press reports it on Monday. On Tuesday, Jessica Young is taken."

"You're thinking he's angry. Someone else is getting the credit for McNair."

Crowder nodded. "Makes sense. He goes to great lengths to leave not a trace of evidence behind and Sanders gives himself up on a silver platter. It's embarrassed him and he's angry."

"Mad enough to add another victim."

"And perhaps pissed off enough to make a statement with her."

"What do you mean?"

"The other two were beaten so badly and malnourished that after three days they almost died. Basically, he left them for dead."

"So you're thinking this time he might actually *leave her dead.*"

"It's the logical next step for a psychopath. The more deviant the acts become, the greater the thrill."

"A week to solve McNair, which means all three cases if your serial rapist theory is correct."

"Right. A week to solve the crimes … but much less to save that girl."

Chapter 10

The call from the evidence technician came to Crowder just after one o'clock while she was finishing her preliminary report on the Amy Stillman murder.

"A Ford transit van 2015 to 2018. The body configuration was identical all years. This one, a 2017 model, was the extended version with dual sliding-side-cargo doors. It's a popular model. What distinguished it were the accessories. Sixteen-inch steel rims and a running board."

"Registration?"

"Louisiana."

"Owner?"

"We only got a good look at two of the numbers on the license plate from a single shot on one of the recordings. We generated a computer algorithm to scan the registrations of all Ford transit cargo vans with the two numbers."

"And?"

"Four possibles, all white. But only one with the accessories. Is your computer on?"

"It's on."

"The registration information is on the way."

Crowder closed the screen with the report she'd been working on and opened the email with the vehicle and owner information: vehicle identification number WDD6GGG5GF137; tag and registration number C69539; owner, Ellis Samuel Weymouth d/b/a Weymouth Plumbing, 2624 Willow Road, Edgard, Louisiana 70049.

She opened the bottom drawer of her desk and took out her Smith & Wesson police-issued pistol and shoulder holster. It fit comfortably under her blazer.

So did the accessory she strapped on her right calf.

Steele drove while Crowder googled Weymouth Plumbing on her cell phone. "Same address as on the registration form," she said. "Self-employed tradesman. Good. Only one place to go."

"We're about thirty miles from Edgard," Steele said, bringing the directions up on the GPS.

"About the same from Baton Rouge," Crowder said. "Might explain why he's bouncing between the cities. Easy access to his victims. Hides them in a small town. I bet he lives alone in some isolated rural area outside Edgard. No houses close enough to hear calls for help or screams of little girls."

They made their way out to the interstate in one of the department's unmarked vehicles and exited, a half hour later, onto a two-lane road into Edgard. They drove the last mile through woods on a narrow shoulder-less road with sporadic asphalt and abundant potholes. Many of the numbers on the cottages' mailboxes had been painted on crooked, making them hard to read.

They parked about a hundred yards from their destination. Best to approach on foot. Before getting out Crowder reached for the thin metal coat hanger on the backseat. For Crowder, surprise was a hidden weapon. She was proceeding without a warrant. Getting one was futile. No judge would sign off on a warrant without a direct link between Weymouth and the victims. His van passing in front of the schools wasn't enough.

She didn't care.

She wasn't there to solve three crimes.

She was there to save one girl.

They moved quickly and stealthily along the road. The house soon came into view. The adhesive numbers 2624 on the mailbox were evenly spaced. A fresh coat of yellow paint on the one-story framed house glistened under the mid-afternoon sun, its neat, clean appearance out of place. The front window shades were down. A prefabricated metal shed sat alongside the house at the end of a loosely graveled driveway.

Weymouth's vehicle was parked in front of the shed. *Weymouth Plumbing—Your Plumbing Problems Are Our Plumbing Problems* was printed on the sides of the van. Crowder put a finger under one of the signs, confirming that it was magnetic and easily removable. The van doors were locked. Crowder unraveled the coat hanger, bent it into a V shape, slipped it into the bottom of the window just above the passenger-side door latch and worked it down until it engaged the latch. A gentle tug upwards released it, and the door unlocked.

Steele got in and unlocked the other doors. Crowder opened the sliding door and studied the contents of the cargo area while Steele checked under the front seat and in the glove compartment.

The cargo area was spotless. No tools. No snakes or plungers. No pipes or pipe fittings. No toilet flappers. Not a single plumbing supply. Only a small wooden crate with a half-full bottle of bleach, a scrub brush and a box of latex gloves.

"He's our man," Crowder said to Steele when they huddled up alongside the van. "It's spotless—his obsession to clean up after his messes. Let's take a look around the house. I'll take the front. You take the back."

Steele headed to the rear of the house while Crowder moved to the front door. She tried opening it.

Locked.

So were the front windows.

Steele came from around the side of the house. "Everything's locked. Shades pulled down tight except for the kitchen window. Doesn't look like anyone's home."

"Cover me from behind the van. If he tries to get away, he'll go to it."

"And you?"

"I'm going in to take a look."

"We need a warrant, Jo. Maybe the vehicle and the cleaning detergent will be enough."

"You know they aren't enough. Maybe, just maybe, I'll hear the girl scream. That's the probable cause I'll need to enter."

"You sure you don't want some company when you go in?"

"It's best you back me up on this, partner."

Steele moved to his position behind the van and drew his pistol.

Crowder still had the coat hanger in her hand. She needed it to release the lock on the front door. She heard the screams of a little girl—if only in her mind. Silent cries for help. Left no other choice, she entered.

The closed shades made it dusk-like inside, the only illumination being the daylight streaming through the kitchen window like a flashlight beam. The living room and dining area were clean and neat. On a white-linen cloth covering a table for four rested a single place setting and a crystal bowl filled with fresh fruit in the center. A glance inside the bedroom revealed a made queen-size bed—not a stitch of clothing in sight.

The kitchen was pristine. The canned goods in the cupboard sat neatly in rows, the labels turned forward, organized alphabetically by food group. A look in the refrigerator revealed a similar pattern. Not a morsel of leftover food. Not a single Tupperware. A clean, ironed, white, terry cloth dish towel hung from the handle of the oven.

Crowder paused when she reached an interior closed door in the kitchen. A thumping sound came from behind it. She cupped her ear against the door to better hear the pulsating vibration—like the beat of disco music.

A turn of the doorknob released the deadbolt. She opened the door a crack. A flash of light, then another … and another. Blinking flashes from a multicolored strobe light somewhere in the basement—a split second for her to see but not long enough to know what she was looking at.

The music beat louder as she opened the door wider—the eerie tempo reminiscent of the background sound of a horror movie. The strobe flashed on and off like an airport beacon. She reached for her fully-loaded Smith & Wesson, unlocked the safety, and pulled back the slide, loading the chamber. Then she slid through the half-opened door, closed it behind her, and slowly descended the staircase.

At the bottom she found a large room with wall dividers but no doors. The first section had the least amount of illumination. She felt the wall with her hands as she moved through the room. Her knee struck a bathtub. Next to it a thin garden hose and nozzle lay rolled up inside a sink. Moving along, she touched her way to the first opening.

The light shone brighter.

The music beat louder.

The room was smaller than the first one, and the greater illumination revealed shackles, rope nooses, whips, and hand

and leg cuffs dangling from hooks on one wall. Garments hung in a row on another wall. Crowder traced the design of the clothing with her fingertips; the first one felt like a skirt; above it, a blouse. The next a jumper; inside it, a shirt. The third garment similar to the first; the fourth similar to the second.

School uniforms.

She felt two more as she moved her way to the next opening.

She peered in.

A room much larger than the others. On the right, a box spring and mattress on a four-poster bed, rope restraints around each post.

She slowly entered the room, pistol raised.

To her left, a camera on a tripod.

In between, a cube-shaped cage against the far wall. Large enough to hold a good size animal—or a small child.

A chair—a recliner with its back to her—partially blocked Crowder's view inside the cage. On a table to the side of it sat a bong, a cloud of smoky vapor swirling above it. The sweet smell of cannabis permeated the air. She inched forward, pistol raised, barrel pointed at the back of the chair.

The music pulsated like the beat of "The Tell-Tale Heart." The lights flashed like flames from a bonfire in the woods on a dark, moonless night.

Within a few feet of the chair, Crowder saw over the back of it into the cage—a girl, kneeling, her arms folded tight across her chest.

Naked.

Whimpering like a sick animal.

Her eyes pleading for mercy.

Crowder took a deep breath and released it slowly. She moved a step to her left. And then another. Her last full stride placed her to the side of the chair, her gun pointed into it.

"Police, don't move," she yelled, her finger itching to pull the trigger.

The last thing Crowder saw before the bat struck her across the arm of her shooting hand was an empty chair. The blow, from behind, knocked her sideways to the floor and the gun from her hand. A second blow struck the floor inches from her head—a split second later, she rolled over, reached for his ankle and jerked it forward. The maneuver caused him to lose his balance. The bat fell to the floor, and he stumbled backwards into the shadows.

An adrenaline rush overcame the pain that radiated through her right arm and hand like a jolt of electricity. She felt for her gun. It was nowhere near her, but the bat was. She picked it up and moved away from the flickering glow of the strobe.

The light-flashes danced in harmony with the beat of the music; the girl's cries—"Help me; help me,"—eerily providing the lyrics.

Crowder knelt on the floor hunched over, staring into the darkness that enveloped the outer perimeter of the room.

Where is he? Does he have my gun?

He came out of the shadows and into the blinking light just enough for her to see the glistening metal of the barrel of her gun in his hand. Holding the bat close to her chest, she rolled over her shoulder into a kneeling position and swung the bat at the gun. She caught enough of the barrel to knock it from the hand that held it. The bat dropped to the floor and rolled away.

He retreated into the darkness.

Instinctively, she made a dash to the cage. The girl, her face frozen in terror, knelt by the door, her tiny fingertips protruding through the openings in the wire. Crowder fumbled with the latch until it released. When she pulled the gate open, the girl fell into her arms. With the girl's arms clenched around her neck, Crowder slid on her bottom into the darkness until she ended up in a corner of the room.

She whispered softly into the girl's ear. "Be quiet, very quiet, Jessica, while I put my jacket on you." As soon as the girl released her grip, Crowder removed her blazer and worked each of the girl's arms into the sleeves, then buttoned it. The girl wrapped her arms around Crowder's neck for dear life, and Crowder hugged her until she stopped shivering.

He was somewhere in the darkness—on the other side of the strobe light.

Then the music stopped.

The lights went out.

Nothing but silence.

And darkness.

She heard a click; a second later, a floodlight beamed in her face. The flash of light blinded her. She squinted to reduce the glare—to see what was in front of her.

The child's grip around her neck tightened.

When her vision regained its focus, Crowder saw him in the light for the first time.

Tall. Lean. Naked. Hairless.

The white mask of a mime covered his face.

Mannequin in appearance, he stood there completely still, left arm by his side, right arm and hand fully extended, the barrel of Crowder's gun pointed directly at her head.

Or was it pointed at the head of the little girl curled up in her arms?

He stood about twenty feet from her, just to the right of the light shining brightly in her face. From that distance, a headshot misses fifty percent of the time unless the shooter, like Crowder, was proficient in using it. He didn't have his own gun. Persons into sadomasochism seldom used firearms. They preferred torture over a bullet in the brain, a thousand cuts over a beheading, repeated floggings over a single fatal clubbing of the head. Their way of death was slow—breaking bones, one by one; whipping someone raw with a cat o' nine tails; starvation; dehydration; isolation and humiliation until the victim was stripped of the will to live.

Indecision was Crowder's worst enemy.

Don't wait ... act now.

She reached for the accessory she'd strapped to her calf before leaving district headquarters and gripped the pearl handle of her two-shot derringer—a safety feature she'd added to her weaponry after the last time she'd been shot—a bullet that almost killed her. She had no backup pistol then.

She had one now.

A shot from a derringer is designed for close-up targets. In the hands of a novice, it will miss a target more than twenty-five feet away nearly every time. In the hands of Crowder—a dead shot with most handguns—the chances increased substantially. But there were no guarantees. Not even when your life and the life of a little girl depended on it.

She calculated the probabilities like a computer analyzing data.

Light source about ten feet behind him to his right.

Room exit about ten feet behind him to his left.

He stood smack dab in between.

She tightened her grip around the girl with one hand and around the handle of her derringer with the other. In the blink of an eye, she shot out the light with her first pull of the trigger, and a millisecond later, with her second pull, she shot into the darkness where a man had been holding a gun with dead aim on her and the girl.

Crowder dropped the derringer, scrambled to her feet with

the girl clenched firmly in her arms, and darted in pitch black to where she thought the doorway should be. Shots rang out behind her as she made her way blindly through the rooms to the staircase.

Her foot struck the bottom step of the staircase, tumbling her forward as a bullet whizzed by. Breaking her fall with an outstretched hand, she quickly regained her balance and, with the girl clinging to her chest, climbed the steps to the top as another shot splintered the wood of the step just below. A turn of the knob and a push on the door and they were out. She slammed the door shut with the heel of her shoe, grabbed a kitchen chair with one of her hands, and jammed the back of it under the doorknob.

Steele darted into the kitchen pistol drawn.

"Are you all right?" he yelled.

She didn't waste words on an answer. Seeing he was headed for the door, she said, "Don't go down. He has my gun. He may have a shot or two left."

"I called for backup when I heard the shots," Steele said. "I'll watch the door."

"I want the girl out of the house," Crowder said. "She'll be with me in the car. I'll call for an ambulance."

Ten minutes later, two state-police patrol officers and two deputies from the local sheriff's office arrived at the scene. They entered the basement and found Weymouth's naked dead body on the floor five feet from the staircase, a hole in his chest from Crowder's second shot.

The girl left in an ambulance after a lot of prodding from the paramedics and some softly spoken assurances from Crowder to release her grip around her neck—it helped that she gave the girl her gold shield to hold in her hand.

The paramedic's examination of Jessica at the scene revealed that she was dehydrated but had no visible physical injuries. The ER physician who examined her afterwards found no evidence of rape. The child advocate assigned to the case reported that Jessica's captor had her remove her uniform and undergarments an hour before Crowder saved her, a sure sign he was soon to begin his ritual of physical and sexual abuse. The girl was discharged into the care of her parents after a child psychologist evaluated her for post-traumatic stress.

At no time did Jessica Young release her grip on Crowder's gold shield, and it remained in her hand when she left the hospital.

Crowder's weapons were retrieved from the scene and bagged as evidence. Crime scene investigators from the Louisiana State Police and the NOPD scoured the house for evidence. They found a total of seven school uniforms. The photographs Weymouth had taken documented who'd worn them and what had been done to them.

One set of photographs was of the girl abducted in Baton Rouge. Another set was of the McNair girl. The photos in the camera on the tripod were of Jessica Young in the early stage of her abduction. They found abundant other evidence proving that Weymouth was a serial rapist responsible for at least seven abductions, six rapes, and possibly the deaths of one or more of the girls in the photographs not yet identified. Only time would tell.

Crowder and Steele drove to the Louisiana State Police headquarters in Baton Rouge to give their statements and then headed back to district headquarters to await the internal affairs inquiry into violations of department regulations and protocols with respect to the detectives' warrantless searches, Crowder's forcible entry into Weymouth's home, and her use of deadly force in apprehending him.

Crowder knew she'd be brought up on charges when she used the coat hanger to open Weymouth's locked vehicle and door to his home. When she'd reached for her pistol and the accessory in her desk drawer, she knew she might have to face up to the consequences of her actions if she had to confront Weymouth and shoot him dead.

But Crowder never did anything half-way or half-ass.

Not with the life of a little girl on the line.

Not with the life of an innocent man hanging in the balance.

What she did may not have been the legal thing to do.

But, for Crowder, it was the right—and only—thing to do.

Chapter 11

Crowder's desk phone was ringing off the hook when she returned to district headquarters. Every crime-beat reporter wanted the scoop on Weymouth's apprehension—and his death—in the shootout at his home. She threw messages from earlier calls in the wastebasket, including Gardner's simply stated missive—*fuck you*—which brought a smile to her face that lasted until she saw O'Malley's note: *My office as soon as you return—alone.*

O'Malley was finishing up a phone call when Crowder entered his office. She knew the scowl on his face wasn't from a bad case of indigestion. He motioned for her to sit down in the chair in front of his desk. "That was Hellman," O'Malley said. "He wants you brought up on charges and placed on administrative leave pending your hearing. I told him it was up to the superintendent."

"And?"

"Don't know yet. He's at a budget hearing before the state legislature in Baton Rouge. I do know this—the mayor wants to give you a medal and name a public high school after you."

"I did what I had to do."

"But couldn't you have done it with a warrant?"

"Not enough time."

"Are you sure you didn't hear the girl screaming before you broke into the house?"

"Only in my head."

O'Malley sat back in his chair in a more relaxed position, the scowl gone. He began to chuckle. "I'd have paid good money to have been there when Hellman was told you tanked his slam-dunk case. He's got omelet all over his face, and you put it there. He'll want more than a pound of your flesh."

"Gardner too," Crowder said. "I had a love note from him on my desk when I got back."

"As far as I'm concerned, you and Weymouth saved the taxpayers a lot of money by shooting it out in the basement of his home. That was a hell of a shot in the dark you made. Why shoot out the light first?"

"To distract and disorient him. It took his mind off his aim just long enough for me to get off the second shot while the girl and I faded into the darkness."

"You'll need a weapon and a gold shield. I hear you made the young girl an honorary detective."

"She earned it," Crowder said as she stood to leave. "We still need to identify the girls in the other uniforms."

"I'll put Gardner on it as his penance for screwing up. I need you to concentrate on the Stillman murder. Hellman sees Attwell as the prime suspect."

"Right now Attwell's the only suspect, but rape is all we have on him. Turns out he was drinking most of Saturday night at a bar two blocks from his home. Murdering the girl? I'm not buying it. Whoever did it was smart, meticulous, had knowledge of anatomy, pharmacology, and wanted to make a statement by leaving the girl at the doorstep of a church. Attwell would have clubbed her over the head or strangled her and dumped her body in the bayou."

O'Malley opened a desk drawer and reached for a gold badge. "You'll be needing this," he said, tossing a gold shield to Crowder, who caught it with an outstretched hand. "I can't do anything about your weapons until internal affairs clears you in the Weymouth shooting." He opened another drawer, pulled out a pistol, and laid it on his desk. "Use mine until you get yours back."

Crowder stood to leave, grabbed the gun, and headed to the door.

As she holstered the pistol, O'Malley said, "Crowder, as far as I'm concerned, you're back on duty—no conditions but one."

"What's that?"

"Try hard not to shoot anyone."

Two officers from Internal Affairs interviewed Crowder and Steele separately. Both detectives took the position that getting search and arrest warrants would've resulted in a delay that jeopardized the girl's safety. Crowder took responsibility for making all decisions. So did Steele. The decision on whether to suspend or reprimand them for violations of departmental protocols would be made by the police superintendent after a review board hearing.

It was after six when the detectives left district headquarters and headed over to Benny's Sports Bar, a regular hangout for cops, lawyers and beat reporters.

Crowder followed a two-drink limit during the week, but tonight was different. Her daring rescue of Jessica Young was all over the evening news. Jessica's parents had been interviewed and publicly praised the New Orleans Police Department for its competency and Detective Crowder for her heroism.

The bar was abuzz with chatter and the rounds kept coming, every cop wanting to buy Crowder a drink. After her third beer, the shots started. She lost count.

She knew tomorrow would be a long, mostly unproductive day dealing with the effects of a hangover.

Chapter 12

The ringtone of the cellphone on her pillow blared into Crowder's ear like the horn of a passing freight train an hour before sunrise. She'd slept in the clothes she'd worn the day before; her bout of dizziness and nausea when she'd returned home after midnight had made the safest path one directly to her bed, where she'd lain frozen until she passed out.

Crowder reserved binge drinking for celebrating important collars and convictions—and for wrestling her conscience over having used lethal force to take out a perp. She remembered the three men she'd shot and killed every morning when she holstered her weapon before leaving for work. She lay with her head half off the edge of the bed, one arm dangling over the side, the other tightly holding a pillow like it was a life preserver. A single eye opened and fixed on O'Malley's gun on the bedside table, a reminder of the man she'd killed the day before.

Number four.

She felt the onset of a hangover headache—no doubt triggered by the sudden shrill sound of the ringtone and by Fred's barking. The dog had wisely chosen to sleep on the floor when Crowder stumbled into her bedroom and plopped down on the bed like a felled sequoia.

Findings of *reasonable and necessary* force by internal affairs and the police review board did little to erase the memories of having ended the lives of the men she'd killed. After her first kill—two shots into the heart of a drug dealer who chose to shoot it out with her instead of leaving the matter to his on-call lawyer to handle—she'd had a recurring dream in which she was deer hunting with her father and saw the face of the man she'd killed on the face of the buck she'd shot in her dream.

"It's normal to ruminate over taking someone's life even in self-defense," Crowder remembered the police psychologist telling her afterwards. "It will pass with time."

It didn't.

Not completely.

The other kills also shared a common nexus—men shooting at her or someone else. One had put a couple of bullets in the chest of her former partner; he'd have taken more if Crowder hadn't put a slug between the eyes of the shooter and saved his life. The other, a year before Weymouth became number four, cashed in his chips in a shootout with Crowder in an alley; Crowder took a slug in the leg before emptying her clip into the shooter's chest.

Crowder let the call go to voicemail. The ping that followed was most certainly a text from the caller. She rewarded the persistence by reaching for her phone and reading the text: *Call in immediately. O'Malley.*

O'Malley answered her call. "We have our number two. Holy Angels Catholic Church on North Monroe Street in the Lower Ninth Ward. Steele will meet you there."

The body of the young girl lay in the open arms of the statue of the Blessed Virgin Mary beneath a white sheet. The marble sculpture rested on a pedestal that bisected the two sets of doors at the entrance to the church.

It was Wednesday of Easter week. The church sign posted the cancellation of services for the day.

Crowder followed the same routine as before—reports from the first responders, inspection of the body, a statement from the city street cleaner who noticed a hand dangling beneath the sheet and called it in, and a meeting with the pastor of the church, who didn't know the girl.

The similarities between the two murders made it instantly apparent to Crowder that they were committed by the same person—a naked teenage girl, a St. Mary Magdalene medal around her neck, a sutured incision across her lower abdomen. Tell-tale signs of a recidivist.

Forensics once again came up empty.

The autopsy performed later in the day revealed almost identical findings—a pregnant young teen whose fetus and reproductive organs had been removed, with puncture marks on her thigh and neck, and trace evidence of propofol in her blood.

A police photo of the girl was on the local news stations and social media within a couple of hours and in the printed news the following morning. The girl's description—mid-teens, average height and weight, no tattoos or distinguishing marks—was unremarkable in all ways but one, a mane of striking bright-red, curly hair.

After leaving the scene, Crowder returned to district headquarters to wait for the call from Sessions with his autopsy findings. After they spoke, she called Sister Ann to arrange a meeting with her and Sister Agnes.

Crowder had a hunch.

Armed with the police photos of the girl, she showed up for a two o'clock meeting at the convent while Steele worked with missing persons to identify the murdered girl. She met the nuns in Sister Ann's office. The nuns examined the photos of the dead girl while Crowder studied their faces to see their reactions. The nuns looked at each other and made the sign of the cross, Sister Agnes whispering, "May she rest in peace."

Sister Agnes was the first to speak. "The name she gave was Brittany Connors, her hesitation in giving it suggesting she may have made it up. But we never pressure the girls who come see us."

"Did she come to the clinic because she was pregnant?" Crowder asked.

Sister Ann interrupted before the nun could answer. "Let me answer that question for Sister Agnes. That way she doesn't have to disclose confidential information in a patient's file."

"Thank you, Sister Ann," the nun said.

Sister Ann continued, "With some coaxing from Sister Agnes, the girl came to the convent after being seen at the clinic. The girl told me she was on the run, but when I asked her why she ran away from home she said, 'I didn't.' After that she wouldn't provide me with any more personal information."

"Any idea where she's from?"

"No, but she said she'd hitchhiked here."

"Did she tell you where she was staying in New Orleans?"

"I believe she was staying with the man who was managing her because she told me that she'd been working the streets the past seven months, and when she found out she was pregnant, she was afraid to tell her 'man'—a term the girls use to describe their pimps. That's why I believe she was willing to seek refuge at the convent."

"Why did she go to the clinic?"

"She went there seeking an abortion. When she was informed that they didn't perform them, she came here. She stayed two nights and left yesterday evening shortly after Monsignor Rossi met with her at the convent and counseled her."

Crowder's eyebrows lifted. "So the monsignor saw her yesterday. What time?"

"After dinner, around seven, in my office."

"And did the monsignor tell you what they discussed?"

"He left before I had a chance to speak to him."

"Did you see the girl after they met?"

"She was gone when I checked her room about an hour after the monsignor left."

"Does the monsignor normally counsel the girls who come to the convent for refuge?"

"Some. The minors, mostly. He counsels them to return home to their parents, or if they've fled an abusive environment, to a trusted relative or friend."

Crowder looked at Sister Agnes and asked, "Was the girl seen again at the clinic, after the first visit?"

"No. She was seen only the one time."

"Is there a medical file for the girl?"

"Everyone seen at the clinic must complete a health questionnaire and provide the usual personal information. Of course some are reluctant to give us their personal information, and we doubt the accuracy of much of it."

"Are all of the patients' medical files kept in the same location?"

"They're kept in cabinets in the office. The files are arranged alphabetically by patient name. The records aren't computerized. All information is either typed or handwritten on preprinted forms."

"I'll need the original files for the two girls. I'll be back with a subpoena tomorrow."

"I understand," Sister Agnes said. "I'll have them ready for you."

"Are there any pregnant girls currently staying at the convent, Sister Ann?"

"No."

"Good. Let's keep it that way for now. Send anyone who comes to the convent or clinic who's pregnant to a women's shelter operated by social services. There are several in the city."

"Yes, we're familiar with them," Sister Ann said.

"And I want you to lock away the files of any pregnant girls who come to the clinic. Only Sister Agnes and Dr. Latham should know that they were seen here. Agreed?"

"Agreed," the nuns said in unison. Crowder had successfully recruited two nuns to go undercover with her to catch a serial killer.

As Crowder stood to leave, Sister Ann asked, "Detective Crowder, are the girls and women staying at the convent in any danger?"

"I don't think so. Whoever is doing this is selecting his victims from a very narrow subset—pregnant young girls who've been seen at the clinic and sought refuge at the convent. If we cut off the supply source, we may have an end to the killings."

~

Crowder left the clinic and returned to district headquarters. When she arrived she found Steele sitting at his desk staring at his computer screen. A peek over his shoulder revealed that he was looking through the missing persons photos. "Any luck?"

"There are currently 330 missing persons in Louisiana. Mostly adults. This is my second look through, and we have no match. I'm having missing persons check the national databases."

"If they come up empty, try the juvenile detention centers. See if they have any runaways. I have a hunch the girl was on the lam. She hitchhiked here, so start with the ones in Lake Charles and Baton Rouge. She was street smart; she may have had a juvenile record."

Steele looked over at Crowder. "I got your message about returning to the convent. What's up?"

"We have our first lead."

Crowder briefed Steele on her meeting with the nuns who'd identified the murdered girl. "It's more than a coincidence that the girls were seen at the clinic and sought refuge at the convent only to suddenly take off without telling anyone."

"So you're thinking that the murderer had knowledge of the girls' circumstances and picked them out."

"That's the only logical explanation," Crowder said. "Those who knew the girls were pregnant include two nuns who were at the convent on the evening the girls went missing, and Dr. Latham and Attwell who were somewhere else when the first murder was committed."

"What about Father Julian?" Steele asked. "He's still a suspect. He knew about the girl's circumstances and lied about not knowing her."

"I know, but he can probably be excluded because the two murders are linked, and he wouldn't have been aware of the second girl's circumstances."

"So who are we looking for?"

The expression on Crowder's face darkened. "Someone who knew about the girls' pregnancies and where they were staying, someone who had contact with them shortly before they went missing, and someone who the girls would've trusted enough to leave the convent and meet up with."

So far only one person fit the description.

Chapter 13

On Friday morning Crowder placed a call to the archbishop's residence to arrange a meeting with Monsignor Rossi. The housekeeper informed her that the monsignor's official duties required him to accompany the archbishop to a conference of bishops being held in Baton Rouge that day and that his responsibilities for the balance of Easter week made a meeting before Monday impossible. Crowder didn't like the brushoff but agreed to a Monday meeting at Rossi's office at the archbishop's residence.

An hour later, O'Malley called Crowder into his office to discuss the status of the homicide investigations. After she summarized the common findings that proved both victims were murdered by the same person, the true purpose of the briefing became apparent.

"Why is it so important to involve the archbishop's personal assistant in the investigation?" O'Malley asked.

"Rossi's the last one to have had contact with both victims," Crowder said.

"Do you honestly believe the monsignor's a suspect?"

"That's what I'll find out when I meet him on Monday. Too

much connects him to those girls. The girls left the convent without a place to go. Why would they do that? Makes no sense unless someone they trusted asked them to leave."

"That would make the monsignor a monster. Do you know anything about him—about his relationship to Archbishop Santini?"

"It wouldn't be the first time a priest committed crimes of violence against young girls—or boys."

O'Malley was aware of the scandals that embroiled many Catholic dioceses in litigation over pedophilic abuse by parish priests. The financial settlements bankrupted some dioceses and resulted in the closing of churches and parochial schools.

"As sad as it is that clergy abuse occurred here and elsewhere, murdering pregnant teenage girls, aborting their fetuses and removing their reproductive organs is the work of a deranged psychopath with a grudge against the church, not one of its brightest superstars."

"I haven't excluded it being a defrocked priest, a psycho-seminarian, or some religious fanatic nutcase out to show God's wrath over adolescent promiscuity. It's partly the reason I want to pick the monsignor's mind."

"Tread very carefully. The archbishop's relationship with the monsignor is unique. Rossi was abandoned by his mother as an infant. Santini became his guardian. Sent him to live with his family in Rome. They are one of the wealthiest, most-influential families in Italy. Rossi was the pope's personal secretary before becoming the archbishop's second in command."

"Are you saying I shouldn't meet with Rossi?"

"I'm saying that the archbishop told the superintendent that the monsignor knows nothing that could be of value in the investigation. He had a telephone conversation with one of the victims and a meeting with the other. In both instances, he merely counseled them to return to their homes and have their babies. The superintendent is satisfied, and so am I."

Crowder pivoted to another part of her plan. "I want to have patrol officers in plainclothes in unmarked cars staking out the Catholic churches in the city for the balance of Easter week. It's a long shot, but one of them might see something suspicious— like our murderer leaving another body at a church."

"There are more than thirty Catholic churches in the city. You're proposing stakeouts for tonight and tomorrow. Do the math. The overtime will take us into next year's budget."

"We really have no choice," Crowder protested. "These murders are symbolic. The killer chose Easter week to prey on pregnant girls and leave their dead bodies at churches in the city. We might not be able to stop him, but we might be able to catch him."

O'Malley removed his glasses and massaged the sides of his head with his fingers. "All right. You can have your stakeouts," he said, his sigh audible to Crowder. "Has the second girl been identified?"

"We're working on it," Crowder said as she left O'Malley's office, content with having gone one for two with O'Malley on the mound.

At least, for now.

~

"Her name is Beverly Calloway," Steele said, his eyes fixed on his computer screen. "She walked away from the Townsend Juvenile Detention Center in Shreveport seven months ago. They knew it was her as soon as I described her curly red hair. They sent a photo."

Crowder picked up the crime-scene photos on Steele's desk

and compared them to the photo on his computer screen.

"Parents been notified?"

"The mother's in drug rehab; the father's doing time for armed robbery. The social worker said there's an aunt who'll claim the body."

"The girl really never had a chance," Crowder said, pinning one of her photos to a cork board next to one of Amy Stillman, the common denominators being dead-looking faces and St. Mary Magdalene medals.

The cork board had a poster pinned to it with the dates the girls were abducted and the locations of the churches where they were found. Arrows connected the common paths they took prior to their abductions. For Amy, the arrows went from a church to the convent, to the clinic, to the convent, to a church; for Beverly, the arrows went from the clinic, to the convent, to a church. Crowder picked up a felt-tipped marker and wrote in the name *Rossi* between the words *to the convent* and *to a church* for each victim.

Steele, seeing this, said, "It's a stretch, Jo. The archbishop's right-hand man? What motive could he possibly have?"

"I'll know better when I finally get to meet him and see if he can account for his whereabouts when the girls went missing."

"Did Cap authorize the stakeouts?"

"He had no choice. We have no leads. All we can do is wait and watch the churches."

~

Crowder conducted her briefing of the stake-out officers in the lecture hall at the police academy—sixty-eight cops in civilian clothes in pairs of two assigned to the thirty-four Catholic churches in the city. She instructed them to park their vehicles a block away from the churches, to seek the cover of night on foot, and to wait until the body was out of the killer's vehicle before making the arrest.

Friday night passed uneventfully—the usual reports of shots fired, petty thefts, and night-walking working girls and drug dealers transacting business on the corners of streets in the high-crime neighborhoods.

Crowder felt apprehensive about Saturday night—the killer's last chance to close Easter week with another symbolic expression of murder and mutilation. Choosing to spend the night at her desk, she sat there, reflecting on the cold, calculated nature of her plan. Baiting the killer into a trap at the expense of one more victim—some scared, pregnant teen offered in sacrifice—for the greater good.

Deployment to scenes where hostages had been taken came to mind. SWAT team marksmen surrounding the building at the ready when negotiations broke down, instructed to shoot to kill if a clear shot presented—even at the risk of a less-than-mortal injury and the death of a hostage as retribution. A miss invariably meant that the SWAT team would storm the building, guns blazing, risking the lives of hostages caught up in the crossfire.

Calculated risks.

Collateral damage.

Acceptable losses.

The bottom line—another girl's life would be lost if her plan was to work.

A simple matter of life … and death.

Catnapping her way into Saturday morning, her intuition told her that the call would come before sunrise—the business of a vampire was conducted in the still black of night before the dagger-like rays of a rising sun appeared above the horizon.

The clock on her computer screen read 6:20 a.m. She walked to the window to witness the breaking of dawn. Twenty minutes later the shadows of twilight evaporated into the brilliance of an Easter Sunday sunrise. Thirty-four Catholic churches would soon be bustling with parishioners celebrating the resurrection of God's only son—the congregants' prayers, psalms, and joyous hymns resounding like echoes in a canyon.

Would another white sheet be found at one of them?

Daylight broke in pin-drop silence. No reports of suspicious activity. No one seemed interested in leaving a dead pregnant teen at the doorstep of a church to close out Easter week in style.

Crowder's feelings were in conflict: disappointment that a killer wasn't caught; relief that another girl wasn't killed.

The conflict would soon resolve itself.

O'Malley's text came at 7:26 a.m.: *Number three is lying in front of the archbishop's residence.*

Chapter 14

The archbishop's residence was a large antebellum Georgian brick mansion in the most fashionable neighborhood of New Orleans. On the historical register of Louisiana landmarks, it sat on two lushly landscaped acres, a jewel in a precinct of expensive homes of the state's most prominent professionals and business owners. The three-story rectangular structure was perfectly symmetrical to the naked eye: large, evenly spaced windows on each side of an imposing arched colonnade; chimneys jutting out of the four corners of a pitched roofline, and a cupola-enclosed widow's walk located dead center. Aged neatly trimmed sycamores stood sentry along the property line. A circular driveway worked its way around the front of the house, and a garage and gardener's cottage nestled behind it, hidden from view. A backstreet alley provided access to them.

The private estate had been bequeathed to the diocese by its last resident—a wealthy oil baron whose only son chose the priesthood over the family business and celibacy over heirs to the family's fortune.

The usual responders to homicide scenes were busy at work when Crowder arrived. Crime scene investigators combed the grounds, looking for a footprint, a dropped glove, a discarded piece of chewing gum, a piece of fabric caught on a thorny hedge—anything left behind that might be dusted for a print or tested for DNA.

The signature white sheet covered the victim.

Steele stood beside the body, talking to Travis Jones and a patrol officer. Crowder joined them. The officer told Crowder that he'd responded to the 911 call and that the archbishop and monsignor were kneeling beside the body praying when he got there.

"Who found the body?" Crowder asked.

"The monsignor," the officer replied. "He found her when he showed up shortly before seven. He didn't remove the sheet. He didn't want to disturb the scene."

"And the archbishop. What did he have to say?"

"Only that he was unaware of the body until the monsignor arrived to take him to St. Stephan's to perform Easter services. They went outside to pray for the girl after the monsignor called it in."

"Are they inside?"

"No. They left a few minutes after I arrived."

Crowder's brow furrowed. "You let them leave the scene before a homicide detective could talk to them?"

"I didn't. I told them to wait inside and to make arrangements to be here when you arrived. About five minutes later, the superintendent called me and told me to let them go and that you could get their statements later."

Crowder was seriously pissed off. Witnesses' minds are best picked when fresh. This was the second time Rossi avoided being questioned. Had he been there, she could have asked him to look at the girl while she was still at the scene. She would've pulled off the sheet so he could see her pale, blue-tinted skin—

the color of death—and the sutured incision—the doorway the killer entered to do his post-mortem mutilation. She'd have watched his face and studied any changes in his expression.

Perhaps he'd look shocked and turn his head away after only a fleeting glance at the body—the compassionate reaction of an innocent man. Perhaps he'd look woeful and act priestly by saying an immediate prayer—the dutiful act of a cleric preparing a soul for the afterlife. Or perhaps he'd have the stone-cold look of someone who'd seen the girl before—the unemotional, detached response of a psychopath who'd laid the mutilated body at the doorstep of his boss's home.

Now decorum would limit her to showing Rossi photographs of only the dead girl's face.

Or would it?

Screw decorum.

"Travis, make sure you get a couple of glossies showing the girl from head to toe to me as soon as possible."

"Sure, Jo. You'll have them in a couple of hours."

"Time of death?"

"Around midnight based on her rectal temperature."

"Just like the others."

"A creature of habit," Steele said.

"Not really," Crowder said.

"Why not?"

"He went to Plan B and decided not to leave the body at another church even though we went clandestine on the stakeouts and no one but us knew anything about the surveillance."

"Almost like he knew we were watching the churches."

"Precisely," Crowder said as she walked to the front door and pressed the doorbell several times. No one answered.

"Was the bishop alone last night?" she asked, shooting a glance at the patrol officer.

"Don't know," he replied. "Like I said, the two of them left in a rush in the monsignor's vehicle."

"There's a lot we don't know. Sid, let's take a look around the property."

The two detectives worked their way around the back of the house, peering in windows on the first floor. The garage doors at the rear of the house were closed and the exterior shutters of the cottage windows latched shut.

Steele quelled Crowder's temptation to unlatch a shutter and take a look inside when he said, "I know what you're thinking, Jo."

"Maybe, for another day," she said as they walked out the rear driveway that led to a narrow, mostly tree-lined, alleyway. She looked to her left and right. There were no houses for a full block in either direction.

The detectives proceeded around the house to the front, passing nicely gardened areas, a couple of fountains, and several large statues of religious figures. Their gazing into the first floor windows revealed opulent furnishings, Persian carpets on polished hardwood floors, sculptures on pedestals, and artwork hanging on heavily crown-molded, wood-paneled walls.

When they returned to the front of the house, Crowder said, "Odd, don't you think?"

"What?"

"Only the archbishop appears to have been home last night. There must be a staff—a housekeeper, cook, maybe a gardener—taking care of the mansion and the archbishop. Yet the killer chose his house on a day the archbishop was home alone."

"I see what you mean. Just like he knew not to leave the girl's body at a church; he knew it would be safe to leave her at the archbishop's home."

"Right. And who was the person most likely to know the

archbishop would be alone?"

Steele didn't need to name him. "But he wouldn't have known about the surveillance."

"We can't exclude the possibility that he did," she said as she walked to her pickup truck and headed back to district headquarters.

~

The crime scene photos of the dead girl were on her desk by noon. While Steele checked out the dead girl's identity, Crowder met with Sister Ann and Sister Agnes and showed them a head shot photo of the girl's face. They'd never seen her before.

Steele called her cell phone while she was driving back to district headquarters. "Bingo," he said as soon as his partner answered. "A girl fitting the description of the victim went missing last night. The parents came down around midnight to file a report. They left a school photo of the girl. It's her."

"Let me have the parents' names and address. I'll head over there now."

"Carlos and Angela López. 2712 Piper Street. Their daughter's name is Angelica. They call her Angel."

Crowder arrived at the Lopezes' home in the city's Latino district at two o'clock. The modest two-story row home was well kept: the exterior appeared freshly painted; geraniums and begonias in full bloom cascaded over two first-floor window boxes. She parked on the street a half block from the house and walked to the front door.

Notifying family members of the death of a loved one was especially difficult when the victim was a child subjected to a senseless act of violence. Seeing no doorbell, she opened the screen door and knocked several times. The door opened just enough for a child to peek from behind it. Her wavy dark hair, sweetly intense brown eyes and round face matched the victim's features—only a half-dozen years younger.

"Who's call-ing?" she asked in a soft, sing-song voice.

"I'm a police officer. Are your parents home?"

The girl's face lit up like a struck match. "Have you found my sister?" she asked excitedly.

Just then a middle-aged man appeared behind the girl and opened the door wide. His saggy face and weary eyes had the tired look of someone who'd stayed up all night worrying about how he was going to pay his mortgage, car loan, and credit-card debt after losing his job—or someone whose teenage daughter had suddenly gone missing. "I'm Angelica's father, have you found our daughter?" he asked, his tone more of a plea.

"I'm Jo Crowder, a detective with the New Orleans Police Department. Can we talk privately—you and Angelica's mother?"

"Of course, come in. My wife, she's in the kitchen."

Following the man in, Crowder watched him direct his younger daughter to a room where a television played a children's movie.

"Stay here, Rosa … until we come for you," he said, his tone solemn like he was about to get some very bad news.

Mrs. Lopez was sitting at the kitchen table staring at a framed photo of a young girl. It lay beside a full cup of coffee, a box of tissues next to it, several balled up in a hand.

Crowder recognized the face of a distraught mother. She'd seen it before—the face of someone who'd spent most of the day crying.

"Bad news is best delivered the right way," O'Malley had told Crowder when she became a detective and joined the homicide division, "which means right away."

115

Crowder always followed his advice.

"I'll bring you coffee," the woman offered tiredly, slowly rising from her chair.

"No, please don't get up, Mrs. Lopez. I'm here to speak to both of you about your daughter."

The husband pulled a chair away from the table for Crowder and then sat in a chair next to his wife.

When the woman sat down, Crowder delivered the news. "A girl meeting your daughter's description was found this morning." She paused only long enough for Mr. Lopez to reach for his wife's hands now folded on the table. "The girl was the victim of a homicide," she continued. "I'm so sorry to have to tell you that the girl was your daughter."

Mrs. Lopez buried her face into her husband's shoulder and sobbed while saying things in Spanish. Crowder didn't need a Spanish to English translator to know the outpourings of a mother's anguish. Mr. Lopez held his wife in his arms and spoke to her in a soft, comforting tone.

When the woman got her crying under control and again sat upright in her chair, Mr. Lopez, speaking in English, asked, "Who do this to our Angel?"

"We believe it's the same person who was responsible for the deaths of the two girls found at Catholic churches in the city this week."

"This monster, what did he do to her?"

Rather than go into the gruesome details, Crowder chose a safer course—one that would avoid a total emotional collapse by Mrs. Lopez and allow the detective to get information about her daughter in the hours preceding her abduction. "We'll know more when Angelica is examined by the chief medical examiner."

"W-when, when will we be able to see her?" Mr. Lopez stuttered, almost in a whisper.

"Soon. Someone from social services will meet you at the medical examiner's office after Angelica has been examined." Crowder avoided the word autopsy and the grim reality that it involved cutting open their daughter and removing more of her internal organs.

Crowder wrote down the Lopezes' contact information in a small notepad she carried in the pocket of her blazer and then moved on with the interview. "When did you last see Angelica?"

"Last night, after dinner," Mr. Lopez answered. "She say she going to a movie with a friend, Miguel, Miguel Diaz."

"Did you see her leave with him?"

The Lopezes exchanged glances, shaking their heads in the negative. "We finish our dinner here in the kitchen," he explained. "She get up from the table and leave in a rush. She say she not want to be late. We hear the door shut when she leave."

"Tell me about Miguel Diaz."

Her crying having abated, Mrs. Lopez now spoke: "Miguel, he live two blocks from here. He grow up in the neighborhood, just like Angel. We know his parents. He like a big brother to Angel. They see each other a lot. But not like boyfriend and girlfriend. He twenty. She only sixteen." Mrs. Lopez spoke until she was too choked up to continue.

Crowder jotted down notes.

Mr. Lopez picked up on the narrative. "Angel say that Miguel have her home by ten-thirty. When she not home by eleven, we call her. But she not answer. We call Miguel's mother who say Miguel take Angel to a movie, but he not back yet. We wait some more, and she not back by midnight. That's when we go to police station and say she not come home."

Crowder figured that Angelica, like the others, was pregnant and that the parents were unaware of it. Looking at Mrs. Lopez, she asked, "Was Angelica sexually active?"

"I tell her, 'You wait until you older.' She turn sixteen just last week. She not go out on dates except when Miguel take her out. She a good student in school, and she stay out of trouble, my Angel."

"Does your daughter have her own room?"

"*Si*, since she was twelve. Before, she share a room with Rosa, her sister."

"It may help us in our investigation if I could see your daughter's room and perhaps go through her things, if that's all right with you."

"*Si*," Mr. Lopez said. "If it help find who do this to her."

Mrs. Lopez began to tear up. Continuing the interview would be unnecessarily painful for her. Crowder would return later to look through the girl's room—for clues that might lead to her killer. For now, she'd leave the Lopezes to mourn the loss of one daughter, to tell another daughter that her sister was dead, and to plan a funeral.

PART TWO

The Suspect

Chapter 15

A surprise visit on Easter Sunday was a good tactic—especially when the persons you're calling on are the parents of a person of interest. Miguel Diaz's home was a short walk from where Angelica Lopez had lived. On her way, Crowder's mind sifted through what she knew about Angelica's actions in the hours before her abduction: Diaz was supposed to have dropped her off at her home around ten-thirty; if he'd driven away before she was in her house, Angelica's murderer would've had only a few seconds to stick a syringe full of propofol in her neck and drag her to his vehicle; but if anything suspicious was going on—an unfamiliar vehicle parked on the street; a stranger lurking on the sidewalk—Diaz would surely have waited until she was safely inside her home.

The puzzle pieces didn't fit.

Mrs. Diaz, a stout, soft-spoken woman with a thick Spanish accent, answered the door and informed Crowder that her son wasn't home. "Is it about Angel?" she asked, a worried expression on her face.

"Yes, ma'am. May I come in and speak to you and your husband?"

"Hector, he not home. He help at the soup kitchen on Sundays. He be back soon. Come in. We wait for him."

The woman led Crowder into a room that served as both a den and dining room. A sofa, two dissimilar armchairs, and an unpolished coffee table formed a horseshoe around a big-screen television set on a table. A small dining-room table sat in close proximity to it. That there were only three chairs around the table suggested to Crowder that Miguel was an only child.

Crowder accepted an offer of a glass of iced tea, and the two engaged in mostly small talk during the ten minutes that passed before Mr. Diaz arrived home. She did learn that Miguel's older brother was in a nursing home—the innocent victim of a stray bullet in a shootout between rival gangs five years earlier. It explained why the fourth dining-room chair had been placed against a wall.

After she introduced herself to Mr. Diaz, Crowder got to the point of her visit. "I understand that your son took Angelica to a movie last night."

Mrs. Diaz did the speaking. "*Si*. Miguel and Angel, they friends for a long time."

"When did you last see Miguel?"

"Last night. He leave the house around seven."

"And the last time you saw Angelica?"

"Good Friday. She come over to see Miguel in the afternoon. She stay for a while, and then she go home. Miguel, he have dinner with us, and then he go to library to study."

"What library?"

"At the college he go to. He study to be a nurse."

Nursing student. The killer had a good knowledge of anatomy and pharmaceuticals. A data point Crowder stored away.

"When did Miguel come home last night?"

Mr. Diaz spoke for the first time. "We both in bed before

124

he come home," he said. "We not see him until we come home from Easter mass."

"What time was that?"

"Around ten-thirty. He was in kitchen drinking coffee. He leave right after that."

"Why didn't he go to church service with you?"

"Miguel lose his faith when his brother ..." the father said, abruptly pausing and lowering his head before proceeding, "was shot and hurt real bad. He blame God for what happen to Roberto. He angry for a long time."

"Does your son own a car?"

"*Si*. He buy it himself. He save for it."

"So he's working while going to school."

"*Si*. He works as a nurse."

"At a hospital or doctor's office?"

"A clinic."

"Which clinic?"

"St. Joseph's Clinic."

A person of interest was now a prime suspect.

~

Crowder returned to district headquarters late in the afternoon. She'd called Steele on her way over, gave him an update on her interviews, and asked him to run a background check on Miguel Diaz. Steele was at his desk on his computer when she arrived.

"Anything?" Crowder asked, handing her partner one of the two coffees she'd brought.

"Clean," Steele said, replacing the chewed-on stirrer in his mouth with a new one. "Not even a traffic violation. No juvenile record."

"Did Sessions send over his autopsy findings?"

"Travis faxed them over an hour ago." Steele handed a single sheet of paper to Crowder, who read it, making mental notes of the important findings—a ten-centimeter sutured abdominal incision, reproductive organs absent, fetus removed, puncture marks right femoral artery and left jugular vein, trace propofol in blood.

"Forensics?"

"Nothing to link Diaz to the girl's abduction."

"But enough to bring him in for questioning. He had the means, the opportunity, and, if the baby was his, a motive."

"When do you want to pick him up?"

"It's Easter Sunday," Crowder said. "He'll know soon enough that he's a suspect because he was the last one to have seen her alive. I asked his parents to have him come in tomorrow morning at eight. They told me he doesn't have to be at work until ten and has a class to attend Monday evening. He'll show."

"Any chance he'll be active tonight?" Steele asked.

"I don't think so. He'll know we're watching him."

"How's that?"

"I have a black and white parked in front of his house with a description of his car. He'll either take off when he sees it or know to stay put tonight. Attempting to flee would be another strike against him."

"Let's call it a night," Steele said. "Jenny's cooking Easter dinner so we're staying in." Jenny was Steele's significant other and live in, a relationship that began in earnest a year ago. "What about you?"

"I'm headed over to Tom's."

Steele got up, reached over to turn off his computer, and grabbed his jacket from the back of his chair. "Jo," he said.

"What, Sid?"

"If Diaz doesn't have an alibi for last night, he could be in a whole lot of trouble."

~

After dinner at Tom's townhouse, Crowder and her brother retired to the living room with their glasses and what remained of a second bottle of Merlot. Jenny had insisted on finishing up in the kitchen, so the siblings saw it as an opportunity to talk shop.

"Any word from the review board?" Tom asked while refilling his sister's glass.

"No. But Hellman wants my head on a pike."

"You know, if you'd told them you heard the girl screaming, everyone would have looked the other way."

"I gave it some serious thought. But once you go down that path, it's hard to go back."

"Hellman's labeled you a rogue cop."

"That's me, all right—Dirty Harriet."

"He's in the minority. Most of the prosecutors and every defense attorney I've had contact with this week wants to put a medal around your neck."

"I'm not looking for that. But I don't know what I'd do if they put me behind a desk. Catching bad guys is what I do."

"It's in your blood—just like Dad," Tom said. "When he retired from the state police and was elected sheriff, he was out of his office more than in it, working the investigations on the streets with his deputies."

"But he was by the book, Tom. He would've handled it differently."

"I'm not so sure. He just might've kicked in the door, gun in hand."

"Or he may have followed the rule of law and gotten a

warrant."

"And what? Go back and find the girl beaten and violated? No, he'd have done what you did and, like you, owned up to it. He'd have been proud of what you did." Tom reached for his sister's hand and looked into her eyes. "Just as I'm proud of what you did."

Crowder squeezed her brother's hand to show her appreciation. Inwardly she agonized over the consequences she faced if the review board followed the book and she was booted out of the homicide division and given a desk job. She compartmentalized her anxiety and moved to another subject. "We have a suspect in the serial murders."

"Who?"

"Miguel Diaz. Turns twenty-one next month. A third-year nursing student who wants to be a doctor. He'd know how to do what was done to those girls. The Lopez girl was fifteen when she got pregnant. They were friends. If a DNA match shows him to be the father, he could have been prosecuted for statutory rape."

"How is he linked to the other murders?"

"He worked at the clinic where the first two victims were seen. Had access to their medical files. He would've known they'd be staying at the convent."

"Does he have an alibi?"

"I'll know tomorrow morning."

A desk sergeant led Miguel Diaz into an interrogation room—a sterile uncomfortable place with windowless walls and an obvious two-way mirror on one of them. The chair in which Diaz was told to sit faced it.

Once in the purposefully intimidating room, many suspects accepted the reality that they'd been caught and, after being Mirandized, remained silent except to ask for a lawyer. The innocent ones cooperated and spoke freely in responding to questions. The boldly skeptical ones, sensing entrapment, demanded to be arrested or released. A small number, after being confronted with evidence of their crimes, accepted their fate and confessed.

Crowder wanted to know where Diaz fell in the spectrum. Before entering the room, the two detectives peered through the two-way mirror, studying their prime suspect in what the local press and cable news stations had labeled the *Easter Murders*. Steele, recorder in hand, walked into the room first and sat in one of two empty chairs on the side of the table opposite Diaz.

Crowder, speaking as she followed him in, took the other. "Mr. Diaz, I'm Detective Crowder and this is Detective Steele." She nodded her head slightly in Steele's direction. "Did your parents explain why we asked you to come down and give us a statement?" Crowder waited for an answer. It didn't come. "It's about Angelica Lopez," she said, breaking the silence. "Do you mind if we record your statement?"

More silence.

Steele turned on the recorder.

Crowder put the usual preliminary information on the recording—date, time, place and person to be interviewed—and then said, "Mr. Diaz, we've asked you to come here today to answer questions about your relationship with Angelica Lopez and your involvement with her yesterday. Are you willing to answer our questions?"

Crowder studied Diaz's facial expression and demeanor. He looked at the mirror on the wall behind the detectives, his hands folded on the table. He didn't appear frightened, nervous

129

or agitated.

A few moments later, he asked, "Is that a two-way mirror?"

Crowder had had suspects ask that question before. She'd always been honest in answering it. "Yes. It helps us monitor the conduct of witnesses and suspects, and of police officers like Detective Steele and me when we're asking questions."

"Does that mean you consider me a suspect in Angel's death?"

"You are a person of interest. According to Angelica's parents and your parents, you took her to a movie last night and may have been the last person to have been with her before she was abducted."

"And, if I was, does that make me a suspect?"

"If you can explain your whereabouts last night and Sunday morning, and we can verify what you tell us, you'll not be a suspect—only a witness who's assisting the police in their investigation into your friend's death. But I must caution you about agreeing to answer our questions."

Crowder then proceeded to give Diaz his Miranda warnings, watching his facial expression and body movement as she gave each one.

He didn't grimace.

He didn't furrow his brow.

He didn't flinch.

He very calmly said, "I have nothing to tell you and would like to leave now."

Crowder didn't have enough on Diaz to arrest him. Being the last person known to have seen the murdered girl alive wasn't enough to arrest him. But it was enough to get a search warrant.

That would be her next step.

Diaz was hiding something.

She intended to find out what.

Chapter 16

When Diaz left district headquarters, Crowder asked her partner to work with an assistant district attorney to obtain a search warrant for Diaz's room at his parents' home and his car, while she headed over to the clinic to speak to Dr. Latham and Sister Agnes. So as not to arouse Diaz's suspicion, they agreed to meet at the convent at two. They gathered in Sister Ann's office.

After explaining the circumstances of her visit, Crowder was blunt. "Miguel Diaz was with the girl the evening she was abducted." Looking at Latham, she asked, "How extensive is his knowledge of medicine and drugs?"

"He's been working at the clinic since it opened a little more than a year ago," he said. "He was already a licensed practical nurse and entering his final year of nursing school. Hiring him accomplished two goals. He could help us treat patients and he could satisfy his clinical nursing requirements."

"Do you do surgical procedures at the clinic?"

"Nothing that requires general anesthesia. Only minor procedures. We might drain a cyst, biopsy something suspicious, suture a wound and occasionally remove a bullet."

"Do you stock propofol?"

"We use it for conscious sedation when doing endoscopic procedures. My specialty training was in anesthesiology. So I'm allowed to administer it."

"Where's it kept?"

"In our medicine cabinet in the supply room."

"Is it locked?"

"Only when the clinic is closed. It's left open during the day."

"I suppose you and the staff have immediate access to syringes, suture materials, IV lines, things like that."

"We're stocked much like an urgent-care center but without diagnostic radiology equipment. We send our patients to the hospital for diagnostic tests and inpatient care."

"So who works there other than you, Sister Agnes and Miguel Diaz?"

"I have two colleagues who share duties with me and two part-time nurses. But, basically, it's been the three of us, and a receptionist who's also our typist."

"Do all of you have equal access to the medical files?"

"Of course. The patient's chart is brought into the examining room for all new and returning patients."

"Who does Miguel see at the clinic?"

"All patients, male and female, unless the woman is here for a gynecological examination. Sister Agnes and I do those."

"I suppose Diaz is proficient in drawing blood and injecting drugs."

"Of course. He's studying to be a surgical nurse. He wants to be a physician someday. It wouldn't surprise me if he succeeds. He's quite intelligent. He reads a lot—medical journals I've given him."

"Is he seeing someone—a girlfriend?"

Latham chuckled. "Miguel? He's way too busy with his studies and work at the clinic. He's at the top of his class in nursing school, may end up being valedictorian. He also cleans the examination and treatment rooms, and sterilizes the equipment after the clinic closes. He's paid a stipend from the diocese. The monsignor made sure it was generous enough to take care of his living expenses while he's in school."

"Does he have a key to the clinic?"

"No," Sister Agnes replied. "But I leave the key with him when the clinic closes. He drops it off at the convent when he finishes cleaning up."

"Who else has keys?"

"Doctor Latham ... and the archdiocese, of course."

"Does the monsignor come to the clinic often?"

"Yes, quite frequently. He and the archbishop come to the convent to look in on the Reverend Mother, who is elderly and disabled from a stroke. When they do, he usually stops in and looks at the files."

"Why does he do that?"

"He reviews the drug overdoses, gunshot wounds and stabbings," the nun explained, "as well as the non-accidental children's injuries to be sure they've been reported to the state police as required by law."

Latham abruptly chimed in. "You don't honestly believe that Miguel had anything to do with the deaths of those girls. I would find that hard to believe."

Unlike Latham, Crowder wouldn't be the least bit surprised if Diaz killed those girls. He was quite capable of sticking a syringe in a girl's jugular vein and a needle in her femoral artery, cut her open, remove a fetus and reproductive organs, sew her back up, and drop her dead naked body at the doorsteps of churches and the archbishop's home.

Things aren't always as they appear to be.

Plenty of killers had appeared to family, friends, neighbors and co-workers to be kind, friendly, law-abiding citizens—until they weren't: the seemingly happily-married man with the pretty wife and honor-roll kids who hired a hit man to kill the missus for the insurance proceeds that subsidized his failing business and new life with his secretary; the Dean's List college athlete, on full scholarship, who binged out on raping and strangling coeds; the sweet old landlady whose boarders mysteriously went missing until their poisoned, decomposed bodies were discovered in her basement.

The list goes on … and on.

The Ted Bundys of this world can fool a lot of people for a long time.

By all outward appearances, Miguel Diaz was a normal young man, who'd never been in trouble with the law—a devoted son, an excellent student, a skilled nurse caring for homeless people, drug addicts, crime victims, and the myriad outcasts and misfits who inhabited the poor neighborhoods of a crime-ridden city. Yet his father could see that he'd changed. He'd lost his faith in God and religion, in the Catholic Church that was so much a part of his family's life—but not his, not since God sent a bullet into his brother's brain, turning it into cauliflower. His father had told Crowder it made his son angry—anger that could easily have grown like a malignancy until it killed off his soul.

It all fit. Miguel Diaz selected victims one and two on the days they were seen at the clinic. He'd have had access to their files and known that they were staying at the convent. The third victim he'd known for many years. They hung out together. She trusted him—enough to allow the adult male friend with whom she was infatuated to impregnate her. By then, experienced in murdering and mutilating teenage girls, Angelica Lopez was a no-brainer for Diaz. He could have killed the first two to make the Lopez girl look like another randomly selected victim of a serial killer—his cover for a diabolical plan to execute her all along. The little bitch wasn't going to ruin his life—a statutory rape conviction would effectively end his career goals and life as he knew it. It's hard to complete nursing school, and give a valedictory speech, from the state penitentiary.

When Crowder's reflections ended, she answered Latham: "That's what we're trying to find out." She switched to another subject. "What about security? Is there an alarm system at the clinic?"

"Yes," Sister Agnes replied. "The archbishop insisted on one after we had several break-ins—street addicts hoping to find narcotics."

"Who has the codes to the alarm?"

"I do, Doctor Latham, Miguel, and, of course, the archdiocese."

"Does Miguel have a place at the clinic where he puts his personal things?"

"The nurses and physicians all have lockers in a room at the rear of the building. We keep our personal items in them," the nun explained.

"Are they locked?"

Sister Agnes looked surprised. "We've never felt a need to lock them."

"Are names on the lockers?"

"Yes. The names are on strips of adhesive tape on the front of the lockers."

The urge to walk over to the clinic and take a look in Diaz's locker was short lived. She knew that his workplace space was just as private as the bedroom at his parents' home and required a warrant to search. She'd be back tomorrow with one.

Although Crowder had a bona-fide suspect in Diaz, she was solving a puzzle and was looking for puzzle pieces. Interviewing Rossi and the archbishop might provide some. But would she get the chance?

She'd soon find out.

～

O'Malley's text came while she was on her way over to the archbishop's residence to speak with the clerics, a meeting that had been scheduled for three in the afternoon. It read: *I hear you have a suspect. We'll talk more when you brief me here at 3 p.m. Don't be late.* When Crowder called the archbishop's home to see if the meeting was still on, the archbishop's housekeeper told her that "a meeting was no longer necessary."

Another brush off.

Once back at district headquarters, Crowder stopped at Steele's desk and learned from him that his efforts in obtaining the search warrant had forewarned O'Malley that Diaz was a prime suspect.

The timing of her meeting with O'Malley was more than coincidence.

"Tell me about Diaz," O'Malley asked when she entered his office.

Hellman occupied one of the chairs in front of O'Malley's desk. The scowl on the district attorney's face telegraphed his resentment toward her.

Crowder chose a wall to lean against. "A twenty-year-old nursing student doing his clinical training at a clinic in the Lower Ninth Ward. He had access to the girls' medical files. May have gotten the third girl pregnant. Has a grudge against God and the church."

"What kind of grudge?" Hellman asked, giving Crowder a cold-eye stare.

"Older brother he looked up to got caught up in rival gangs' crossfire five years back. A bullet in the head turned him into a Cabbage Patch doll. He's been institutionalized ever since."

"How old was Lopez?" Hellman asked.

"Fifteen when she got pregnant."

"We'll add a statutory rape charge to the murder charges," Hellman said with the excitement of someone who'd just won a ticket to the Super Bowl.

"Where did he take the girls?" O'Malley asked.

"Don't know," Crowder said. "He owns a vehicle which opens up the possibilities. The clinic is one possibility. He had access to the key. He could have made a copy of it, or simply left the back door open. He had the passcode to the alarm system. The fifteen hours the clinic is closed between six in the evening and nine the next morning was more than enough time for him to abduct the girls, take them to the clinic, do what he did, and clean up afterwards."

O'Malley moved forward in his chair. "I hear he clammed up when you questioned him."

"The guilty ones always do, or ask for a lawyer," Hellman said.

"We still need some hard evidence linking him to the girls' abductions," Crowder said. "Tomorrow we'll take a look in his bedroom, vehicle and locker at work."

"This time I see you've taken the time to get a warrant," Hellman said smugly.

Crowder didn't dignify Hellman's sarcasm with a response.

Chapter 17

A meeting with the clerics was put on the back burner while the search warrant was being executed. Crowder and Steele, with copies of the warrant in hand, showed up unexpectedly at Diaz's home at seven in the morning. Diaz was still home, which meant that his car could also be searched at the same time.

Steele and a CSI technician searched Diaz's car, a six-year-old sports utility vehicle, for prints, blood, fibers, hair and anything else that suggested the victims had been in it.

Crowder spent her time searching Diaz's room. She found medical textbooks, including ones on anatomy and surgery, and another on pharmaceuticals—a quick scan of the index at the back revealed that it included the drug propofol. In a textbook on general surgery, she looked at the table of contents, then eyeballed the chapter *Gynecological Procedures and Surgeries. Page 206.* Flipping to the page, she found a subchapter on Cesarean sections. Subheading topics included preoperative evaluation, abdominal preparation and skin incision. One photo showed Crowder something she'd seen only three times before—a ten-centimeter horizontal incision located in the lower abdomen just above the pubic bone.

An anatomical model of a head with a skull that opened to reveal the lobes of the brain sat on the dresser. Posters of male and female bodies hung on each side of the closet door showing the internal organs and the arterial and nervous systems.

An evidence technician had followed Crowder into the room and photographed objects of importance—the physiology charts and relevant information in the journals and texts. Seizing the items was unnecessary because possession of the material didn't necessarily inculpate Diaz in any crime.

What Crowder found in a desk drawer was different.

She took a black, zippered carrying case out of the drawer and opened it. A booklet and CD lay on top of a block of spongy material with pre-made cuts of various shapes and sizes. The front page of the booklet and the label on the compact disc described the contents as a suture practice kit. According to the booklet, the suture pad was "designed to replicate the anatomical structure of the three layers of human tissue: skin, fat and muscle, and provide the best simulation of human tissue possible." Tools included forceps, retractors, surgical blades, serrated scissors, and suture thread. Crowder bagged the kit as potential evidence. The instruments would be tested later for blood and DNA. The suture material would be compared to what was used to close the victims' incisions.

One piece of evidence sat in plain view—on a desk beside a laptop computer.

A photo.

A boy with his arm around a girl.

The boy—Miguel Diaz.

The girl—Angelica Lopez.

The photo did nothing more than confirm the suspect and victim's affection for each other—a well-known fact. It didn't prove that Diaz planted the seed in the womb of a then-fifteen-year-old girl. But Crowder knew that in Hellman's hands the photo would be used to paint a picture in the jurors' minds that Diaz, an adult man, took advantage of an impressionable underage girl and "got her into trouble," and then killed her to "get himself out of trouble."

Crowder did a quick analysis of the case against Diaz. The circumstantial evidence and absence of a verifiable alibi were enough for an indictment, but not enough for a conviction. An experienced criminal-defense lawyer could easily shred the state's case—cutting away at each and every thorny issue, like wielding a machete and hacking through a hedgerow of rose bushes. What was lacking, and fatal to a successful prosecution of Diaz, was a piece of evidence directly linking him to the abductions and murders.

Crowder met up with Steele outside Diaz's home. "Anything in his SUV?" she asked.

"No blood or sperm. Some prints on the interior and exterior door handles, console and glove compartment. Several strands of hair were found on the front seat carpet. We'll get the DNA and compare it to the victims."

"The Lopez girl was known to have been in Diaz's car, so a match to her isn't necessarily incriminating," Crowder said. "But a match with one of the other girls would be hard evidence of abduction. Let's head over to the clinic and take a look in Diaz's locker before he gets to work."

The detectives arrived at the clinic with a CSI technician before it opened. Sister Agnes led them to a room at the rear of the clinic where eight metal lockers lined up against a wall.

Crowder went to the third one from the left—the one with

DIAZ taped on it.

The CSI technician took photos of Diaz's locker before the detectives inspected the contents. Two gender-neutral tunics hung on hooks; a pair of clean rubber-soled slip-ons lay at the bottom of the locker.

Typical nurses garb.

Crowder pulled out the tunics and checked the pockets. Nothing in the first one. But in the second, she felt something round and metallic through her latex gloves—a coin perhaps; maybe a dime. She also felt a thin chain. She pinched the chain with her fingers and lifted the item out.

What she saw, she and Steele had seen three times before.

Around the necks of three naked girls—all very much dead.

The item was photographed and bagged as evidence.

On the top shelf of the locker sat a nurse's bag and a small toiletries travel case. Crowder inventoried the contents of the nurse's bag: stethoscope, thermometers, blood pressure cuff, pencil light, tape for wrapping sprained ankles, a couple of rolls of sterile gauze, boxes of Band-Aids of varying sizes, a roll of medical adhesive tape, a packaged IV line, scissors and several bottles of over-the-counter medications and ointments.

Nothing out of the ordinary.

Next, the toiletries travel case. Crowder opened it, revealing the usual items. She placed them on the table: travel-size can of shaving cream, two disposable razor blades, toothbrush in a plastic holder, small tube of toothpaste, deodorant, mouthwash, hairbrush ... cell phone.

"Strange he'd leave his cell phone in his travel case," Crowder said, picking it up and looking at it more closely. She pulled out her notepad and thumbed through it until she got to the information she needed.

That piqued Steele's interest. "What's up, Jo?"

"I'll know in a minute."

Using her cell phone, Crowder dialed a telephone number she'd written in her notepad. She put her phone on speaker so that Steele could hear the ringing of the number she'd called, then held the cell phone from Diaz's travel case in one hand and hers in the other. Steele and Crowder's eyes locked on Diaz's phone. When the number Crowder called rang, the ringtone on Diaz's phone remained silent. After four rings, they heard a click on Crowder's cell phone and a voicemail message came on: "You've reached Miguel Diaz. Please leave a message."

Crowder hung up.

She wasn't finished.

Once again, she made reference to her notes—this time locating those from her interviews of Angelica Lopez's parents. She dialed the cell phone number she'd jotted down. When the number Crowder called rang, the phone from Diaz's travel case began to ring. After the fourth ring, they heard a click, and a voicemail message came on. Crowder didn't recognize the voice, but she knew who was speaking. It was the pleasant, sweet-sounding voice of a young girl who said, "This is Angel, I can't take your call right now. Please leave a message and I'll call you back in a flash."

"State's trial exhibit number one," Steele said.

Crowder handed the phone to the technician who placed it in an evidence bag.

The cell phone was the first solid piece of evidence linking Diaz to Angelica Lopez's murder. She had her cell phone with her the evening she was abducted. Her parents had tried calling it, and she hadn't answered. Crowder now knew why.

Crowder still wasn't finished.

She pulled a pencil light from a pocket of her blazer and picked up the hairbrush. Diaz had close-cropped black hair.

But when she shined the light on the brush, several clusters of long strands of hair appeared to be caught up in the bristles. She moved the light back and forth, and gently tugged at the strands, detaching a few, then walked to the window. As a brilliant morning sun shone through, Steele looked over his partner's shoulder at the strands of hair.

What they saw in the beams of sunlight were strands of bright-red, curly hair.

The arrest warrant was issued by one o'clock while Miguel Diaz was being detained at district headquarters. They had enough evidence to bring Diaz in for questioning and hold him until a magistrate could sign off on the arrest warrant.

Crowder gave Diaz the opportunity to give a statement and explain how Angelica Lopez's phone ended up in his possession. She didn't mention the strands of red hair found on his brush, knowing that it was best not to show her hand until the strands could be matched with those of the red-headed victim, Beverly Calloway.

Didn't matter.

He refused to speak to her and insisted on having a lawyer. "The guilty ones always do," she remembered Hellman telling her. But Crowder knew that regardless of guilt or innocence, a suspect in a capital murder case should never give a statement without his lawyer present and only with the advice of counsel, which universally was to shut your mouth and let your lawyer do the talking.

Diaz was arrested at district headquarters, booked and placed in a holding cell. By four o'clock in the afternoon, he stood before a magistrate and, with an assistant public defender by his side, was officially charged with one count of first-degree murder in the death of Angelica Lopez. At Hellman's urging, bail was set at half-a-million dollars, effectively keeping the suspect behind bars until his case came to trial.

Later, when Hellman had a better understanding of the hard evidence—and if the DNA of the hair matched the other victims—Diaz would be charged in connection with all three murders, with an additional count of statutory rape of the Lopez girl thrown in for good measure. With Hellman heading the prosecution team, one thing was certain—the case would move to trial at breakneck speed.

Back at headquarters, Crowder briefed O'Malley on what the searches had uncovered. By then, O'Malley had been informed of the findings of the review board, and of the Superintendent's decision with respect to the internal affairs investigation of Crowder's conduct in the Weymouth shooting.

"Good news," O'Malley said. "Technical violations of department regulations for searching Weymouth's car and entering his house without a warrant, but the only discipline recommended for you was a written warning. Steele got off with a verbal. The review board found that the perp's MO placed the girl in imminent danger, requiring the decisive action you took to rescue her. Your use of lethal force against Weymouth was entirely justified."

"And how is Hellman taking all of this?"

"Not well. He sent a written directive to the superintendent demanding that he take decisive action and boot you out of the homicide division."

"And?"

"Already talked to Sullivan. He intends to adopt the findings and recommendations of the review board … as is."

O'Malley opened a drawer, reached for Crowder's weapons

and placed them on the desk beside a gold shield. "Take off tomorrow. You've earned it."

"Can't," she said, returning O'Malley's gun and gold shield to him. "I'm waiting for the DNA results on the hair samples."

"Did we get the fetal blood analysis back on the Lopez girl? If Diaz is the father, we'll have an airtight case against him for murder and rape."

"Hellman had Gardner take care of it."

Chapter 18

The twelve-feet long by ten-feet wide attorney's room with the whitewashed, windowless walls and uncovered overhead fluorescent light had the number four inscribed above the steel door. The door's small reinforced glass window was the only visual connection between the room and the guard who stood sentry outside.

The room where an attorney met with an incarcerated client at the Hole was spacious compared to the noticeably smaller cell where Diaz was imprisoned pending trial.

Diaz sat in one of four pedestal chairs equally spaced around a small rectangular-shaped metal table that, like the chairs, was anchored to the floor. The bolting down of the furniture was considered a necessary upgrade by the warden when, for the fourth time in a month less than a year ago, a prisoner, unhappy with the services defense counsel was providing, or just plain fed up with a criminal justice system he felt was stacked against him, took out his frustration on his attorney by upending a table and bludgeoning him with the chair on which he'd been sitting.

Andrew Schulman, a public defender who specialized in capital murder cases, sat across from Diaz. Schulman was a card-carrying member of the ACLU—American Civil Liberties Union—and a longtime board member of LACP, the acronym for Lawyers Against Capital Punishment. With twenty-two capital murder trials in his eighteen years of public service, he'd won only two acquittals. Success, however, was not only measured by not-guilty verdicts, it was also measured by lives saved. Fifteen of his clients who stood trial for capital murder were either allowed to plead guilty with life sentences, or were found guilty of a lesser degree of murder or manslaughter, and so spared the lethal injection—wins by anyone's standard.

Capital punishment exacted a toll on even the most experienced, battle-tested criminal defense lawyer, and Schulman was no exception. Five times he'd stood beside his client in court and heard a judge impose a sentence of "death by lethal injection," but only once had Schulman's client been strapped on a black-padded gurney in the execution chamber at the state penitentiary. There, his client, convicted of beating his pregnant wife to death with a baseball bat, had been euthanized like a broken-down horse—after being injected with a cocktail of paralytic drugs that coursed through a vein to his brain until he flatlined.

For Schulman, one execution in his lifetime was enough.

Unfortunately, four other clients, their appeals exhausted, still awaited a date with the executioner. The holdup was a federal court-ordered stay of execution of the seventy defendants who sat on death row in the Louisiana state penitentiary while a lawsuit challenging the state's protocols and procedures for lethal injections snaked its way through the appellate courts.

Seated at one end of the table was a former FBI agent who spent his retirement years giving polygraph tests to criminal defendants, company employees suspected of embezzlement and government workers seeking top-secret security clearances.

Even though the consensus among experts was that properly administered polygraph tests were more than ninety percent accurate in showing whether someone was lying or telling the truth, the courts had uniformly ruled that such tests were inadmissible at criminal trials.

But Schulman had other reasons for having Diaz submit to the test.

Rarely did a client of his admit to him that he'd committed a murder. They either flat-out denied it or gave some bullshit explanation or excuse: I wasn't there; the other guy did the shooting; I killed him in self-defense. He'd heard them all. Only after the weight of forensic evidence, like fingerprints or DNA, came to light, or a jailhouse snitch turned state's evidence, did his clients fess up to what they'd done—universally, to avoid a date with Doctor Death.

Offering the polygraph to Diaz was a way of getting the attention of a prosecutor if the results showed his client had no involvement in the murders. Unless the prosecutor was a hard ass interested only in racking up convictions, it raised enough doubt to reopen an investigation or allow for a negotiated plea to a lesser charge. When Diaz told Schulman he had no involvement in any of the murders and was willing to take a polygraph test, Schulman had a good feeling that his client might be telling the truth. It was worth the gamble. No one would know if the results were unfavorable.

The examiner made final adjustments to the equipment to which he'd hooked Diaz—a blood pressure cuff, a pulse oximeter, and a chest monitoring strap.

"Is your name Miguel Diaz?" he asked without looking at Diaz, his eyes fixed on a computer screen.

"Yes," he replied. Diaz couldn't see the computer screen that recorded changes in pulse, blood pressure and respiration, and would tell the examiner whether he was lying or telling the truth.

Schulman could see the screen from where he sat and was familiar enough with the equipment to know when the polygraph recorded an increase in blood pressure, a quick pulse, and shallow breathing—all signs that a person could be lying. But whether the changes were significant enough to show untruths was often too subtle for him to discern, and ultimately were for a skilled examiner to determine, not an untrained lawyer.

"Do you live in New Orleans, Louisiana?"

"Yes."

"Are you legally married to anyone?"

"No."

"Are you studying to be a lawyer?"

"No."

"Are you studying to be a nurse?"

"Yes."

The examiner asked questions, knowing the answers and seeing the subject's bodily reactions to answering questions truthfully with a straightforward yes or no.

"Do you know Angelica Lopez?"

"Yes."

"Have you ever kissed Angelica Lopez?"

"Yes."

"Have you ever had sexual intercourse with Angelica Lopez?"

Schulman's eyes fixed on the screen, which so far registered no noticeable changes in his client's vital signs.

"No."

The lines on the screen didn't noticeably move. *Good.*

"Did you see Angelica Lopez the Saturday before Easter of this year?"

"Yes."

"Did you take Angelica Lopez to see a movie the Saturday

149

night before Easter of this year?"

"Yes."

"Did you take her to her home after the movie?"

"Yes."

"Were you at your parents' home between the hours of midnight and six o'clock the next morning—Easter Sunday?"

"Yes."

"Did you kill Angelica Lopez?"

"No."

"Do you know who killed Angelica Lopez?"

"No."

"Have you ever killed anyone?"

"No."

The examiner tapped the computer keyboard several times and said, "You can relax, Mr. Diaz. The test is over."

As was customary, Schulman never asked the examiner for his preliminary findings while his client was still in the room. Diaz was returned to his cell, and Schulman left the prison with the examiner. Once the two were in his car, Schulman said, "Well?"

"He's telling the truth. He didn't kill that girl or anyone else."

"What about having had sexual intercourse with her?"

"Nope. He's kissed her for sure. And he admitted that, but sexual intercourse—no way."

"So he was entirely truthful throughout?"

"Not exactly. He was being untruthful when he said he took the girl to the movies and returned her home afterwards."

"Strange," Schulman muttered. "So he saw her Saturday but was either with her somewhere else, or only saw her for a short time, and she was on her own after that."

"And he wasn't at his parents' home when the girl was

abducted and murdered. He lied when he said he was."

"So he was likely with someone else who could potentially be his alibi." Schulman was perplexed by his client's lack of candor. Why did he make up the story about being with the Lopez girl Saturday evening? Why didn't he tell him who he was with on the night she was killed?

He was hiding something.

Schulman intended to find out what.

Chapter 19

Crowder didn't take O'Malley's advice about taking the day off and showed up at her desk the next morning to close out a manslaughter case—a battered wife who'd put a carving knife between her husband's shoulder blades after he'd beaten her for the umpteenth time. For the last time, she thumbed through the crime scene photos that showed the bloodied husband lying on his stomach in bed in his boxers, the knife still in his back.

The bastard had it coming.

The wife's story had been that she couldn't take it any longer. The abuse had begun on their honeymoon ten years earlier when he'd slapped her around for "looking like a whore" after she'd dressed for dinner. She'd never met his first two wives. Wished she had. Both were the objects of his misogyny but were smart enough to divorce him before he caused permanent injury. The third one wasn't so lucky. After two concussions, a fractured humerus, several broken ribs, and a decade of bruises too numerous to count, she finally mustered the strength of will to fight back.

Crowder flipped through the photos of the woman taken on the day of her arrest—a black eye swollen shut, bruises on her face from a barrage of blows, and a split lip. What the photos didn't show was the internal abdominal bleeding from being repeatedly kicked in the stomach.

She'd argued hard with Hellman for an involuntary manslaughter charge; he'd wanted a murder charge and a life sentence. He relented, but only because Crowder testified at the preliminary hearing that the woman was so physically, mentally and emotionally traumatized that it appeared she'd acted in self-defense. The woman's lawyer knew then that a murder conviction was unlikely. So did Hellman, particularly after Crowder located wives one and two who were prepared to testify about their ex-husband's brutality during the course of unhappy marriages.

She knew Hellman wouldn't soon forget the slight.

It made him look bad. After all, he was the hard-ass prosecutor whose take-no-prisoners view of criminal law was to exact extreme justice whenever possible, irrespective of the circumstances. Now, the woman would be allowed to plead to involuntary manslaughter and be given a sentence of five to ten, and a likely early parole date.

A call from the forensic analyst who'd arranged for the DNA analysis of the hair from the brush found in Diaz's locker interrupted Crowder's reflections about the case.

"The red strands are from victim number two, Beverly Calloway," he said.

"And?" Crowder asked, sensing there was more to follow.

"There were also strands of hair matching the other two victims."

"What about Diaz?"

"It's strange. No other person's hair was found on the bristles."

"What about prints on the handle?"

"Clean."

"And the medal?"

"Same."

"Lopez's cell phone?"

"Only the girl's prints."

Careful to wear gloves, but careless to leave evidence of his crimes in an unsecured locker where he worked.

"What about the suture practice kit?"

"No blood. Only prints and DNA found were his. The suture thread was thicker than what was used on the victims."

The facts were forcing Crowder to fit square pegs in round holes. Suddenly, she felt uneasy about the direct evidence that linked Diaz to the three murders. Only the murderer would be in possession of the Lopez girl's cell phone. Only the murderer would have brushed the hair of the victims, perhaps to keep the strands of hair as mementos of the special occasions. Psychopaths were known to keep something that belonged to their victims— like the stuffed head of the buck the hunter kills and hangs over the fireplace at his cabin in the woods.

Still, it was stupid for Diaz not to remove the evidence from his locker right after she'd spoken to him at district headquarters Monday morning when he'd become a person of interest. And out of character—psychopaths who are serial killers are careful to a fault, which is why they can kill over and over again before being caught, or not caught at all. Up until then, he'd planned every detail to perfection: nabbed the girls without being seen; immobilized them with a syringe full of propofol delivered with precision into the jugular vein; bled them like a Kosher butcher; removed body parts like a battlefield surgeon, and disposed of the bodies under the cover of darkness, leaving not a single clue behind.

Stupid and out of character.

Steele showed up at Crowder's desk with two coffees in hand

just as the call ended. "The report's on its way over to Hellman," he said, handing a coffee to her and sitting in the chair in front of her desk. He propped his feet up on the edge of her desk, blew on his coffee, and took a sip.

"I know. I just got briefed. The hair on the brush links Diaz to all three victims, and his possession of the cell phone seals the deal for the Lopez girl's murder."

"Hellman will be doing cartwheels."

"Yeah. Things are falling in place. The fact that we found the evidence at the clinic raises the likelihood that he did his dirty work there. Since it's a sterile environment and Diaz was responsible for cleaning the place, it'd be unlikely that forensics would find any blood evidence there.

"All very reasonable and logical to conclude, Jo."

"Almost too reasonable and logical."

"How can something be too logical and reasonable?"

"Think outside the box. Why would Diaz be careful in not leaving his prints on the medal, cell phone and hairbrush but leave the incriminating evidence at the clinic among his personal things for the police to find?"

"'Most criminals will make mistakes that lead to their arrest if they continue to commit similar crimes with similar MOs'— do you know who told me that? You."

"I know, but these weren't mistakes—they were colossal blunders well beneath the competence of a skilled psychopath who'd committed complex crimes without leaving a trace of evidence behind. All he had to do was toss the items in the trash. Yet he risked everything by keeping them where they could be found. Something else …"

"What?"

"Because there are no prints, there's no direct link between Diaz and these pieces of evidence other than being found among his things at the clinic. What if these items were found in Dr. Latham's locker? Diaz, wearing gloves, could easily have put them there to implicate someone else."

Steele suddenly followed Crowder's outside-the-box thinking. "Someone, the actual killer, could have planted the evidence in Diaz's locker."

"Precisely," Crowder said. Her mind was analyzing the facts from more than one perspective, which was why she'd solved so many cases that in the hands of other detectives would've ended up as unsolved, cold cases, or, far worse, convictions of someone innocent. "Like what happened in the Westbrook case."

Veronica Westbrook, a sociopath, murdered her wealthy identical twin sister and assumed her identity, stealing millions from her. She'd then staged her sister's suicide by fabricating and planting evidence that logically and reasonably led the victim's family and the police to believe that she'd died from self-inflicted carbon monoxide poisoning—a story that Crowder proved false.

"You're right, Jo. That case had death by suicide written all over it until you figured out that all wasn't as it appeared to be."

"Right. Everything about the case was too logical and reasonable to accept unless you asked yourself this simple question, 'Could someone have planted the evidence?'"

~

Hellman sat back in his chair after finishing up the forensics report on the evidence found in Diaz's locker, then Gardner showed up with another report in his hand.

He sat down, reached over and placed the report on the desk in front of Hellman. "Bad news," he said. "The fetal blood is A positive."

"So."

"The blood types of Diaz and the Lopez girl are O positive. According to the report, it's impossible for both parents to be of the same blood type and produce a child with a different blood type."

"Damn it. I'd have bet your next year's salary that Diaz was the father. Who else knows about the report?"

"No one. The lab sent it directly to me. It was faxed over ten minutes ago. I came right over."

"Good. Let's keep it that way."

"So what should we do?"

"Call the lab and tell them you've been told the blood sample we sent them was tainted. Do it over the phone. Nothing in writing. Request a letter from the lab confirming that fetal-blood testing cannot accurately identify the DNA of a father when the blood sample has been contaminated. Make sure they put our case file number on the letter."

"And the report?"

"The only thing from the lab I want to see in our case file is the letter.

"Diaz's lawyer is entitled to have evidence that's exculpatory," Gardner said, smiling crookedly at Hellman.

"If there's no report from the lab in the file, only a letter saying the test can't be done, there's no exculpatory evidence to produce."

"Diaz's lawyer will think the Lopez girl's blood sample was contaminated and couldn't be tested."

"And I'll still be able to argue that Diaz's relationship with the girl was intimate, as the photo of the girl and him that was found in his room suggests. She didn't date boys. The only person she ever went out with was Diaz. Who else could have gotten her pregnant?"

"Diaz will have to take the stand and deny paternity."

"Precisely. And when he does, I'll destroy him on cross examination if he has no alibi for the evenings the girls were abducted and killed. His parents didn't see him in his room. So they can't swear he was home on the nights of the murders."

"What about Crowder?"

"What about her?"

"She's still the chief investigator on the case. What if she digs behind the letter we get from the lab and finds out about the report?

"She won't be working the case much longer."

"You'll need a reason. O'Malley won't agree to it."

"He'll have no choice."

Chapter 20

"We have some decisions to make, Miguel," Schulman said to his client who sat in the same chair in the same attorney's room where he'd been polygraphed.

"I passed the test like I said I would," Diaz said before Schulman could give him the results.

"On all the important questions, your answers were truthful. You had nothing to do with the murders, and you aren't the father of Angelica Lopez's baby."

"So why am I still here?"

"Like I told you before, the results of a polygraph test, irrespective of whether a person is lying or telling the truth, are inadmissible at criminal trials."

"So why did I take the test?"

"I now know that, if necessary, I can put you on the stand at trial and let the jury hear your side of the case. It will depend on what evidence the state has that links you to Angelica's murder. Right now, all they have is your parents and Angelica's parents' statements that the two of you went to a movie Saturday night which I know is a lie."

"What do you mean? We saw a movie at a theater at the

mall. It was over around ten o'clock. I dropped her off at her house fifteen, maybe twenty minutes later. I was supposed to meet up with someone at the Havana Club on Jackson Street. I was there until midnight. She didn't show. I went home and was in bed by twelve-thirty."

"According to the polygraph, you weren't with Angelica at a movie Saturday night."

"He must have made a mistake," Diaz said defensively.

"Did anyone see you and Angelica together at the movie?"

"We didn't see anyone we knew, so no."

"What about at the Havana Club."

"It was crowded. I sat at the bar by myself."

"What about on the other two nights? The first girl was abducted the Saturday before Palm Sunday, and on Tuesday, the second girl was taken. Where were you on the nights those girls were murdered?"

"Same place I've been going the past month and a half— the library at the nursing school I'm attending. Southeastern Louisiana University in Hammond, which is about an hour from New Orleans."

"Can anyone verify that?"

"Not really. I study alone. I graduate next month and will be taking my nursing boards in June. I'm studying for them. I'm usually there until the library closes at eleven. I'm not home until after midnight."

"I checked the inventory of what was taken from you when you were arrested and booked. I didn't see a cell phone among your personal items."

"I threw it out the night before I was arrested."

"Why did you do that?"

"It'd fallen out of my pocket and I accidentally ran over it with my car."

"So far, Miguel, you have no one to corroborate where you were on the nights the girls were murdered and your cell phone conveniently comes up missing. So your whereabouts and voicemail messages can't be determined from your phone."

"It is what it is."

"You're an intelligent young man. Did you know that the police can get your cell phone records, track your calls, and get the substance of your text messages?"

Diaz remained silent. Schulman could see his client's brow furrow and his eyes squint as though he had just been given some very bad news.

"I'll need to see your billing statement. You can tell me who you called and who called you during Easter week. It's best I know what the state will soon find out."

"What happens next?" Diaz asked.

"Your preliminary hearing is next Tuesday. Max Hellman, the district attorney, is personally prosecuting your case. Not a good sign. He only takes cases he believes are easy convictions. But at least we'll know after the hearing whether there's enough evidence against you to go to trial."

~

O'Malley had set the briefing on the investigation of the *Easter Murders* for ten o'clock Friday morning. Crowder handed her report to him. He leaned back in his chair and flipped through the twenty-two-page document, only occasionally stopping to scan its contents. She and Steele took seats in chairs in front of his desk.

"Cliffs Notes version," O'Malley said, looking at Crowder, who then summarized the important evidence. When she finished, O'Malley said, "So it looks like you'll be ready for the preliminary hearing next Tuesday."

"Why the rush?" Crowder asked. "We still don't have the results of the fetal blood test. Maybe the baby wasn't Diaz's."

"That's no longer an issue. The test couldn't be done. The blood sample was contaminated."

"But if he wasn't the father, someone else had a motive to kill the girl."

"There's no way Diaz isn't connected to all three killings. He had the Lopez girl's cell phone and hairs from the victims on his brush. That's more than enough evidence to convict him. He even had the same religious medal he'd put around the dead girls' necks in the pocket of his nursing scrubs. The identical MO means that if Diaz is connected to any one of the murders, he's connected to all of them. It all fits."

"It all fits because of what was found in his locker. It fits too perfectly. If you take that evidence away, and Diaz had no motive to kill those girls, you have no case.

"Are you suggesting someone planted the evidence?"

"Diaz's prints weren't found on the medal, the brush or the cell phone, but they were all over the other toiletries in his travel bag. And none of his hair was found on the bristles of the brush. What better way for the actual murderer to steer the investigation away from himself?"

"And just who might this person be in the dime-store crime story you're writing?"

Crowder was determined to keep the investigation open to other possible suspects, and she had one person in mind. She'd inserted his name on the poster board on the wall by her desk before Diaz became a person of interest.

"Someone who had access to the same information Diaz had, access to the clinic where the girls were probably taken and murdered—someone who knew that Diaz had a locker at the clinic where evidence could be planted."

"Careful, Crowder," O'Malley warned. "Right now we have a solid case against a prime suspect. Hellman wants to move the case to trial next month. You're already on his shit list. Don't sabotage his case at the preliminary hearing with unwarranted suspicions."

"Who's been assigned the case?"

"Allen. Having the most seniority on the court, he decided to take the case himself. So behave yourself."

Crowder returned to her desk to find Steele in a chair with his feet propped up on it, strumming an imaginary guitar. "The kid must have ditched his cell phone," Steele said. "It wasn't on him when he was booked. I called it this morning and the call wouldn't go through."

"Did you get his billing statement and text messages?" she asked.

"The subpoena was served on his service provider yesterday afternoon. I called their legal department and was told they'd fax it over later today."

"As soon as we get the record of his calls, have someone match the phone numbers with the ones on my contacts sheet." She paused to hand Steele a sheet of paper with names and telephone numbers on it. "Let's see who he was talking to the week the girls were murdered."

Steele got up to leave. "Will I see you Saturday night at the Bayou? We open for a new act from Nashville."

Steele played bass guitar and was lead singer in a band with two other cops and a female tambourine player that opened for the main acts at clubs in the New Orleans metro area. The weekend gig was at the Bayou Club.

"You bet. Do you want me to pick up Jenny?"

"No. She's working Saturday. She'll meet you there after her shift, around eight-thirty."

"Has Hellman told you when he wants to prep you for the prelim next Tuesday?" Steele asked, changing the subject.

"Not yet. He's got our report. He knows how to reach me."

"It'll bug him to no end that you'll be sitting at the prosecutor's table at the prelim and the trial. You know how you get under his skin."

"He's stuck with me. He'll just have to live with it."

Little did she know how wrong she was.

Chapter 21

The Bayou Club, on Bourbon Street in the heart of the city's entertainment district, was a popular nightclub for locals, including lawyers and cops. Steele's band was performing when Crowder arrived around eight. She took a seat at the bar and ordered a Chardonnay. The stool next to her was unoccupied. She threw her sweater over the back of it to reserve it for Jenny.

Typical Saturday night crowd. The couples took the tables, the singles sat at the bar or stood near it, milling around in groups and sharing workplace gossip. Sitting at a far end of the bar gave her a good view of the patrons that included a prosecutor and defense lawyer she'd once dated, both with women younger than her by their sides.

A man sitting alone at the opposite end of the bar fixed his gaze on her. But just to be sure, she nonchalantly looked over her shoulder to see if he was staring at someone else. Just three guys looking for love. *Good.*

He smiled.

She smiled back.

He was tall, six-two or six-three, late thirties or early forties, dark curly hair, neatly brushed. His cardigan sweater mapped out an athletic build.

It'd been quite a while since she'd shared her bed with someone other than Fred. He was a reporter with The Times-Picayune, who'd covered her last murder trial three months ago. He'd come onto her like a flea on a feral cat's ass. Her "no comment" replies to his daily barrage of questions had done little to diminish his interest in seeking her out and seeing her socially. She'd finally relented and agreed to meet him for a drink while the jury was deliberating on the murder charge.

The euphoria of a murder conviction in a case where she'd been the chief investigator always aroused her sexually. One thing led to another. The day after his account of the murder conviction had appeared as the lead, front-page story, his euphoria and hers had conjoined in a steamy night of uninhibited sex. It was in her nature to be proactive in her professional work, and it extended to her occasional romps in the sack. She'd liked the way her cuffs looked on him. So had he.

He wasn't the first who had.

And he wouldn't be the last.

The man on the other side of the bar, his gaze still fixed on her, raised his glass and tipped it in a toast.

She toasted back.

He left his stool and navigated his way through the crowd; a couple of the men and a woman acknowledged him as he passed by. His course didn't deviate and he soon stood by the empty stool beside her.

His steely blue eyes were piercing and confident. A quick glance at his left hand revealed no ring. She'd remembered times when men came on to her and her inspection of their left hand had revealed the distinctive, tell-tale sign of a married man on the prowl—the whiter than normal circular band of skin on the finger where a wedding band had been temporarily removed.

His evenly tanned hands showed no such band of white.

"Seat taken?" he asked cheerfully, his smile revealing perfect teeth.

Crowder knew she wasn't drop-dead gorgeous; but she was pretty ... even sexy by some standards. Short, pixie-styled dark hair, large hazel eyes, a lean, muscular build on a five-feet, five-inch frame from years of workouts in the gym, and a blemish-free complexion brought on many a man's stare.

"It will be if you take it," she replied playfully.

He sat beside her as the bartender, seeing his glass was nearly empty, came over to him. "Another?" he asked.

"Yes, and a refill for my friend." He looked at Crowder. "Andrew Schulman," he said. "But, please, call me Drew."

Crowder recognized the name. The criminal defense attorney who'd recently moved from Shreveport to New Orleans to head the homicide section of the public defender's office.

And Miguel Diaz's trial counsel.

"Jo Crowder. But, please, call me Detective Lieutenant Crowder," she said cheekily.

He smiled. "I've always wanted to meet you. Your reputation preceded you when I moved here earlier this year. I was in the courtroom when you took on Hellman in the Sanders' rape case. Very courageous of you to assert yourself that way. Your instincts saved that man from being wrongly convicted."

"I had information Hellman didn't have."

"He would've pressed on anyway if you hadn't tracked down the serial rapist responsible for the abduction of those girls."

"So how's your client holding up?"

"It's always more difficult on the accused—and his lawyer—when he's innocent."

"I have yet to meet a defendant accused of capital murder who didn't profess his innocence even when there was a mountain of evidence proving he did it."

"I know, but Diaz passed a polygraph. Mac did the test."

"Bill MacLaughlin?"

"You bet. He's the best around. He says the kid had no involvement in the three murders and never had sexual relations with the Lopez girl."

"Polygraphs are inadmissible. Guilty people have been known to pass them."

"A small percentage. But Diaz is squeaky clean, no arrests—not ever. The kid's quiet. A loner, but not in a creepy kind of way. A good student. Works hard at the clinic. Wants to be a physician someday."

"Ted Bundy wanted to be a lawyer and was in law school when he began murdering more than thirty women."

"What if Diaz consents to being polygraphed by your examiner? Would Hellman agree?"

"You'd have to ask him. That's above my pay grade."

"But it makes you wonder, doesn't it?"

"Did you get the forensics reports on Friday?" Crowder asked. "They were sent over."

"I read them. If you know your client's innocent, the medal, DNA hair matches, and cell phone are all easily explained."

Crowder knew where Schulman was going with this. She'd already considered the possibility before knowing Diaz passed a polygraph. "How's that?" she asked, playing dumb.

"Diaz's prints weren't on any of the incriminating evidence against him. But the murderer of the three girls most certainly had to have touched the evidence."

Schulman was swimming in her stream of consciousness. She wanted to shout out the answers but knew she had to remain silent. It wasn't her place to doubt the prosecution's case, or the evidence her investigation uncovered. Now that the case was in Hellman's hands, it was for him to dictate the course of the investigation.

Yet she'd doubted Sanders' involvement in the McNair rape, and her actions led her to Weymouth and saved an innocent man. She took a long, last swallow of her second glass of wine, and stifled the urge to speak.

"Jo, I hope you don't mind me calling you that. I feel we're both professionals sharing information with a common goal—seeing that the right person who murdered those girls is brought to justice."

Crowder liked hearing Schulman call her by her first name. But she needed to keep him at arm's length while the case against Diaz was pending. "Just so long as it's Detective Crowder in the courtroom, counselor. The murderer touched the evidence for sure. But Diaz could have been wearing gloves."

"But why leave such incriminating evidence in an unsecured locker for you to find? Diaz had to know he was a suspect as early as Easter Sunday. Yet he doesn't go to the clinic and dispose of the only direct evidence linking him to the girls' murders."

Crowder had asked herself that exact same question. "I gave him a chance to clear everything up the Monday morning after the Lopez girl was murdered. I just needed a verifiable alibi for the days of the abductions. He refused to provide one."

"He says he was alone at places where no one could corroborate his presence—the library at the college he's attending; a bar where he was stood up by a girl who'd said she'd meet him there."

"Does this girl have a name?"

"He didn't get it. It was more of a casual suggestion that they'd meet. He's shy. It was probably only wishful thinking on his part."

Just then, Jenny showed up at the club. Crowder waved to

her and she came over. Schulman finished his scotch and soda and motioned to the bartender for the bill. "Both, please," he said to him, so that he could pick up her tab.

"No. Separate checks, please," Crowder said. "I wouldn't want someone to think you were trying to bribe me."

"Then, I'll see you on Tuesday," he said sticking a twenty and a five under his bar tab.

"Who's the hunk?" Jenny said when Schulman was out of earshot.

"Someone who was just dying to meet me."

The two exchanged small talk until Steele came over during the break to have a drink with them.

"I was just introduced to Diaz's lawyer," Crowder said to Steele.

"So that was Schulman I saw with you. I wondered if he'd show. He called you Friday after you left for the gym. I took his call. He wanted to speak to you about the prelim on Tuesday. I told him you'd be here tonight. Does he want to plea bargain and save his client's life?"

"No. He wants the charges dropped—you see he's in the unique position of defending an innocent man."

Steele laughed.

Crowder didn't. She found nothing funny about the possibility that Diaz was being framed for crimes he didn't commit.

Chapter 22

A text message from O'Malley came to Crowder while she sat at her desk Monday morning reviewing Diaz's cell phone calls and text messages: *You and Steele. My office. Now.*

The two detectives took seats in front of O'Malley's desk. From the stern look on his face Crowder figured O'Malley was pissed at someone, probably her.

"Crowder, you're off the case."

"Which case?"

"The Easter Murders."

"Why so?"

"Conflict of interest."

"How's that?"

"You can't be sitting at the prosecution table as chief investigator when the case goes to trial with your brother sitting between you and Hellman."

"The bastard found a way to get me off the case."

"I know. He said he could use the trial skills of his chief prosecutor at what he believes will be the trial of the decade."

"What about Sid? He could take over from here."

"I tried that. He's the collateral damage. Hellman wants his own team on this—Jack Gardner and Al Jones. Gardner will be chief investigator."

"Tweedledum and Tweedledee," Steele hummed under his breath but audible enough for everyone to hear.

"Tom tried to talk Hellman out of it. He told him that your investigation broke open the case and that your presence at trial was worth more than his courtroom skills. Hellman will be sitting first chair but Tom will be handling the bulk of the courtroom work. Hellman will, of course, handle the press conferences and take credit for the conviction."

"What about the prelim?"

"He's got Gardner reviewing your report and the forensics on the case. He assures me he'll be up to speed."

The detectives returned to Crowder's desk to commiserate.

"It could backfire on Hellman," Steele said. "He'll never get from Gardner what he'd get from you. Gardner never looks beyond the dust on the surface of anything. You dig out the grit between the fibers of the carpet."

"I have to admit, it was a strategic move on his part. He gets rid of me, a royal pain in his ass, and gets an experienced prosecutor like Tom, who he'll need to guarantee a conviction."

"Do you want me to send Diaz's cell phone records over to Gardner."

Crowder was reviewing the records for the second time as he spoke. "Not just yet. I'm still looking through them."

"And?"

"There were calls between Diaz and the Lopez girl during Easter week, but none on the Saturday she was abducted. Most of the calls were between Diaz and the convent or the clinic, or to and from his parents." She focused her attention on Easter week. "Sid, look at this." She put the phone log on her desk and turned it for him to see. "There's a pattern of calls beginning on the Friday before Palm Sunday. The calls were only a minute or two in duration, always between seven and eight in the evening." Crowder looked at her contacts sheet. "The phone number is not one that's been identified."

Crowder picked up her phone and dialed the number. It rang. No one answered. No voicemail. She hung up.

She called again.

She let it ring for five minutes.

This time someone picked up. "Sigma Alpha Epsilon. Who's calling?"

"This is Detective Jo Crowder of the New Orleans Police Department. Who am I speaking to?"

"Barry Williamson; I'm a member of the fraternity here at Tulane University."

"Is this your private phone?"

"No. You've called the house phone; I just happened to hear it ring."

"Do you know a Miguel Diaz?"

"Can't say that I do. There's no one by that name who lives here."

"How many residents are there at this location?"

"Eighteen. All upperclassmen. It's one of the perks we get from membership. The freshmen and sophomores live in dorms on campus."

"Where are you located?"

"At Emerson and Weldon, about a five-minute walk to the main campus. 1200 Emerson is the exact address."

"And who is the president of your fraternity?"

"Tyler Van Horn. Hey, are we in some kind of trouble? Maybe you should talk to Tyler."

"Yes. That's my intention. Will he be there today?"

"Sure. He may be in a class now, but we have a meeting of

the brotherhood tonight after dinner. The meeting's at seven."

"Good. Inform him that I'll be there at six-thirty."

"Detective Crowder, should we be worried?"

"Not unless you've done something wrong," she said, ending the call.

~

The fraternity house was a well-maintained, stately old mansion on a tree-lined street. An assortment of high-end sedans, SUVs and late-model sports cars were parked in the driveway and on the street. The place had smart rich kids written all over it.

Crowder and Steele showed up at six-thirty, figuring on seeing Van Horn before the meeting of the brotherhood began. They were led into a small office where the business of the fraternity was conducted. A desktop computer sat on a desk, a cabinet full of catalogs, assorted books, and ledgers behind it. A coat of arms hung on a wall with the Greek letters of the fraternity embossed in gold leaf between two lions.

Tyler Van Horn was a diminutive, thin man in his early twenties with neatly combed blond hair. Sitting in an oversized chair made him look like a little boy pretending to be his father. His horn-rimmed glasses gave him a studious look. He wore a collared shirt and a V-neck cashmere sweater with the fraternity's coat of arms sewn in on the top left; a Phi Beta Kappa pin hung just below.

Crowder handed Van Horn her card and Steele's. The detectives remained standing even when he offered them the chairs in front of his desk. Crowder could see the cocky, confident expression the young man had on his face temporarily fade away when he looked at the cards and saw that he was talking to two homicide detectives. "How can I help you, detectives?" he asked, the hint of a quiver in his voice.

Crowder took the lead. "We're trying to locate someone who may have information of importance in a homicide investigation."

Van Horn's eyes widened as though shocked that someone from the fraternity could be involved in a murder investigation. "Do you believe the person is one of our members?"

"Yes. Someone who knew the prime suspect."

"What makes you think that?"

"Calls were placed from his cell phone to the house phone at your fraternity during the week certain murders were committed here in New Orleans."

"You mean those girls who were murdered during Easter week?"

"Yes. The person arrested, Miguel Diaz, called the fraternity house throughout the week, between the hours of seven and eight in the evening."

"He might have called. But no one would have answered," Van Horn said, the cockiness returning.

"Why so?"

"The fraternity house was closed that week. Spring break began the Wednesday before Palm Sunday. All the brothers were gone by three in the afternoon. I was the last to leave, shortly after five. I returned the Tuesday after Easter to open up again."

"So no one should've been living here that week?"

"That's right."

"When you returned on Tuesday, did you notice anything unusual—like someone might have been staying here, perhaps an intruder?"

"No. I turned the alarm on when I left and turned it off when I returned. I saw nothing out of the ordinary—certainly nothing to suggest that someone broke in and was living here that week."

"Who has a key to the house?"

"The officers have keys."

"Their names?"

Steele pulled out a notepad and pen to write down the names.

"Dougie Bronson, vice-president; Bryce Tipton, treasurer; and Larry McNeal, secretary. No one else has a key."

"Who knows the code to the alarm?"

"The same ones who have keys. Our charter requires that at least one officer be present at the house whenever school is in session."

"Any reports of the alarm being triggered during Easter week?"

"No. And our security system is a state-of-the-art one installed two years ago."

"Do you know the man accused of the murders?"

"Of course not. And it's unlikely he'd know anyone here."

Crowder saw Steele shoot a quick glance at her and knew what he was thinking: *What a xenophobic little shit.* She'd play with him and expose his prejudice. "Why do you say that?"

"What I mean is that the newspaper account of the man arrested was that he was Latino and a student at a public college. Tulane is a private university. This fraternity is more or less a homogenous group."

"I see, like homogenized milk," Steele interjected. "Are the members of the fraternity barred from socializing with minorities?"

Van Horn wore his inbred snobbiness like a badge of honor. "Our charter is very specific about our mission—to select the very best of the best. We are the oldest fraternity in the state. Our alumni include Pulitzer Prize winners, Rhodes Scholars, members of congress, a couple of senators and three governors. We have the most members of Phi Beta Kappa and the highest GPA of any fraternity on campus. We are birds of the same feathers here at Sigma Alpha Epsilon."

Crowder sensed that Steele wasn't finished: "Well then," he said, "I suppose we should speak to the other officers before they fly away."

Van Horn's face reddened from embarrassment. "All b-but one will be at tonight's meeting," he stammered. "I'll delay the meeting and you can speak to them here in my office."

"Who's not here?" Crowder asked.

"Bryce Tipton."

"Why not?"

"He got sick over spring break and is home with his family recuperating. You may know the family. Bryce Tipton is Senator Tipton's son."

Crowder thought as much. Bryson Tipton II was Louisiana's two-term United States Senator, one of the wealthiest entrepreneurs in the state, and the current head of a family whose ancestry dated back to the American Revolution.

Van Horn excused himself and went to locate the two officers who'd returned to the frat house after spring break. The young men were carbon copies of Van Horn—snobby elitists. Neither knew anything about Diaz and found it hard to believe that any of their members would associate with him.

Crowder and Steele headed home—Crowder in her six-year-old pickup truck, Steele in his '68 VW Beetle.

~

That night in bed, Crowder reflected on the unexpected turn of events. The text from her brother summarized how he felt about the changes made to Hellman's prosecution team: *At least one Crowder got lucky today … because she doesn't have to put up with Hellman's bullshit. Wish me luck, Jo. I'll need it.*

Luck. He'll need a lot more than luck, she thought as she turned off the light.

Sleep didn't come for another hour as she lay in bed reviewing what she knew from Diaz's phone calls and text messages. Someone answered Diaz's calls to the frat house. The few text messages were mostly back and forth texts between Diaz and his father about his brother's condition—he'd visited him twice at the nursing home where he was institutionalized. The only text message between Diaz and Angelica Lopez was on Good Friday. It cryptically read: *I'm to meet him on Saturday.*

Who was *him?*

Only Diaz knew the answer.

Chapter 23

When she arrived at work Tuesday morning at eight, she found a subpoena on her desk: *State of Louisiana v. Miguel Diaz, Criminal Action No. P-6792. Subpoena compelling your appearance in the Orleans Parish Criminal District Court in New Orleans, Louisiana, at the date and time indicated below.*

How could this be? She was no longer on the case. Gardner would be testifying about the evidence uncovered during the searches, the results of the forensic tests, and the circumstances showing probable cause to arrest Diaz. A further review of the document, however, indicated that she had been subpoenaed by defense counsel.

But why?

She'd soon find out.

Crowder showed up at eleven to a crowded courtroom and took a seat in a back row. Beat reporters from every major newspaper and local television station in the state filled the front rows. National cable news networks had live feeds outside the courthouse for the press conference that Hellman had promised following the hearing.

Crowder eyed the prosecution team assembled at their table—Hellman, her brother and Gardner; two paralegals sat in chairs behind them with boxes full of court filings and exhibits stacked three high.

Across the room, Schulman sat with his client who had his hands folded on the table, staring ahead at court personnel—the clerk, court stenographer, and bailiff.

Why Schulman wanted her at the hearing remained a mystery. He hadn't requested that she be sequestered outside the courtroom until called to testify—a customary practice in most criminal proceedings. She figured that he wanted her to hear the state's evidence. But how could her testimony possibly help Diaz?

Her gaze moved back and forth between Schulman and her brother. The chatter among the news people and the spectators was focused on the evidence that might be introduced at the preliminary hearing. The state's burden was to show probable cause to believe that Miguel Diaz abducted and murdered three pregnant teenagers. If the state's evidence was deemed sufficient by the judge, the case would proceed to a jury trial.

When the bailiff announced, "All rise," Judge Allen entered the courtroom and moved quickly to his chair behind the bench. Predictably, Hellman delegated the task of introducing the state's evidence to Tom Crowder, who showed why he'd never lost a murder trial by methodically moving through Gardner's testimony and establishing the relevant facts—the discovery of the victims' bodies, the evidence collected at the crime scenes and the evidence seized during the searches.

Schulman surprised everyone in the courtroom by waiving cross examination of Gardner. Nor did he question the forensic analyst who tested the hair evidence, or the medical examiner who testified about the cause and manner of the victims' deaths. When the prosecution's case was completed, the judge announced a brief recess after which the defense would have the opportunity to introduce evidence and testimony.

~

Schulman, like most defense counsel, routinely cross examined the state's witnesses at a preliminary hearing—looking for inconsistencies, casting doubt on the chain of custody of incriminating evidence and disputing the accuracy of important tests. And he, like most others, typically called no witnesses—not wanting to subject them to a prosecutor's cross examination— and usually introduced little or no evidence—not wanting to show his hand until trial.

Schulman wasn't doing what was routine, typical or usual because this case was different—he was representing an innocent man. He didn't need to go through the motions—doing what defense counsel customarily did when representing a guilty-as-hell client.

He surveyed the gallery as they rustled about in their seats. He'd seen Crowder in the back of the courtroom shortly after she'd arrived while her gaze was in the direction of the prosecutor's table. This time, when he looked in her direction, she was staring at him with eyes that were asking, "What can I say that can possibly help your client?" Schulman smiled at her, showing just enough of his pearly whites to make Crowder blush.

Schulman liked Jo Crowder. He liked her a lot. He liked her the first time he ever laid eyes on her—in the courtroom in the Sanders case when she personally took on Hellman. He knew then that he'd pursue her. He'd made sure to seek out Tom Crowder and speak approvingly of his sister's chutzpah before Judge Allen.

He needed that same flagrant boldness from her now if Diaz had any chance at all.

He'd never before represented a client who was being framed by a serial killer who was so meticulously clever that his chances of being caught and brought to justice were as certain as his client's chances of being wrongly convicted and sentenced to death. He needed the help of an honest cop. Someone unafraid of doing what was right, regardless of the consequences. He hoped that person was Crowder.

A young man's life hung in the balance.

He'd do whatever he had to do, whatever the risk ... whatever the cost.

Would she?

~

Hellman scanned the gallery, gloating over what had taken place. In Tom Crowder's hands, the evidence introduced at the hearing was more than enough to find probable cause and have a jury trial. It all played out in Hellman's mind. A trial in one month— Diaz convicted and sentenced to death. Another trophy upon his mantel, one that would erase the public's memory of the botched Sanders prosecution of an innocent man, guarantee his re-election as district attorney, and give him his shot at becoming the city's next mayor.

The facial droop of a stroke victim replaced the confident grin on Hellman's face when he saw Crowder seated in the back of the courtroom. When their eyes locked, she pulled out the subpoena from the inside pocket of her blazer and waved it in her hand. Hellman turned and leaned into Crowder's brother to speak privately. Gardner leaned in from the other side and the three heads met in a whispering tête-à-tête.

"What's going on?" Hellman asked. "Your sister's in the back of the courtroom with a fucking subpoena in her hand."

"I have no idea. Schulman must have served her this morning."

"Schulman's a prick," Gardner added. "But your sister could've given us a heads up, for Christ's sake."

"But she's off the case. Remember, Jack?" Tom Crowder said, the faint hint of a smile on his face.

"Let's hope she doesn't fuck things up," Hellman said as the bailiff announced the return of the judge.

Chapter 24

"The defense calls Detective Lieutenant Jo Crowder," Schulman announced to Judge Allen.

Crowder sauntered to the witness box, shooting a glance in the direction of the prosecution team on her way.

"Detective Crowder, some preliminary questions. You are a detective in the homicide division of the New Orleans Police Department and have been for the past six years."

"Yes."

"And you've been the chief investigator on at least ten capital murder cases that have come to trial in this district."

"Yes. Twelve to be exact."

"Those cases ... those twelve cases ... all resulted in convictions, correct?"

"Eleven guilty verdicts."

"Oh." Schulman said, as though surprised by her answer. It was well known that Crowder was the only homicide detective with a perfect record of convictions in capital murder cases.

Crowder explained. "One case ended in a mistrial. The defendant tried to escape from a third-floor window of this building, slipped on the ledge, and fell into the street. The public bus that ran over him ended the need for a trial."

Schulman liked gallows humor and couldn't suppress a slight chuckle. "So would you agree that among all the homicide detectives in the district of Orleans Parish, you are the most experienced homicide investigator with the most successful prosecutions for first degree murder?"

"If you say so, counselor," she answered, being politely coy.

"Were you here when Detective Gardner testified?"

"I was."

"And he testified primarily from the chief investigator's report in the case—a report you prepared."

"Yes."

"And you are the person most knowledgeable about the investigation that led to Miguel Diaz's arrest, and about the evidence that was found in his locker."

"Also, true."

"Detective Crowder, did there come a time when you learned that Miguel Diaz passed a polygraph test that showed he had nothing to do with the murders he's accused of?"

Tom Crowder started to rise to object but Hellman reached for his arm stopping him and rose instead. "The state doesn't know anything about the defendant's polygraph test, the results of which are inadmissible in criminal trials."

"Mr. Schulman," the judge said, seeking his response.

"That may be true under present interpretations of rulings in our state courts, but there are cases pending in three states challenging those rulings."

"That's true, Mr. Schulman, but I'd be bound to follow judicial precedents of this state which hold that the results of polygraph testing, whether they show a defendant to be telling the truth or lying, are inadmissible in a criminal trial."

Hellman stood just long enough to interject. "Precisely,

Your Honor."

"I agree, Your Honor," Schulman conceded unfazed. "But I'm entitled to make a record prior to trial to preserve my client's rights on appeal should he be convicted, and this matter ends up in the Louisiana Supreme Court with an opportunity to revisit and reverse those judicial precedents."

"Mr. Hellman, defense counsel is correct. He's entitled to make a record. And evidence may be introduced at a preliminary hearing that may be inadmissible at trial as long as it has some relevance in showing whether or not there's probable cause to believe a defendant committed a crime. Proceed, Mr. Schulman."

Hellman slouched back in his chair.

Schulman continued, "Detective Crowder, were you advised that Mr. Diaz passed a polygraph examination?"

"I was. You informed me of that."

"And that he was willing to submit to another polygraph if district attorney Hellman wanted his own test?"

"Yes, and I told you that would be up to the district attorney."

"And I informed you of that on Saturday while you were still the chief investigator assigned to this case, correct?"

"Yes."

"I'm curious about something, why did Detective Gardner testify today instead of you?"

"I was taken off the case."

"By whom?"

"District Attorney Hellman."

Hellman fidgeted in his seat. Schulman was making it look like he purposely took her off the case because there was evidence she believed might exonerate Diaz.

"Polygraph examinations are highly reliable when properly given, correct?"

Hellman jumped from his chair. "And unreliable when given

by someone not properly trained or experienced."

"I suppose that's true Mr. Hellman," the judge said, "depending upon which side in the case is paying the expert to give the opinion." The judge's comment brought a few chuckles from members of the gallery. "Proceed, Mr. Schulman," the judge said, brushing off the objection.

"Do you agree with Mr. Hellman that the reliability of a polygraph test for determining whether someone is lying or telling the truth depends on the training and experience of the examiner?"

"Yes. The better trained and more experienced the examiner, the more reliable the results."

"Detective Crowder, isn't it true that many law enforcement agencies use polygraph testing to interrogate suspects and witnesses, and to screen new employees?"

"Some."

"Some?" Schulman repeated as though surprised by Crowder's answer. "The FBI uses polygraph, correct?"

"Yes."

"And the NSA—our government's intelligence agency—to determine whether their employees are lying or telling the truth about past criminal misconduct."

"Yes."

"And the CIA.

"Yes."

"Miguel Diaz's polygraph was given by Bill MacLaughlin. Do you know Mr. MacLaughlin?"

"I do. He was formerly with the FBI."

"And was trained as a polygraph examiner while a special agent for the bureau."

"Yes. I'm familiar with his credentials."

"Would it surprise you to know that, while he was with the

FBI, he administered more than a thousand polygraph tests?"

"No. It wouldn't surprise me. He's highly qualified. When he retired from the bureau, the Louisiana State Police employed him to administer polygraph tests to suspects and witnesses."

"The arrest warrant in this case was supported by your sworn affidavit, correct?"

"It was. It's customary for the chief investigator on a case to provide the facts justifying a suspect's arrest."

"You say facts, but you really mean evidence that suggests facts. Like the hair of the victims being found on the brush in Miguel Diaz's locker suggests that the murderer brushed the victims' hair at some point in time during the commission of the crimes."

"Yes. The evidence points to that fact."

"Were Mr. Diaz's fingerprints found on the brush?"

"No one's prints were found on it."

"And the medal?"

"Same answer. No prints."

"What about Angelica Lopez's cell phone?"

"Only the girl's."

"What does the absence of prints suggest to you?"

"That he was wearing gloves."

"By 'he' you mean the person who placed the brush, medal and cell phone in Miguel Diaz's locker, correct?"

"Yes. That's correct."

"Detective Crowder, if the polygraph test administered by former special agent MacLaughlin proves that Miguel Diaz had nothing to do with the murders, what is the only logical, reasonable explanation for how the brush, medal and cell phone ended up in his locker?"

Crowder knew the answer Schulman wanted and it made perfect sense. But he'd set her up when they spoke at the bar and then blindsided her by calling her as a defense witness. She'd make him work for the answer. "It's for a jury to determine what conclusions are logical and reasonable."

"But when you prepared your affidavit in support of the arrest warrant in this case, *before* you knew that Miguel Diaz passed the polygraph test, you came to the logical, reasonable conclusion that he put the incriminating evidence in his locker, correct?"

"Yes. I concluded *at that time* that he put them there," Crowder answered, detecting a slight smile on Schulman's face for the emphasis.

"So, I ask you again, if Miguel Diaz told the truth on the polygraph test, what is the only logical, reasonable explanation for how the most incriminating evidence against him got into his locker?"

Outwardly, Crowder remained poker-faced; inwardly she was smiling. Schulman very expertly was getting her to testify that Diaz was innocent. She was ready to reward him for the effort. "Someone else placed those items there to frame your client."

There was a stir among those in the courtroom. Fingers pounded the keyboards of reporters covering the hearing. Some spoke openly to colleagues, one of them could be heard saying, "They have the wrong man;" and another said, "The serial killer's still out there," their comments audible to the judge who banged his gavel and admonished the offenders.

Crowder knew Schulman was hoping for exactly that reaction—and one or more headlines suggesting that an innocent man was being framed. Schulman had milked her like Elsie the cow—for all he could possibly get from her. And she didn't hold back. But there was one question more she knew he'd want to ask her, and she knew she'd give him the answer he wanted.

"If you were still the chief investigator in charge of this case, would you be investigating the possibility that someone else had murdered those girls and planted the brush, medal and cell phone in Miguel Diaz's locker to frame him for murders he did not commit?"

"Objection," Hellman barked out even before he stood up. "Pure speculation to ask this witness what she might do if she was still in charge of the investigation, which she's not. This hearing is to consider the evidence that's been introduced against this defendant, not some fictional criminal that defense counsel's made up."

Judge Allen knew that any answer by Crowder could not be considered by him. Hellman was right. The preliminary hearing wasn't the trial. Its only purpose was to determine whether there was enough admissible evidence for a jury to conclude that Diaz murdered the three girls. And, given the evidence, his ruling had to be that a jury could convict Diaz of all three murders.

Schulman's eyes remained fixed on Crowder's as he awaited the judge's ruling on Hellman's objection.

"Yes. The objection is sustained. You need not answer that question."

It didn't matter that he directed the detective not to answer the question. What mattered was what her answer would've been had she been allowed to answer.

And, for the time being, Schulman could only hope he knew her answer.

A twenty-minute recess followed the conclusion of Schulman's questioning of Crowder. When Judge Allen returned, he issued his ruling that there was enough evidence for a jury to conclude that Miguel Diaz was the cold-blooded murderer of three pregnant teenagers.

Chapter 25

A half-dozen local and national cable-news networks had correspondents stationed outside to greet Hellman and Schulman when they left the courthouse. Crowder chose to slip out a rear exit reserved for correctional officers and prisoners. Schulman had slowed his pace to allow his adversary to do a quick step out the front doors first, the cocky smirk on Hellman's face broadcasting his eagerness to be interviewed.

As Schulman had hoped, the news people flocked to him instead. He stood as far away from Hellman as the front steps of the courthouse permitted, surrounded by cameras and boom mics, while Hellman stood alone at a lectern he'd had a subordinate place in front of the courthouse.

Proclaiming his client's innocence to a national audience, Schulman touted the reliability of the polygraph, and denounced the district attorney's refusal to polygraph Diaz or reopen the investigation and find out who planted the evidence that led to his arrest. He suggested that the reason Crowder was taken off the case was because she suspected that Diaz was being framed. He ended the news conference by imploring the NOPD to find the serial killer and prevent a miscarriage of justice.

When Schulman walked away, the news people descended upon Hellman like vultures on a carcass. Before he could give his prepared statement boasting about his plan to bring Diaz to trial in record time, the airspace was flooded with accusations. Schulman slowed his pace just enough to hear some of the questions.

"Why won't you accept the polygraph results of an FBI special agent?"

"Why doesn't your office polygraph Diaz and see if he's telling the truth?"

"Why aren't you giving the kid a chance to clear himself?"

"Why did you take your chief investigator off the case? Are you afraid she might catch the real killer and make a fool out of you like she did in the Sanders case?"

"What do you have against Latinos?"

Schulman couldn't suppress the urge to gloat. The smile on his face lasted until he got back to his office. He reflected on the events of the day—a good day for his client.

Although the polygraph evidence was inadmissible at trial, the press and news networks had taken the bait. The storyline that Miguel Diaz was an innocent victim being railroaded through the criminal justice system by a prejudiced, ruthless prosecutor was far more intriguing than a murderer having been caught and certain of being convicted. Genuine or fake, the most sensationalized version of the facts was always reported— here, that a cold-blooded serial killer was still on the loose who might kill again.

It had Breaking News written all over it.

There would be a perceived need for commentary from news anchors, guest commentators, and forensic experts about polygraph testing, about the wrongly arrested, convicted and executed, about overly aggressive, blood-thirsty prosecutors interested only in convictions, not justice, and about the disparate impact of capital punishment on minorities. All would be fair game on the cable news networks.

Schulman had played his hand with an ace up his sleeve. He knew Hellman would never agree to polygraph Diaz. If he'd agreed and Diaz passed the test a second time, he'd have no choice but to dismiss the case and look foolish for having precipitously closed down the investigation and prosecuted Diaz. Schulman knew from the Sanders case that looking foolish wasn't an option for Hellman.

His euphoria was short lived, however. Diaz still faced a jury trial. In New Orleans, and in most other large metropolitan cities where violent crime was out of control, an acquittal in a murder trial was a rarity. If Hellman and Gardner weren't willing to reopen the investigation, he'd need to convince someone else to do it.

Crowder was his client's only hope.

~

Crowder watched the newscast of the courthouse press conference at district headquarters. Schulman's gamble had paid off. He'd bet on her to follow the logic of Diaz's only defense—that his telling the truth on the polygraph meant that he didn't murder those girls and was being set up to take the fall. Crowder served as the perfect foil in Schulman's melodrama, and he played her like a fine-tuned Stradivarius.

She had to admit. His balls were showing their brass—not unlike her rolling the dice that day in the courtroom in the Sanders case. Like her, Schulman did whatever was necessary to protect someone from being prosecuted for a crime he didn't commit.

Hellman was probably fuming over her performance at the hearing. Not telling him about the polygraph left him unprepared at the hearing. Hellman was blindsided, sucker punched by Schulman, and she'd let it happen. He'd be gunning for her. Her speculation became fact when she received a text from her brother: *Schulman was brilliant. You did what you had to do. Watch your back.*

Soon afterward, Steele showed up at her desk and sat down with the grin of a Cheshire cat painted on his face. "Hey, partner, expect a call from Cap. He just finished with me. I had to tell him that we were still looking into the case … that we had some unresolved issues. Hellman accused you of trying to tank his case—wants a firewall built between you and the case file."

"Did you tell him about the phone records and text messages?"

"No. He didn't ask what we had. I didn't offer."

"Good. I'll handle it from here."

Crowder passed Jack Gardner as he was leaving O'Malley's office and she was entering it.

"He kinda looks like he ate some bad crow for lunch," she said, closing the door behind her and taking a seat.

"Hellman has put the kibosh on reopening the investigation. He has all he needs to convict Diaz. Doesn't want Gardner having to testify at trial that there's enough doubt in the state's case to keep looking for the serial killer."

Crowder went on the offensive. "Diaz's sure looking like the perfect patsy. The evidence had to be planted if you believe the polygraph. That justifies reopening the investigation. Maybe we'll find out that Diaz committed the murders. Liars have been known to pass polygraph tests. Wouldn't be the first time."

"You're right, of course," O'Malley said. "But the trial is next month. You have four weeks to prove Hellman's wrong."

"What about any evidence we might have or find, what of it?"

"No sense speculating on what you should do with it, only on what you shouldn't do with it."

"Clear as mud. But I get your drift."

"I want to be in the dark until you can enlighten me, if you get my drift."

Crowder could hear herself chuckle as she got up to leave.

Or was it O'Malley she heard?

She understood O'Malley's drift perfectly well.

Chapter 26

Schulman put the log of cell phone calls in front of his client and handed him a pen. "I need you to write down the names of the persons you spoke to beginning the Saturday before Palm Sunday and ending when you *accidentally* ran over your cell phone with your car."

"And what if I don't remember?"

"Then guess. I only have to call the numbers if I want to know."

Diaz spent the next couple of minutes inking in the names. Looking over what his client had written down, Schulman saw a single call from Angelica Lopez on Good Friday and then the repeated calls to "Tulane" during Easter week, including the days the girls were murdered.

"So what did you and Angelica talk about on Friday? The call was six minutes long. That's a long conversation if you were only telling her you wanted to take her to a movie on Saturday."

"Just normal stuff. What movie she wanted to see on Saturday."

"But we know from the polygraph that you didn't take Angelica to a movie Saturday night. You lied about that."

"I don't remember specifically … just stuff."

"Was it about her being pregnant?"

"Might have been. She was scared. She didn't want her parents to know."

"Well that cat's out of the bag. They know now. And they, like everyone else, believe you got her pregnant and had a motive to kill her."

"Can't they do a blood test to determine paternity? It would show I'm not the father."

"The state tested Angelica's fetal blood. The sample was contaminated, so the lab couldn't get the DNA that would've proved you weren't the father. That's unfortunate, because now Hellman can use circumstantial evidence to prove you were the father. He'll show that you were the only boy—or should I say, man—that she'd ever gone out with. Angelica's parents will testify how close the two of you were, and how much Angelica liked and trusted you."

"She didn't tell me who the father was. Angel was a good girl. She didn't date. It was a one-time thing, and she got pregnant."

"Did Angelica's girlfriends have boyfriends?"

"Angel was a lot like me. She didn't have a lot of friends. We stayed to ourselves."

"According to several of her classmates, she talked about you a lot. She even told one of them she was in love with you … a girl by the name of Juanita Sanchez."

"Angel didn't like Juanita. She was always trying to get Angel to go out with friends of her boyfriend, who was an older dude on the basketball team."

"Was Juanita sexually active?"

"Angel thought she was."

Seeing the words Tulane written down, Schulman asked, "So who were you calling at Tulane University?"

"Someone I'd met. A pre-med student. I thought it would be nice to talk to him about becoming a doctor. But he must have been away on spring break. The person who answered said he wasn't there."

"Ever get in touch with him?"

"No."

"Was he the person who stood you up Saturday night?"

Diaz raised his eyebrows and gave Schulman an icy stare. "No. I told you it was some girl who didn't show," he snapped, not hiding his obvious frustration.

"What's the student's name?"

Diaz slouched back in his chair and crossed his arms. "David," he answered unconvincingly.

"Does this David have a last name?"

"I don't remember it."

"You repeatedly called the same number at Tulane and asked for someone by the name of David and you can't remember his last name?"

"Can't remember."

Schulman knew his client was lying but didn't want to press him for the name. He'd call the number later and try to find "David."

~

Crowder spent the next two weeks speaking to Angelica Lopez's classmates and Diaz's teachers. "Angel" was described as a shy, studious kid who didn't hang out a lot or go out on dates. Several girls mentioned that she had a crush on an "older guy." One, Juanita Sanchez, gave him a name.

Point Hellman.

Diaz's teachers talked about him in glowing terms: intelligent, top of his class, a great nurse in the making, insatiable curiosity. All expressed disbelief that he could have anything to do with the *Easter Murders*.

Point Schulman.

Crowder's several calls to Tyler Van Horn provided no new information about Bryce Tipton's return to school—only that his mononucleosis might keep him out the remainder of the semester. She'd learned from her last call that Schulman had contacted Van Horn looking for someone named David. He told Schulman that no one with that name lived at the house and then shared with Schulman the same information he'd given Crowder.

Crowder figured Schulman thought this "David" could provide his client an alibi. But when she'd checked the case docket sheet, Schulman hadn't identified any alibi witnesses who'd be testifying at trial. Diaz was probably lying to his lawyer about who he'd called to keep that person from being discovered and implicated in a murder case. But why, with his neck on the line, would Diaz protect someone else?

~

They arrived at Crowder's desk in an unstamped envelope with the words "Angel's phone calls" in parentheses just below Crowder's name. Angelica's father had dropped them off at district headquarters. Knowing who his daughter was calling and texting in the weeks before her death might help Crowder identify who fathered Angelica's child and just maybe who may have killed her.

She examined the phone log of calls for March and early April. There were one or more calls a week between her and Diaz in March, ranging between five and ten minutes long. The only call in April was a six-minute call on Good Friday. Most of the remaining calls were to or from Angelica's parents.

Crowder retrieved Diaz's text messages from the cork board and found the text message Angelica sent at 4:22 p.m. on Good Friday, the day before she went missing: *I'm to see him tomorrow.* Comparing the time of the text message to the phone calls Angelica had made, Crowder found a six-minute call between her and Diaz at 4:06 p.m.

She studied the phone log carefully.

And then she saw it.

A call Angelica made just before she texted Diaz.

A call made at 4:13 p.m., one minute after she'd spoken to Diaz.

A call that lasted eight minutes.

A call to a number not on Crowder's contacts list.

Crowder picked up the phone on her desk. She dialed the number. It rang three times before someone answered. She didn't recognize the voice. It belonged to someone she'd never met and had never spoken to.

"Good afternoon, Monsignor Rossi speaking."

Crowder's eyes shot a glance at the poster on the cork board by her desk where she'd written "Rossi" twice before—on the lines connecting the first two murders to common denominators. She'd now be able to insert his name on the lines connecting the third one.

After a brief hesitation to collect her thoughts, she said, "This is Detective Jo Crowder. I think it's time we met."

Crowder was working the Diaz case alone, not wanting her partner caught up in the shit storm that was coming. It was Wednesday, a week and a half before Diaz's trial was to begin. She arranged to meet Rossi at his office located at the archbishop's residence on Friday morning. Thursday was already booked. She'd be driving to the state capital and making a surprise visit on the son of a two-term U.S. senator from Louisiana.

Chapter 27

Senator Tipton's home was located on Lakeshore Drive among a dozen other multimillion-dollar homes. Crowder circled the block when she arrived. The stately three-story colonial with massive columns and wraparound porches sat on five acres of manicured lawns and gardens. The tennis court and Olympic-size swimming pool gave it a country club appearance.

Crowder drove her pickup through the black wrought-iron gates to the front door. A frail-looking, elderly African-American woman in a black uniform and white apron answered the door. After the housekeeper politely asked who she wished to see, Crowder identified herself, showed her badge, and asked to see the senator's son.

"He's in the pool, ma'am," the woman explained in a lazy southern drawl.

"I need to speak to him."

"Yes, ma'am. If you'll follow me."

The woman moved at a snail's pace, giving Crowder the opportunity to take in the opulent surroundings—original artwork on walls below wide, decorative crown moldings, a mural and several tapestries on the larger walls, sculptures on pedestals, and a grand piano in a parlor. Abundant memorabilia sat on tables and in cabinets—the possessions of a well-connected, wealthy family with ties to Louisiana dating back generations.

The pool was located in the back on a large terrace. The mist that rose above the water showed that it was heated. A young man was doing laps when Crowder arrived poolside. His lean, muscular physique cut through the water like a knife through warm butter. The flawless execution of his tumble turns at the ends of the pool and the minimal wake he created as he raced along were proof positive the trophies she'd seen in the glass cabinets on her walk through the house belonged to him.

Crowder took a seat around one of the four tables that surrounded the pool, each with a large blue canvas umbrella providing ample shade from the early afternoon sun.

Several laps later, the young man stopped and quickly looked at his watch before lifting himself easily from the pool. He removed his goggles and cap, his blond curly hair falling naturally into place, grabbed a towel and walked over to the woman seated by the pool.

Crowder stood and introduced herself when Tipton approached, handing him one of her cards. He looked at it before saying anything, then wrapped the towel around his waist and sat down. Before he could speak, a stocky-built, tanned man in his late fifties came out of the house. His military style crew cut and heavy jowls made him easily recognizable. It was obvious to Crowder that the son got his physical good looks from his mother.

"Detective Crowder, I'm Senator Tipton. Hattie, our maid, gave me your card. May I know what business a homicide detective has coming to our home?"

"I want to talk to your son. It was my understanding that he hadn't returned to school because he'd been sick with mononucleosis." Crowder looked at Tipton's son with a slight grin on her face to signal to him that she knew that was a lie.

"I can explain …" the boy said before being cut off by his father.

"That will be enough of that, Bryce," the senator said gruffly. "Now, you go in the house while I speak to the detective."

The boy did as ordered, his head bowed like the kid who'd just been scolded for speaking out of turn. When Crowder was alone with the senator, she said, "Sir, there's a young man going to trial in a week for murder who may be innocent. I think your son has information that could be helpful to him."

"I don't see how that's possible. What could possibly connect my son to someone accused of murder?"

"The defendant may have spoken to him on the days three girls were abducted and murdered."

"You mean the murders in New Orleans during Easter week," the senator declared. "Do you think I want my son involved in any way with a serial killer? You'll have to do better than that, detective."

"Strange, isn't it, that the only one who didn't return to the frat house after spring break was your son."

"He got sick."

"Yeah, I've seen how ill he is."

"He doesn't know this Miguel Diaz," he said emphatically. "He'd never associate with someone like him."

"I know—birds of a feather. I've heard that before."

"And it's true. You judge a man by the people he associates with."

"Where was your son living over the spring break?"

"Here with his family."

"You're prepared to swear to that?"

"On a stack of bibles, if necessary. Now I think we're through here, detective." The senator turned and pointed in the direction of the walkway that led to the front of the house.

"For now, senator," Crowder said while walking in that direction. She stopped a few yards from him to say, "Your son knows how to reach me, if you … or he … has a change of mind … or heart."

The drive back to New Orleans gave Crowder the time to sift through the facts. Diaz had spoken to someone at the frat house. The senator's son? Perhaps. Afraid to openly associate with a poor inner-city Latino boy, what better time for Bryce Tipton and Miguel Diaz to meet than Easter week when everyone was away on spring break … and when they had the house entirely to themselves.

He had a key to the house.

He had the passcode to the alarm.

Bryce Tipton wanted to be with Miguel Diaz.

~

Back at district headquarters, Crowder checked her interview notes and found the name of the company that installed and operated the security system at the fraternity house. A call to the company's technical-support team revealed that the alarm system collected data on when the system was turned on and turned off. The data was stored throughout the month but was lost when the hardware's internal computer clock rebooted the first day of each month.

It was April 30. Crowder had until the end of the day to retrieve the data for the month of April.

She jumped in her pickup and headed over to Sigma Alpha Epsilon. She needed Van Horn's authorization to release the data to the NOPD. She'd prepared a one-page authorization for him to sign.

A surprise visit this time.

The Lilliputian was sitting in the chair behind his desk when she arrived. A good three-inches taller than him, Crowder chose to stand so that the microorganism would have to look up at her.

His twitching eyes proved he felt unnerved by the unexpected visit. "I ... I don't know what more I can tell you, Detective Crowder," he said. "No one was staying here during spring break."

"Correction. No one was supposed to be staying here during spring break. I'll know for sure when I see the April monitoring data collected by your security system." Crowder pulled out the authorization from an inside pocket of her blazer, unfolded it and handed it to him.

He read it, his hand shaking—like he was about to sign his life away. "Maybe I should talk to our national headquarters first," he balked.

"No time. The data will be gone tomorrow. We can do this the easy way or the hard way." Crowder pulled out a pen and held it in one hand; then she reached for the handcuffs in a leather pouch on her belt and held them up in the other hand. "You can either sign the authorization or I can arrest you for obstructing a criminal investigation. Your choice."

"But can't I call the lawyer who represents our chapter to discuss it with him?"

"Of course you can. It can be the first call you make from district headquarters after you've been booked and fingerprinted." Crowder was bluffing. She had no reason to believe Van Horn was obstructing a criminal investigation. But he didn't know that. "Come on. I don't have all day," she barked. She knew that the prospect of having an arrest record would weigh heavily on a Phi Beta Kappa.

He rose from his chair and reached for the pen.

A minute later, Crowder was out the door on her way to the security company's New Orleans office. There, she met with a technical-support team member who agreed to obtain a printout of the April data and fax it to her. He assured her that it would document whenever the alarm was turned on and turned off.

Crowder headed back to district headquarters to prepare for a very important meeting. Tomorrow, she'd meet with a person of interest in her ongoing investigation of the *Easter Murders.*

Chapter 28

The housekeeper showed Crowder to the archbishop's study for her ten-o'clock meeting with Monsignor Rossi. A red leather sofa and three elegantly upholstered armchairs were positioned around a large, ornate, hand-carved, walnut coffee table. Bookshelves lined one wall; religious paintings occupied another two—but it was the photographs on a wall behind a large green leather-top mahogany desk that caught her interest.

Alone in the room, she studied the framed photos. Three were of the archbishop and the pope and two with the pontiff's predecessors. But the photos that occupied most of the wall space were of the archbishop over a span of decades. A common feature in most of the photos was the presence of a child, an adolescent, a young man, and a priest standing beside the archbishop as the years progressed.

The monsignor?

Crowder remembered O'Malley telling her that the archbishop had raised Rossi like a son. She had her suspicions confirmed when a man in a black suit with the white collar of a priest entered the study and introduced himself. "Detective Crowder, I am so sorry to have kept you waiting. His Grace had an urgent matter he wanted to see me about. I'm Monsignor Rossi. Please sit down."

Crowder was impressed by the clergyman's striking good looks and amiable smile. She recognized him instantly as the person in the photographs.

The housekeeper had followed Rossi in and stood by the door while Rossi directed Crowder to one of the armchairs. He took the other. When Crowder declined refreshments, he dismissed the servant.

Crowder had much to cover. She opened the folder she'd brought and put three photos on the coffee table. She watched Rossi's face as she laid the crime scene photos of the three victims before him. She could've used school photos and head shots for an identification but she wanted his visceral reaction to seeing them where the killer had left them—faces a killer would always remember ... and could never forget.

As they sat in silence, Crowder studied Rossi's eyes as they surveyed the photos of teenagers with much in common.

All had been pregnant.

All had been bled to death.

All had been gutted like animals that had been hunted and killed.

And—all had been murdered by the same person.

She studied his face as he studied the corpses. Not a flinch. Not a tic. Not even a blink—two dark orbs frozen open. Lips sealed shut.

Silence as dead as the girls blanketed the room like a London fog.

His hand reached across the table and picked up one of the photos. He held it at arm's length from his face for a full ten seconds, returning the photo of Angelica Lopez to its original position beside the other two.

Breaking the silence, Crowder asked, "How many of these girls do you know, Monsignor Rossi?"

"All three."

"Tell me how you know them."

"The first girl—the one found at St. Stephan's—I spoke to her over the phone the Saturday she went missing. I didn't know her last name then. I only knew her circumstances. We were to meet at the convent. She left before I got there.

"The second girl I met at the convent. She wanted an abortion. I counseled her against it and told her I'd try to get her into a women's shelter where she'd be taken care of until she had her baby.

"The third girl is Angelica Lopez. I was supposed to meet her at her parish church but she didn't show."

"Why didn't you come forward about knowing the Lopez girl?"

"I only talked to her. She called the day before she went missing. She wanted my help. She was going to have a baby and hadn't yet told her parents. She'd told me a friend had given her my number. When she didn't show up for our meeting, I assumed she took my advice and decided to tell her parents about her pregnancy."

"For the record, where were you the nights the girls were abducted and murdered?" Crowder was purposefully blunt when asking suspects if they had an alibi. It caught the innocent ones off guard, and often they stumbled their way into an incorrect explanation of where they'd been. The guilty ones, conversely, knew they might be asked that question and had an immediate, well-constructed answer that necessarily had them being somewhere alone.

"Well, I suppose you need to ask that question to everyone who had contact with the girls. I was home alone in my apartment the night the Lopez girl was murdered." He paused, but only momentarily, and then continued, "The same answer for the other two victims, and for every night of Easter week except Friday when His Grace and I spent the night in Baton Rouge."

"Did Angelica identify the father of her child when she called you on Friday?"

"No. I usually counsel the girls to disclose their pregnancies to the fathers so they and their families can share responsibility for the child—financially and emotionally."

"She knew Miguel Diaz. Were you aware of that?"

"Not until Miguel was arrested and his relationship with the girl was reported in the news."

"Do you have any reason to believe he was the father of Angelica's baby, or had anything to do with what was done to those girls?"

"I suppose it's logical to assume he was the father, if what's been reported in the news is accurate. His relationship to the clinic and convent links him to the other two victims. Does he have an alibi for the nights the girls were murdered?"

"Like you, he has no one who can confirm he was somewhere else."

Crowder saw Rossi flinch for the first time—a break in his armored facade. She could almost read his mind. *And I, too, am linked to the three girls, knew their circumstances, and had contact with them shortly before they were abducted.*

He remained silent.

"There's an obvious connection between the murders and the Catholic Church," she continued.

"It occurred to us that the murderer might have a vendetta against the church."

"Us?"

"His Grace and I discussed the possibility. We've followed the case closely. More so after the third victim was left at the doorstep of this house. It was suddenly up front and personal."

"I don't want to disturb the archbishop unnecessarily. But it was most irregular for a homicide detective not to get statements from him and from you after Angelica Lopez was found here."

"I'm afraid I may have had a hand in that." The words were spoken by a man whose tone was powerful and deliberate, while at the same time, calm and confident.

Rossi stood and looked over Crowder's left shoulder at a distinguished-looking man with wavy gray hair that shone like polished sterling silver.

Crowder instinctively stood and turned.

"Archbishop Antonio Santini," he said, introducing himself. "I'm embarrassed to say that I've been eavesdropping at the door. A theologian's obsession with guilt prompted me to come away from the shadows and confess my transgression."

"Your Grace, Detective Crowder was just mentioning how she should have obtained our statements shortly after that poor girl was found here."

"I know, Thomas," Santini said in a mellow, affectionate tone. He waved a hand for Crowder and Rossi to sit, while he took a seat on the sofa. "I called police superintendent Sullivan shortly after the monsignor found the girl," he explained. "Russell understood the importance of proceeding with the utmost discretion. The media can be most unforgiving when facts can be spun into a sensationalized story."

Crowder knew the archbishop's name drop was purposeful. Unsure how she should address him, she followed her usual practice of resorting to the time-tested generic salutation. "*Sir*, the circumstances of the three murders appear to be more than coincidence: the girls—all Catholics with St. Mary Magdalene medals around their necks; their out-of-wedlock babies aborted; their bodies left at Catholic churches and here at your home."

"Yes. I see plainly the connection," Santini said. "And the murderer—also a Catholic, who'd lost his faith in God—behind bars awaiting trial. I applaud you for having made the arrest so quickly."

"I hope not too quickly," Crowder said reflexively.

Santini's back noticeably stiffened as did his tone. He then spoke like a prosecutor—like Hellman. "My understanding is that there is considerable evidence of guilt. Diaz worked at the clinic, knew the victims, impregnated one of them, was skilled in matters of medicine, had access to the drug used to sedate the girls during their abductions. Those facts, and the hairbrush, medal and cell phone found in his locker, make for a compelling case, don't you agree?"

"It would appear so," Crowder said, appeasing the archbishop. She didn't want to share her ambivalence about the facts in front of Rossi. She was there to see if Rossi, not Diaz, might be involved in some way.

"Although I don't see how we can help, we are here to answer your questions and bring *your* investigation to a conclusion."

His emphasis suggested to Crowder that Sullivan had told him the official police investigation was closed. Still, she'd take full advantage of the opportunity to dig for facts.

"Sir, Monsignor Rossi says he spent the Saturday night before Easter at his apartment. Were you here at your residence the entire night?"

"Yes. The monsignor and I had attended a conference of bishops from our southern dioceses in Baton Rouge on Friday. We stayed the night there, returning around four Saturday afternoon. He delivered me here and went home."

"When did you see the monsignor next?"

"We talked on the phone early that evening. I next saw him Sunday when he came to the house and discovered the girl's body."

"Did you know the girl?"

"No."

"So you looked under the sheet at her face?"

"Well, no. We knelt in prayer by her side. It was obvious that the girl was like the other two."

"So how can you say you didn't know her?"

Santini sat quietly, staring at Crowder through dark, unblinking eyes. Crowder stared back, waiting for a response. Finally, he spoke. "Her photo was in the newspaper, along with the other girls. I didn't recognize her."

"Did you have any visitors Saturday night?"

"No. I followed my usual routine. Evening prayers in the chapel at nine-thirty. In bed by ten."

"Were any of your household staff with you Saturday night?"

"Why do you ask?"

"They may have seen or heard something if they were here."

"No. The housekeeper and cook leave at seven and, unless there are functions being held here, they are given Sundays off. The landscaping and gardening are handled by third-party contractors.

"Do you have a driver?"

"No. I'm still quite capable of performing that function."

"Has Miguel Diaz ever been to your residence?"

"To my knowledge, only once."

"When was that?" she asked, moving forward in her chair as if a secret was about to be revealed.

"When he left that poor girl's dead body on the doorstep of my home," he said glibly.

Put off by his sarcasm, Crowder took a deep breath and

exhaled slowly to release her pent-up tension. "Did you know him?" she asked.

"Of course. I knew everyone at the clinic. The clinic was the monsignor's idea. It had the full financial support of the archdiocese—I made sure of that. I'd often visit the clinic after seeing the Reverend Mother who is under the care of the sisters at the convent."

"Were you surprised by his arrest?"

"Surprised? Of course. He didn't seem the type to run amuck. Then again, appearances can be deceiving. Well, do you have all you need from me, Detective Crowder?" He rose, signaling to her that the interview was over. "I trust you won't keep the monsignor from his duties for much longer," he said as he walked out of the room without closing the door.

"I understand that the archbishop will soon become a cardinal," Crowder said when she was once again alone with Rossi.

"Yes. It was announced last week. He'll be ordained in a ceremony at the Vatican on Sunday. I'll have the privilege and the honor of accompanying him and will be by his side when the Holy Father places the red biretta on his head and the ring of a cardinal on his finger."

Crowder saw in Rossi's face the pride a son feels for the accomplishments of a father he'd looked up to his entire life. Could such a son reject the teachings of his father's church and commit the worst of sins?

Didn't seem logical.

Didn't seem reasonable.

But the same could be said of Diaz.

Crowder left the archbishop's home feeling the same ambivalence about Rossi she'd felt about Diaz.

She'd need to know more, a lot more, about Rossi... and Diaz.

PART THREE

The Fall From Grace

Chapter 29

"I've been informed that the detective's visit today was unauthorized," Santini said to Rossi. The prelates were having an after-dinner sherry in the study. Rossi often dined with the archbishop and had an en suite bedroom at his home. "The investigation was supposed to be closed. They believe they have the murderer, but this ... this detective ... has her doubts."

"Miguel's lawyer believes that the physical evidence linking Miguel to the victims was planted," Rossi said. "Maybe she does too."

"Perhaps planted by the police. It's been done before, Thomas. They know they have their man but not enough evidence for a conviction. So one day, a hairbrush, medal and cell phone show up in his locker."

"The detective's questions make me believe she suspects me," Rossi said, refilling their glasses from a decanter of liquor. "She knows I had contact with all three girls and, like Miguel, I have no alibi for the evenings the girls were murdered. She thinks I should've come forward about knowing the Lopez girl and arranging to meet her the evening she was abducted."

"In retrospect, perhaps I shouldn't have counseled you to

remain silent. What did you tell her about that?"

"That Miguel was arrested so quickly. I didn't think it was necessary. They had the killer in custody."

"Still, she comes here on the eve of the boy's trial and speaks to you—the only other person who knew all the victims and had contact with them shortly before they were abducted."

"Should I be worried, Father?"

"Don't ruminate over it, Thomas. I know you had nothing to do with those murders. The matter is best handled by me."

~

The Louisiana newspapers on Sunday featured the pope's announcement that Santini was to become the sixth American cardinal and that Rossi would be ordained a bishop and the archbishop's successor.

Crowder read the story with much interest.

Santini's rise in the Catholic Church since his ordination as a Jesuit priest at the age of twenty-three had been unprecedented. The son of a prominent Italian family, who were patrons of the arts and whose roots dated back to the Renaissance, Santini was well educated and well connected. His first assignment was pastor of St. Stephan's Cathedral, a national landmark with a rich Catholic heritage. His appointment as the archbishop of New Orleans came at the age of thirty-eight. Now, at the age of fifty-nine, he would become one of the youngest members of the College of Cardinals.

The story also focused on Rossi. As a newborn, he'd been left wrapped in a blanket in a basket in a pew at St. Stephan's with a note from the mother who gave no name—only a plea that her son be raised a Catholic. Santini had found the infant after the last Sunday mass, the baby's cries echoing into the sacristy as he removed his vestments. A search for the mother proved unsuccessful, and after being awarded guardianship, Santini named the child and placed him in the care of the Reverend Mother at the Convent of the Sisters of St. Mary. There, she'd cared for him until he was five years old. With the court's consent, Thomas Aquinas Rossi then went to live with Santini's family in Rome.

Santini had made frequent trips to Rome to visit him. Educated in the finest private Catholic primary schools in Rome, Rossi had become fluent in four languages, learned piano and violin, and consorted with the sons and daughters of the most influential Catholic families in Italy. Summers had been spent in New Orleans with Santini. When he was eighteen, Rossi had come to live with Santini, by then an archbishop.

Rossi had followed in Santini's footsteps. Bachelor and doctoral degrees in theology with high honors from Georgetown University. Ordained a Jesuit priest at the age of twenty-four, he'd gone on to author two books on canon law, teach at his alma mater, and join the faculty of the prestigious Pontifical Gregorian University in Rome. At the age of thirty, he'd been appointed the pope's personal secretary, lived in an apartment in Vatican City, and had been awarded the honorarium of monsignor. When his duties concluded five years later, he returned to New Orleans to serve as the archbishop's personal assistant and understudy.

Heartwarming story, Crowder thought. But, like Diaz, Rossi had no alibi for the nights the girls had been abducted, had a key to the clinic, and the passcode to the alarm. An educated man, Rossi was quite capable of doing what was done to those girls. The medical examiner confirmed that the procedures performed didn't look like the work of a physician or obstetrical nurse. Diaz had practiced suturing wounds, and the girls' sutures were jagged and irregular, the work of an amateur.

Crowder mulled over how best to proceed. If Diaz was innocent, Rossi had to be guilty. As far as she was concerned, her ongoing investigation of the Easter Murders was two-pronged— proving that Rossi murdered those girls, or proving that Diaz couldn't have killed them because he was somewhere else.

~

The fax came in around noon on Monday. The monitoring data appended to it had numerical dates and military times. Crowder scrolled down the chart to the day spring break started. At 17:01:02 of the day before Amy Stillman was murdered, the alarm was turned on shortly after five in the afternoon, just as Van Horn had said. The very next entry that day, the day of the Stillman abduction, the alarm was turned off at 18:45:13—a quarter to seven that evening.

Someone had entered the frat house.

She checked Diaz's cell phone calls. He'd called the frat house twenty-eight minutes later.

That someone had answered the phone.

The next entry, the following morning at ten minutes after six, the alarm was turned on.

That someone had left the frat house.

She went down the columns and found the same pattern throughout Easter week, including the evenings of the days the other two victims were abducted and murdered—the alarm was turned off between six and seven in the evening, approximately a half hour before Diaz called the frat house, and turned on the next morning between six and seven.

Whoever answered the frat house phone when Diaz called had a key to get in, knew the passcode, and stayed the night, leaving the next morning and the house unoccupied during the day.

It was time to put the ball in someone else's hands.

She tore a sheet of paper from her notepad and wrote down a name. She placed it, and a copy of the security company's monitoring data, in a plain envelope with no return address and dropped it in the outgoing mail basket by the photocopier. An hour later a police cadet brought the envelope to the mail room where it was hand delivered that afternoon.

Chapter 30

"Her lungs are clearing; her respiration's stable," Dr. Latham said as he moved his stethoscope from one spot to another across the Reverend Mother's chest and abdomen.

Sister Agnes removed her fingers from the old woman's wrist. "Slow pulse." She pointed the infrared thermometer at her forehead. "Still slightly febrile."

"The antibiotics appear to be working, though. Her fever should resolve soon, but let's check it every eight hours just to be safe."

The elderly nun had turned eighty-five the week before. The multiple strokes that began six years ago had left her with increasing amounts of disability: her body, mostly paralyzed; her head, bent back and rigid. She wore the facial sag of a stroke victim like a mask. Only her right arm and hand remained functional. She hadn't spoken in a year. Communication with the outside world was limited to hand squeezes and eye blinks— one for "yes," two for "no." Feeding by mouth also ended a year earlier when the last mini stroke destroyed her ability to swallow. The feedings were now from a bag of liquid nutrients that hung from a pole next to a breathing machine that was used intermittently to oxygenate her lungs.

The cabinet by her nightstand was a clutter of bags of saline, IV lines, syringes, body lotion, diapers, baby wipes, and medicines, including the morphine given whenever the old woman's urine output slowed from urinary tract infections.

Latham reached for her right hand and looked at her glued-shut eyes. He squeezed her hand gently and said, "Reverend Mother can you hear me. It's Dr. Latham. Are you in any pain?"

The aged nun's eyes opened like each lid weighed a ton. When fully opened, the white of her eyes showed yellow and veiny.

"Squeeze my hand if you hear me."

The woman's bony digits pressed against Latham's palm.

"Squeeze my hand again if you're in pain and want some medicine for it." He waited a full minute but detected no response. "Now with your eyes, tell me if you want something for pain."

She blinked twice for "no" before closing her eyes.

Latham always double checked when asking about the morphine. Her caretakers had to be careful. Too much morphine could cause respiratory arrest. "Thank you for that response, Reverend Mother," he said in a compassionate tone.

Santini entered the room unnoticed and appeared like an apparition at the foot of the bed. "How is she?"

"Under the circumstances, she's holding her own." Latham stepped away from her side and moved closer to Santini. "She's been in a lot of pain, Your Grace," he whispered. "I can see it in the way her eyes flicker and the occasional white-knuckle grip her only good hand has on the sheet."

"And the morphine doesn't help?"

"It does. But she often refuses it. It's almost as if she's in her own little purgatory on earth, and the pain is some kind of self-imposed penance. She's run a good race. Yet I fear the finish line may soon be in sight."

Sister Agnes made the sign of the cross and said, "God's will be done."

"Yes, Sister Agnes," Santini said. "And God's will is to take her when the time is right for her ... the blessed curse of having bestowed free will on us, I suppose. She'll know when the time is right."

"Will the monsignor be visiting her today?" the nun asked. "She looks forward to his visits. He recites scripture to her. The parables are often embellished with all the drama of a novella. Sometimes I wait outside the door and eavesdrop to hear them."

"Yes. The monsignor will be visiting her today. I was to inform her of that when I arrived."

"On afternoons when he visits," Sister Agnes said, "he sometimes lifts her into her wheelchair and takes her to the garden and sits with her. When he returns her to her room and departs, I go to her and see her hand resting upon her heart and her eyes opened wide—her way of smiling." Sister Agnes saw the Reverend Mother's hand go limp and her eyelids fold down like window shades being lowered. "I'll be in to see you for evening vespers," she whispered, gently stroking the old nun's forehead. "We'll leave you alone with His Grace." She turned and followed Latham out the door.

Santini closed the door and walked to the bedside. He couldn't believe how long it had been since he'd had a conversation with her. She had her first stroke shortly after Rossi had left for Rome to become the pope's personal secretary. Their last talk together had been about Rossi's selection for the position.

Connections, he'd told her, were worth their weight in gold, but so were euros.

His family had been a heavy financial supporter of

226

religious art, funding almost a quarter of the cost of cleaning the centuries-old dirt and grime from the ceiling of the Sistine Chapel, revealing Michelangelo's frescoes as they looked the day he finished them. The generous donation the family made to help restore Da Vinci's masterpiece, the Last Supper, just happened to coincide with the pope's appointment of Santini as an archbishop, one of only thirty residing in the United States at the time. The family's transfer of euros to the Vatican Bank to fund the renovation of the Holy Father's summer residence on Lake Albano was reportedly made on the same day the pontiff announced that Antonio Ignatius Santini was to be ordained a cardinal. Another donation would be likely to occur when his protégé, Thomas Aquinas Rossi, succeeded him as archbishop.

The Santini family would make sure of it.

As was his practice when visiting the Reverend Mother, Santini anointed the old nun with holy water from a small bottle he kept in a pocket of his suit jacket. He noticed the Reverend Mother's usual reaction when he made the sign of the cross with his thumb on her forehead—she closed her eyes and tightened her grip on the sheet.

"Thomas and I leave for Rome next week," he said in the one-sided conversation. "My ordination is Sunday. The Holy Father will be announcing the new bishops following the initiation of new cardinals. Thomas is to succeed me here, just as I'd planned."

Santini removed two rosaries from a pocket of his suit trousers and placed one of them in the nun's right hand. He held the other in his hand, looked at her and said, "Now let us pray for our souls."

The prayer beads lay loose in the old woman's hand as Santini prayed aloud.

"The older nuns remember it well," Sister Agnes said to the monsignor as they walked to the Reverend Mother's room at the convent. "She alone fed and bathed you. She had a rocker brought to her room and sang lullabies to you as you fell asleep in her arms. She left only the minimal of your care to the other nuns. It made them wonder whether the convent had been the right choice for her."

"God's will was to bring her and His Grace to me. No child could've had better parents."

"His Grace shared with the Reverend Mother and me the good news of your appointment as the next archbishop of the diocese. At evening vespers, when I mentioned my excitement to her, she laid her hand upon her heart and tears—tears of joy—poured from her eyes. Now, go to her," she said when they reached her room. "It's been a day full of excitement for her. I fear she may not long be alert and awake."

When Rossi entered the room, Sister Agnes stayed back, closing the door behind him. Alone in the room, he brought a chair bedside. Sitting beside her, he spoke softly. "I'm here, my mother, my dear and blessed mother."

The nun's eyes opened wide, and she raised her right arm and rubbed the back of her hand against his cheek.

He took her hand in his and gently kissed it. "God's plan is to keep us together, and I thank him every day for that. No son could have more affection for his mother."

Rossi spoke to the old nun about the ceremonies for the ordinations. He promised to return from Rome with the video that was to be taken to memorialize the occasions and arrange for them to see it together. He could feel her grip on his hand loosen and her eyes close to slits, a sure sign that she was overcome by fatigue and sleep was imminent. He always saved the parable reading for last, knowing that she often fell asleep before he finished.

"Now I've selected a parable that you read to me so many years ago. It's one of my favorites. The Parable of the Prodigal Son." As he recited the story from memory, the old woman's eyes once again widened and her grip on his hand strengthened.

"There was a man who had two sons. The younger one, by comparison to his brother, was a spendthrift who lived for the moment. He said to his father, 'Father, give me my share of the estate.' The brother made no such demand and was content to stay with his father and remain in his service. But the father gave in to his younger son's demands and divided his property between them."

The nun's grip waxed and waned as Rossi recounted the tale.

"Not long after that," he continued, "the younger son got together all he had, set off for a distant country, and there squandered his wealth in wild living." The Reverend Mother's eyes closed, and the soft sound of her snoring told Rossi that the mellow tone of his voice had fulfilled its purpose and she was asleep. As was his usual practice during visits, he finished reciting the parable, said prayers, and gave her his blessing.

He reflected on how paradoxical it was that their roles had reversed and he was the one reading the bedtime story. When he finished, he did as the Reverend Mother had done so many times when he was a child—he kissed her gently on the forehead and pulled the sheet and blanket up to cover her and shield her from an early morning's chill when she awoke.

Chapter 31

Steele's band had a return gig Saturday night at the Bayou Club. Jenny had the night shift at the hospital, so Crowder showed up alone, took a seat at the bar, and ordered a Chardonnay. She wondered whether Schulman would take the evening off, or hunker down in his office to prepare for the trial that was to begin with jury selection and opening statements on Monday.

He'd have put two and two together and known she'd sent him the name and security monitoring data. He'd also have known that she'd broken Hellman's cast-in-stone rule against disclosing helpful information to defense counsel in a capital murder trial, where the slightest breach could tank a solid case.

The D.A.'s instructions had always been, "Only disinformation should be leaked."

Schulman's ploy of revealing that his client had passed the polygraph and then manipulating Crowder's testimony at the preliminary hearing had worked to Diaz's advantage. But Crowder knew that the best Schulman could hope for was to get a juror or two who'd read about Diaz passing the polygraph to conceal their bias from the court and argue for a not guilty verdict, or hold out for an acquittal and force a mistrial.

Crowder threw her jacket over the empty chair beside her, in case ... no ... when ... Schulman showed up. She should be pissed off as hell at him for setting her up like he did, but he was trying to save the life of someone he believed was innocent. That, and his good looks, earned him a fool's pardon.

Crowder looked good. Damn good. The black leather miniskirt and tight-fitting spandex top she'd worn going undercover as a prostitute two years ago still fit. The blood of the creep who'd tried to attack her with a knife was barely visible on the hemline.

The only pushup bra she owned helped to feminize a boyish but attractive figure—her lean, muscular physique the reward for leading an athletic life. She'd left the five-inch stilettos she'd worn parading around as a hooker in the closet, opting for two-inch heels instead. She'd added just enough eye shadow, lip gloss, hair gel and perfume to attract most any man.

She felt the stares of the single men clustered around the bar, and the ones who'd removed their wedding bands before they pounced. No doubt she'd be hit on more than once before the night was over. Whether she'd leave alone or with a companion remained an open question.

Halfway through her glass of wine, she heard a voice speak out over her left shoulder. "Seat taken?" asked a red-headed man who'd broken ranks with his companions on the other side of the bar.

"Yes, by me," another man said, his tone of voice firm and deliberate.

"Sorry, friend," said the redhead. "Thought she was alone."

"Not anymore, friend," Schulman said as he stepped in front of the redhead and pulled out the bar stool. He removed Crowder's leather jacket from the backrest, put it over the back of her stool, and sat beside her. "Didn't order me a scotch and soda?"

"Didn't want the ice to melt in case you were late."

"Are you always so sure about people, detective?"

"Like minds think alike."

Schulman, like Crowder, primped for the occasion. Crowder noticed the recent haircut and wondered whether it was because of the upcoming trial or his interest in her. The fresh nick on his cheek told her that he'd shaved twice that day, the second time for her. He looked sharp in his soft denim slacks, powder-blue pullover shirt that revealed a muscular chest and chiseled biceps when he removed his weathered leather flight jacket.

To Crowder, and probably the other single women staring at him, he looked like he belonged on the cover of J.Crew.

Schulman ordered a drink and a refill for her. "Miguel cried when I mentioned his name."

"Did they spend the nights together?"

"You bet. Tipton drove over from Baton Rouge and turned off the alarm. The call to the frat house was to confirm he was there. Miguel left the next morning around six. Tipton left a few minutes later, turning on the alarm on his way out."

"You have your alibi witness. Have you disclosed him to Hellman?"

"I did as soon as Miguel fessed up. The court will have to allow him to testify. The late disclosure shouldn't be a problem, not in a capital murder case."

"Do you think anyone might've seen Diaz's car parked nearby?" Crowder asked.

"Unlikely. They both parked on side streets a couple blocks away. Still, I had one of our investigators check with residents in the neighborhood, but nothing turned up."

"Son of a U.S. senator. Pre-med honor student. Captain of the swim team. All-American boy having to come to terms with his sexuality at a murder trial. He's gonna fight you on this."

"Hellman, the senator, or the son?"

"Maybe all three."

"The kid will break down when I get him on the stand. Miguel shared with me that they fell in love the first time they met."

"I'm sure you're right. When I went out to the senator's house, I could tell he wanted to talk to me."

"Why didn't he?"

"Daddy sent him to his room for speaking out of turn."

Two drinks later, the conversation turned personal as they shared their life stories—Crowder growing up in a small Louisiana town, the only daughter of a career cop in a family full of badges; Schulman, the only child of two neurosurgeons being raised in an Upper East Side co-op overlooking Central Park.

Crowder's humble beginnings never embarrassed her, just as those born into privilege never awed her. Schulman was not a braggart by any stretch of the imagination. He portrayed himself as an underachiever—"The only son of two Jewish doctors not to become a doctor"—and showed a penchant for wry self-deprecation—"When it comes to music, I have no ear for it ... I'm stone deaf, and I'm a klutz on a dance floor ... bears dance better than me."

Yet she knew from her internet search that Schulman's accomplishments were many. Harvard undergraduate. All-Ivy ice hockey. Fulbright scholar. Harvard Law School. Air Force pilot. Yet he was friendly, funny, and approachable. The best she could do were a few cop and lawyer jokes. He politely laughed as though he'd never heard them before.

After their third drink, the gap between their barstools was indiscernible. Their heads were so close, they spoke in whispers. They stared fixedly into each other's eyes, occasionally remaining silent—allowing their throaty chuckles to telegraph dirty thoughts.

"You know, I was practically begging Tom to fix me up with you. He said you were not presently in a relationship; I made sure to ask."

Crowder had to laugh. She hadn't been in a relationship in more than two years—just the occasional romp in the sack when her libido got the better of her—like it was with Schulman at that moment. "And you?"

"I was married for three years a while back."

"Didn't work out … why not?"

"She was more in love with herself and the tennis pro at the country club than with me. You?"

"Just to the job. There's something about catching bad guys. My dad and uncles being in law enforcement and all. It must be in my genes."

"And you're damn good at it. By the way, thanks."

"Just doing my job—as I see it."

"I'm sure Hellman wouldn't agree. You stuck your neck out for this kid. Not many cops I know would do that."

"It may not be enough. You still have to prove that the evidence was planted."

"I'm working on that."

"So am I."

"Can I walk you to your car?"

"Sure."

This time Crowder let Schulman pick up the tab, and the two left just as Steele's band had finished the set. She caught sight of her partner giving her a thumb's up from the stage. Nice thought. But she didn't need the encouragement.

Neither did Schulman.

When she got to her pickup, she turned and leaned back

against the driver's door. Like hers, the look in his eyes was intensely deep and penetrating.

He acted like he didn't want the evening to end.

Nor did she.

"Your place or mine?" she blurted.

"Mine. It's closer."

~

Senator Tipton—who insisted on having immediate contact with everyone whose candidacy he'd endorsed—made a call to Hellman's cell phone. Their NRA memberships weren't the only thing the two had in common. They had the same views on capital punishment, immigration reform, sanctuary cities, and gay marriage. The only liberal cause they supported was the liberal use of the police department's stop-and-frisk policy that targeted people of color.

"What in the hell is a homicide detective doing barging into my home wanting to speak to Bryce about this serial murderer?" the senator bellowed.

Hellman frowned. *That bitch is still working the case.* "Crowder?" he asked, just to be sure.

"Right. Detective … Lieutenant … Jo … Crowder," the senator shouted into the phone, emphasizing each word.

"Was she alone?"

"All by her lonesome."

"Did she speak to Bryce?"

"No. I kicked her skinny ass off the property before she could question him."

"Did you ask Bryce if there's a connection to Diaz?"

"He said they were friends. He told me that Diaz couldn't have killed those girls. Look, I don't know what's going on here, but I don't want my son connected in any way to a murder investigation."

"Is Bryce back at Tulane?"

"Hell no. I wanted him as far away from Tulane as possible—at least until this kid gets convicted and this mess is all over with. Listen to me. You do whatever is necessary. You hear me?"

"Loud and clear. Do you still have your place on St. Barts?"

"Of course we do. Why?"

"Don't you think Lorraine and Bryce could use a vacation—at least until the trial is over?"

"I hear you loud and clear."

~

Crowder lay in bed Sunday morning feeling satisfied for the first time in a long while. For too long she'd treated sex the same way she'd approached police work—boldly, aggressively, and always the one in control. She acted; he reacted. She was the one on top, not him. For her, nothing was off limits—no holds barred—just like it had been fighting in the octagon.

It was different with Schulman. He was a gentle and respectful lover. His kisses were soft, his caresses tender. He allowed their intimacy to build gradually to a crescendo. When the lovemaking ended, he held her in his arms and whispered sweet things in her ear—about how lucky he was to know her and to be with her.

Crowder thought that a relationship with Schulman might smooth her rough edges, give her someone special to care about, someone to be able to confide in … share secrets with.

She knew Schulman wanted a relationship.

She now knew that so did she.

Chapter 32

The trial opened on Monday with jury selection. Schulman knew that finding an open-minded, unbiased jury in Orleans Parish was a tall order, particularly in a capital murder case with the life of a poor Latino man hanging in the balance.

One-hundred-fifty-five residents of the parish were herded into the courthouse for the spectacle. Twelve would eventually be selected, and four alternates just to be safe—but only after being questioned *ad nauseam* by the judge, the prosecutors and defense counsel about their education, occupation, criminal record, religious beliefs and their views on a host of subjects including abortion and gay marriage.

The first order of business was to part ways with anyone who opposed capital punishment in a state where death sentences were as popular as Monday Night Football.

Seventy inmates sat in cells on Death Row awaiting disposition of their umpteenth appeal challenging the evidence introduced in the case, alleging prosecutorial misconduct, disputing the competency of trial counsel, and contesting the constitutionality of a death sentence. Schulman was there to keep Miguel Diaz from becoming number seventy-one.

At least that was the plan.

Until an hour ago when his office called and told him the process server couldn't subpoena Bryce Tipton because he was sunbathing on a beach in the Caribbean.

All of a sudden, the reality of doom set in.

It would get worse.

Judge Allen suffered angina over the weekend and was in the hospital. Considered a fair-minded judge by both sides of a criminal case, Allen disputed the efficacy of capital punishment and had the highest number of dismissals of criminal convictions for prosecutorial foul play. He believed in reasonable sentences, prison reform and second chances.

Judge Jensen "Stonewall" Jackson replaced Allen.

Another punch in the gut.

"Stoney" was the good-old-boy judge. He'd received the worst rating from the NAACP—the National Association for the Advancement of Colored People—and the ACLU. He had the lowest number of written opinions, preferring to rule from the bench instead, and the highest number of reversals on appeal. He carried a fully loaded .45-caliber Glock in a shoulder holster under his robe, and had pulled it out on occasions when he thought a defendant had become too unruly at sentencing.

Schulman got his first taste of how the trial might go when the bailiff said, "All rise," and Jackson took his seat behind the bench. "I understand you have a motion to present, Mr. Schulman?" he said, a noticeable edge in his voice.

"Yes, Your Honor," Schulman replied, moving to the lectern to address the court. "Defendant requests a postponement of the trial. I just now learned that a witness, a very important witness, left the country before he could be subpoenaed for the trial. He is expected to corroborate my client's alibi on the nights the victims were abducted and murdered."

"Who is this witness?"

"Bryson Tipton III, a twenty-year-old college student, who was with Mr. Diaz at the Sigma Alpha Epsilon fraternity house at Tulane University when the crimes were committed."

Jackson reached into the file for the witness list and found Schulman's belated listing of Tipton. "Is the witness Senator Tipton's son?" he asked.

Schulman suspected Jackson knew the answer and that the senator had probably endorsed him when he campaigned for judge. It was well known that the senator was instrumental in selecting the candidates from his party who ran for judge.

"Yes. The senator's son."

"Why did you wait so long to subpoena him if he's that important?"

"It only came to my attention recently that he could corroborate my client's alibi."

"How can that be possible? Your client had to know who he was with. You've been representing him since the preliminary hearing."

"It's complicated. To explain would require me to disclose privileged communications between an attorney and his client."

"Well, have you talked to your witness—Mr. Tipton—to confirm what he'd say if he testifies?"

"Well, no. At least, not yet."

"So you don't know what Mr. Tipton will say if he were to testify."

"Not having spoken to him, I don't."

Jackson looked over at Hellman, who was seated first chair at the prosecutor's table. "The state's position on a postponement?" the judge asked in a dismissive tone that signaled his displeasure over the eleventh-hour request.

Schulman looked behind him at Tom Crowder, hoping he'd

speak for the state. His relaxed appearance told Schulman that, in a capital murder case, he'd take the reasonable position that a postponement was necessary. Hellman, conversely, looked angry and outraged, shaking his head and arching back in his chair before rising from it. He walked quickly to the lectern with notes in hand.

Suddenly feeling warm and sweaty, Schulman returned to his seat.

"The state opposes a postponement," Hellman began. "The motion comes on the day of trial and involves a witness who has not been disclosed in a timely manner. Defense counsel was dilatory in trying to serve a subpoena on him. Senator Tipton's son was under no obligation to cancel a trip his mother had planned. It's Mr. Schulman's fault that he's not here to testify."

A red light flashed in Schulman's brain. How did Hellman know anything about a trip? The son-of-a-bitch got to his witness or to the senator. If he could prove it, he'd have grounds for a mistrial if the judge refused to grant the continuance. But he couldn't prove it, at least not yet.

And maybe not ever.

Tom Crowder would never do something like that— interfering with a material witness in a capital murder trial.

But Hellman sure as hell would.

Stoney's ruling came as no surprise. "Yes. I quite agree with you, Mr. Hellman. Motion denied."

~

It took only two hours to select a jury—record time in a capital murder case. Judge Jackson blew through the standard questions: about whether they knew someone associated with the case, or read or heard anything about it; about their views on capital punishment, excusing anyone from jury service who was the least bit equivocal about imposing a sentence of death "if the evidence so warranted." To move things along, he limited the questions each side could ask prospective jurors, and summarily dismissed many persons of color "for cause" when there was none. Forty-six potential jurors—mostly white men and women—were left in the pool.

Hellman used his preemptory challenges to send the Latinos home and several of the African-Americans whose children had had run-ins with the police. Schulman ousted some of the rednecks, two cops' wives, and a tattooed dude with a mohawk and nose ring. All that remained after jury selection were mostly white-faced people from suburban and rural areas of New Orleans—a couple of blue-collar housewives with kids in school, a few born-again Christians, several retired seniors, and the rest uneducated, unemployed people on the public dole—the kind of mix of jurors that brought a smile to the face of a prosecutor.

Opening statements were scheduled for the afternoon of the first day of trial. Hellman wanted the limelight, so he addressed the jury. He spoke about the victims, how they were carefully selected by Diaz, how they were abducted and bled to death, how their babies were killed, how their bodies were mutilated, and how evil and despicable a person Miguel Diaz was—a serial killer who'd preyed on vulnerable young girls—a modern-day Jack the Ripper.

Schulman had some tough decisions to make. Did he give his opening statement now or wait until the state rested its case? He'd planned on giving his opening address immediately after Hellman's to blunt its impact. He'd have told the jury that his client was cloaked in a presumption of innocence and that they must acquit him if there was any reasonable doubt of his guilt. He'd have put all his eggs in Tipton's basket—a "brave young man," who'd tell them Diaz was with him when the girls were abducted, and that any embarrassment he'd felt about his sexuality played second fiddle to him coming forward and telling the truth, and saving the life of an innocent man. And most of all, Schulman would have told them that because Diaz was with Tipton, the evidence found in Diaz's locker had to have been put there by the murderer who was still at large.

But everything had changed now that Bryce Tipton had fled the country. Too much was up in the air. He needed to buy time. He had no choice but to reserve giving his opening statement.

The first day of trial did not go well for Diaz.

For the first time in a long while, Schulman doubted himself—questioned his abilities. Suddenly the evidence against his client looked overwhelming. An open-and-shut case. A slam dunk conviction for the prosecution team—just as Hellman predicted.

After the state rested its case, another tough decision had to be made. Should he put his client on the stand? Without Bryce Tipton, the only person who could say that Diaz was somewhere else was Diaz, who'd have to take the stand and tell the jury, the news people covering the trial, and his family sitting in the courtroom that he was gay, and that the son of the United States senator from Louisiana was his lover, even though his lover wasn't there to back up his story. He'd have to deny being the father of Angelica Lopez's baby even though she'd told a friend that she loved Miguel and wanted to marry him.

Diaz would be grilled on cross examination: on the textbook explaining how to perform a C-section, on the photos depicting the size and location of the incision, and on the physiology charts showing the appearance and location of a woman's reproductive organs. He'd have to admit that he had access to the victims' healthcare records and to the propofol, scalpels and suturing materials at the clinic. He'd deny putting the hairbrush, cell phone and St. Mary Magdalene medal in his locker. His only explanation would be that they must have been planted. But by whom? He'd have no one else to blame.

It wasn't that Schulman felt the first day of trial hadn't gone well for his client.

It was that he knew it had been an unmitigated disaster.

Chapter 33

Crowder sat at her desk Monday afternoon working on reports of other criminal investigations, but her mind was elsewhere. If Diaz was innocent, someone planted the evidence against him, and that someone had to be a sadistic, cold-blooded killer.

She pulled out her notebook where she'd written down the possible suspects after the third girl had been killed and before she'd formed the belief that Diaz was the murderer.

Father Julian concealed knowing the first victim, but he wouldn't have known of the others. Doctor Latham knew the first two victims and their circumstances, but he was home with his wife and kids when the girls were murdered. The part-time doctors and nurses who worked at the clinic weren't there when the first two victims were seen at the clinic, and the twenty-four-year-old receptionist was home taking care of a sickly grandmother on the nights of the abductions.

She'd considered Sister Agnes—a fit woman in her early forties, who knew more about the first two victims than anyone, was medically trained, had access to the clinic, and could have learned about the Lopez girl from Diaz over idle chatter at work. The distraught girls would certainly have trusted a nun enough to meet up with her at the clinic.

Could a woman, a nurse practitioner—a nun—be a serial killer?

Crowder had studied serial killers. Men dominated the field. But the number of females was enough to make even Sister Agnes a suspect. More than a handful of nurses had smothered patients with their hospital pillows under the crazed belief they were putting them out of their misery, or for no particular reason at all. Same was true for caretakers working in nursing homes who'd made it a habit of injecting air into the veins of elderly residents, or overdosing them on their medications. And wives—the black widows—who couldn't live with a single husband and the support he provided, moving methodically from one breadwinner to another.

Sister Agnes, a serial killer?

Crowder learned early that you look at the facts in compiling a list of suspects, and then draw inferences from those facts to exclude them, one by one. Sherlock Holmes' maxim came to mind: *When you've excluded the impossible, whatever remains, however improbable, must be the truth.*

Her deduction? It was impossible for Sister Agnes to have killed those girls. She'd have needed a suitable vehicle—the one undeniable fact that excluded her.

The vehicle the convent owned was a 2017 Ford Fusion. The compact car's trunk space and rear passenger seat were too small to have transported the shopping cart Amy Stillman had been left in. A geometric truth—measurements don't lie.

Sister Agnes didn't have a suitable vehicle.

But Rossi did.

A computer check of Louisiana's Office of Motor Vehicle's database showed that Rossi had a Louisiana driver's license and a black Lincoln Aviator registered to him. She'd seen it parked at the archbishop's home when she'd gone there to interview Rossi. Getting a warrant to search his car for latent prints and DNA evidence was out of the question, but Crowder's mind didn't work within the narrow parameters of what she couldn't do. What she could do was track the movements of Rossi's vehicle on the nights the girls were murdered. It would take time and she would need help.

When Steele returned to the homicide division from an assignment, he went over to Crowder, who sat looking at her computer screen. "I saw Gardner on his way back from the Diaz trial," he said. "They finished earlier than expected. He told me they have the perfect jury and the perfect case."

"Perfect, until the senator's all-American son takes the stand and tells the world he's outing himself to save an innocent man's life. The jury will know that took courage and that he's telling the truth. They'll have to conclude that Diaz is being framed."

"That's just it. Gardner says that Schulman had his ass handed to him by the judge."

"What do you mean?"

"Schulman's star witness took off with his mother for some island in the Caribbean before he could be served, and Stoney wouldn't postpone the trial."

"Jackson? I thought Allen was the trial judge."

"He's in the hospital with a heart problem."

Crowder felt a sudden pang of guilt. By going to his home, she'd tipped off the senator that his son could provide Diaz with an alibi. If she'd told Schulman first, he could have surprised Tipton's son with a subpoena before he'd taken off.

"Sid, I've been keeping you away from the case," she said, "but if Diaz is innocent, the last man standing is Rossi. I spoke to him. He had contact with all three victims. Knew they were pregnant. Knew where they'd be. Had a key to the clinic. Knew the security code. It would have been easy for him to frame Diaz."

"You still need some direct evidence tying him to the bodies."

"I have a plan that just might provide it, but I'll need some help."

Crowder went on her computer and accessed the database of the New Orleans Department of Homeland Security's Real Time Crime Center that identified the locations of more than 400 surveillance cameras throughout the city. Police, fire and other first responders used the cameras when called to emergencies and to monitor criminal activity in the city. If there was a camera close to the locations where the victims' bodies were found, one of them may have captured Rossi's Lincoln Aviator—maybe the plate number—when he drove to the two churches and the archbishop's residence to dispose of the bodies.

The print-out she obtained showed 428 surveillance cameras, mostly located on telephone poles at intersections in the city.

With Steele looking over her shoulder, Crowder brought up a map of the city and methodically located the cameras closest to the three locations where the girls were found. "Sid, look here. There's a surveillance camera a block away from St. Stephan's. It's the street that runs along the park—a logical route to take to get to the church. Let's get the tapes for Sunday morning. He most likely left the body at the church between midnight and daybreak.

"The girl was found around six-thirty, according to Father Julian," Steele remembered out loud.

"We'll start at six-thirty and work back to midnight."

They did searches for Holy Angels Catholic Church and the archbishop's home and found cameras at intersections within a two-block radius.

"That's a lot of footage to review in slow motion," Steele

said.

"We'll put cadets from the academy on special assignment beginning tonight. They'll need photos of a black Lincoln Aviator. Once we get the tapes and photos to them, they can work on the computers there and report their results when they finish tomorrow. The cameras are too far away to show someone leaving the bodies. But we might find Rossi's vehicle going to or coming from those locations around the same time."

"Like we did with the surveillance tapes from the two schools to locate Weymouth's truck."

"Right. But this time we're at a disadvantage because it was nighttime. Getting a plate number may not be possible if the intersections aren't well lit, or the angle of the camera lens isn't just right."

"We'll need a plate number to prove it's Rossi's."

"Not necessarily. The Aviator is a recent model that hasn't been out very long. Here, take a look." Crowder brought up images of the vehicle on her computer.

"The rear cargo space would easily hold a grocery cart," Steele said.

"I know. And the Lincoln Aviator is a recent model luxury sports utility vehicle with a price tag over fifty thousand dollars, so there aren't many on the road just yet."

"How many cadets do you want?"

"Six. We'll need three pairs—two for each location, one hour on, one hour off. Tired eyes miss things. I'll meet you and the cadets in the computer lab at the academy at six."

"On it," Steele said, heading back to his desk to make some calls. He had cadets to recruit.

Crowder, meanwhile, put a call into the Department of Homeland Security. She had surveillance tapes to request.

Crowder settled back on her sofa with a cold beer, feet propped up on a coffee table. Fred lay on the floor in the middle of the room gnawing on what remained of a ham bone. After she'd met with the cadets at the police academy and instructed them on their assignment, she'd worked out at the gym and then stopped for Chinese on the way home—enough for two, just in case. She was dead tired. The shower she needed could wait until morning.

Fred growled just before the doorbell rang. She wondered if it was Schulman needing some comfort and companionship after a rough day in court. Now she'd wished she showered. No worries. They could take a sudsy bath together. The prospect of it aroused her. But when she opened the door, her brother greeted her instead. She couldn't hide her disappointment—the smile quickly evaporated from her face. "Oh … Tom. I didn't expect you."

"Nice to see you, too," he said with a laugh. "Expecting someone else?"

"Let's just leave it at this—the bath I'd planned tonight will have to wait until tomorrow."

"Hellman is such a dick," Tom said, walking to the refrigerator for a beer, then going to sit next to his sister. "He knew Schulman wouldn't be able to subpoena Tipton's son. He told me he didn't know, but I don't believe him."

"Do you think he tipped off the senator?"

"It wouldn't surprise me. But proving it is another thing. He told the judge that Schulman's addition of an alibi witness was untimely even though I told him this morning, before we got to the courthouse, that it would be reversible error for the court to disallow the testimony from the senator's son on that basis alone. There's an Allen opinion directly on that point."

"Do you think not postponing the trial until Tipton's son returns is grounds for appeal?" Crowder asked.

"Unfortunately, it's not. It's within the trial court's discretion. There's clear precedent on that as well. The kid's only hope is that Bryce Tipton somehow musters the courage to defy his father and comes back to testify."

Crowder sighed. "I went to see the boy on Friday. He wanted to talk to me. The senator stopped him and told me to leave."

"How did you find out the two of them were connected?"

Crowder summarized how—Diaz's phone records, the security company's monitoring data, Tipton's sudden disappearance from school.

"Could Gardner have done what you did?"

"He had the phone records. Then again, Gardner, if he were twice as smart, would still be an idiot. He knows that Hellman doesn't care about the truth, Tom. He only cares about convictions. It's a lot easier to pin the crimes on a poor Latino kid who's being framed than to pursue an investigation that might implicate the Catholic Church."

"You suspect a priest?"

"I'll know tomorrow."

"I'm calling Sessions tomorrow morning. It's mostly my show the next couple of days— the medical and forensic evidence. Hellman is calling Angelica Lopez's parents and one of her classmates. He had them in the office over the weekend. The parents are prepared to say that the only boy their daughter ever went out with was Diaz and that he was the only one who could've gotten her pregnant. The school friend will corroborate that the girl was sweet on him."

"But there's no direct evidence proving that he fathered the child."

"The lab test was inconclusive because the blood sample

was contaminated. But Stoney ruled we can still argue that the circumstantial evidence supports a reasonable inference that Diaz was the father."

"Why didn't Gardner get another sample from Sessions and have the lab run another test?"

"Too late. The girl was embalmed and buried by the time he got around to requesting it."

"Schulman's back's to the wall, Jo. If he puts Diaz on the stand, Hellman will tear him apart on cross examination. He'll make it look like Diaz killed the other two girls first to make Lopez's murder look like another random act of a serial killer who had an ax to grind with pregnant teenagers." Tom finished his beer in one long swallow, got up, and tossed the can in a recycling bin. "Well, I'm off," he said turning to leave. "Lots of evidence and testimony goes in tomorrow. I need a decent night's sleep."

"Hey! Take some Chinese with you. I ordered more than one person can eat."

"Thanks, but I'll take a pass. Claire's cooking a couple of steaks."

When her brother left, Crowder's thoughts turned to Schulman, and they were not about sharing Chinese food, sudsy baths and romps in the hay. They were about a lawyer whose case was falling apart and whose client's head was about to be handed to him on a serving tray.

Chapter 34

Rossi drove his Lincoln Aviator to the convent to visit with the Reverend Mother. It was that special day when he lifted her into a wheelchair and took her to the convent's immaculately maintained, lushly landscaped walled garden. A strategically located six-decade-old elm tree provided ample shade. A shrine of the Virgin Mary with her statue holding the baby Jesus stood at the center of the garden. Rossi remembered the shrine well. As a child the garden had been his private playground; he'd stood beside the Reverend Mother there to say afternoon prayers.

He'd been gently scolded by the nuns for traipsing through the rectangular bed of perennials and annuals that covered the ground in front of the statue like a blanket, and for trying to catch butterflies and picking blossoms to make bouquets for the Reverend Mother—who always forgave him for his transgressions.

It was a comfortably warm day with just enough breeze to offset the high New Orleans humidity. He covered her shoulders with a handmade shawl of fine-silk challis that he'd brought from Rome. He placed her rosary in her one good hand and prayed aloud as he'd done when he was a child. Her fingers moved from one bead to another in sync with each Hail Mary. When he finished, he stayed with her until her head began to droop, a sure sign she was ready for her afternoon nap. He removed the rosary beads from her hand and wheeled her back to her room.

When he lay her in bed, she became alert once again. Her eyes met his as she raised her one good arm just enough off the bedsheet to point her finger at the dresser in her room.

"Is there something on the dresser you want?" he asked.

She blinked twice for "no" and continued to point, her hand now trembling under the weight of the effort.

"Is there something in a drawer of your dresser you want me to get?"

She blinked once for "yes."

"Is it in the top drawer?"

Two blinks for "no."

"The drawer below it?"

Her single blink led him to it. Inside the drawer he found bundles of envelopes—the many letters he'd written while living in Rome and attending the university. Photographs of himself as a child growing up at the convent sat in neat stacks beside them, many of him with the Reverend Mother—pushing him in a stroller, holding his hand as he took his first steps, swaying him in a makeshift swing that hung from the giant elm in the garden, and standing beside him while he blew out five candles on a birthday cake.

One letter set apart caught his eye—addressed to "My Beloved Thomas." Recognizing the Reverend Mother's handwriting, he picked up the envelope, closed the drawer, and went to sit in the chair beside her bed. He removed the two-page letter from the envelope and began to read it.

Rossi felt the eyes of the Reverend Mother studying his face as he read to himself:

My Dearest Thomas,

I write to you with a heavy heart. I can bear no longer the weight of a sin that has blackened my soul. To reveal what I know of your birth may bring much distress to you and to your Reverend Father who has raised you as a son.

But if I hope to one day see the face of God, I must cleanse my soul of a lie that I had chosen to live for so many years.

Rossi stopped reading, studied the envelope, and quickly scanned the letter, looking for some indication of the day it was written. Surely it had to have been written years earlier before her strokes deprived her of the ability to compose a letter.

He continued:

I witnessed your birth. I delivered you with the help of Sister Margaret Mary who has since passed away. The young girl, your mother, couldn't have been more than sixteen years old. She was brought to us by your Reverend Father while he was the pastor of St. Stephan's. He'd told us to tell no one and to take care of your mother until you were born.

Your mother was already in labor. We found a room remote from those of the other sisters, and she gave birth that very night. Her labor was long and difficult. We feared she might not survive the birth, but she fought hard to have you, and God rewarded her for her courage.

Rossi stopped momentarily to reflect. *Who was she, this mother of mine?* She'd been shrouded in mystery for so many years. As a child, he'd dreamt of her, but the face of the woman he saw was always the face of a middle-aged nun.

He read on:

When your Reverend Father saw you for the first time, he took you in his arms and kissed your head and your little hands. I could see plainly that his plan was to provide for your needs. He told me to take you to another room and provide for your care while he counseled your mother about what to do with her child if she couldn't care for him. He was praying over her when I returned. While the Reverend Father was with your mother, she expired—from an untreated underlying illness, he believed.

He'd told me that she gave no name, was parentless and living on the streets, and unsure who the father might be. I recall as though it was today that, at the height of her labor, she cried out for your Reverend Father to save her baby and forgive her for her sins. Later, when she first held you in her arms, I could see in her face that her love for you was deep. She wanted you, my dearest Thomas, of that I'm sure.

Rossi paused to look endearingly at the face of the Reverend Mother, her eyes wide open and glistening. He said, "For you to have shared such tender moments of the mother who gave life to me makes my heart overflow with love for her … and for you."

He returned to the letter:

Your Reverend Father believed it was best for you to be spared the anguish of knowing the circumstances of your birth and for him to raise you as a son. Sister Margaret Mary and I were made to swear an oath to bury your past with your mother, whose death was hidden from the authorities. I know now that was an unholy oath before God because God knows only truth, and only through truth shall we know God.

Forgive me, Thomas.

He sat back and reflected on the day of his birth—and his mother's death. The revelations in the letter left him with many unanswered questions. He needed to know more—a lot more.

There was only one person who could provide the answers.

Chapter 35

The screening of the surveillance tapes would not be completed until late afternoon, so Crowder headed over to the courthouse to listen to Dr. Session's testimony on the morning of the second day of Diaz's trial. She'd had a special interest in the forensic autopsies he'd performed ever since she became a homicide detective.

Ordinarily, she'd be sitting in the seat Gardner occupied.

She arrived just in time to hear her brother announce to the court and jury that he was calling Sessions to the witness stand. She took a seat next to Travis Jones.

"So you find the killer and arrest him, and Jack Gardner takes the credit and replaces you as chief investigator. What's not right with that picture?" Jones whispered to Crowder.

"He can have the credit. I just wish he had the right guy sitting next to defense counsel."

"What do you mean?"

"Diaz has a solid alibi on the nights the girls were murdered, but the alibi hightailed it out of the country before he could be subpoenaed."

"No postponement?"

"It's a long, sad story."

Tom Crowder expertly questioned Sessions and put before the jury the gruesome facts of how the three victims were shot full of propofol, bled to death, cut open and mutilated. According to Sessions, the nearly identical autopsy findings, incisions and suturing were the consistent mark of a serial killer. The jurors gave a collective gasp when his testimony turned graphic, and several of the women became teary-eyed when the crime scene photos of the girls' dead, naked bodies were circulated to them.

Hellman's cocky smile coincided with the dilated-eye look of hate on the jurors' faces as they periodically turned to glare at Diaz.

When the direct examination concluded, Schulman stood and asked the only questions he knew would be answered favorably for his client.

"Dr. Sessions, none of your autopsy findings connect Miguel Diaz to the girls' abductions or to how they were sedated, correct?"

"That's correct."

"Nothing you uncovered from your autopsies links Miguel to how the three girls were made to bleed to death."

"Also correct. My findings do not prove who did these things to the three victims, only what was done to them."

"And nothing in the lab work you did on the three victims indicates that Miguel fathered their babies?"

"The fetal blood testing of the first two victims established that Miguel Diaz was not the father of their babies. The third, of Angelica Lopez, was inconclusive."

"Why was it inconclusive?"

"The blood sample was contaminated."

"What contaminated the sample?"

"It was unclear from the lab report what contaminated it."

257

"Why not retest with another sample?"

"By the time the request was made she'd been embalmed and interred."

"So the failure of the state to promptly secure a proper blood sample deprived my client the chance of proving that he did not father Angelica Lopez's baby."

"Well, I suppose that's true."

"And, to be clear, nothing in the testimony you've given today implicates Miguel Diaz in any of the victims' pregnancies, their deaths or the deaths of their babies."

"That's correct. I'm here to explain what happened, not who made it happen."

Crowder had to admit. As good as Tom's questioning was, Schulman's cross examination took the wind out of his sails, mitigating the effect of Sessions' testimony. She'd tell him the first chance she had.

"Any redirect?" the judge asked.

Tom Crowder stood but did not return to the lectern. He had a single question—one that would give him the last word with the jury.

"One question, your Honor. Dr. Sessions, the fact that the fetal blood test was inconclusive doesn't mean that Mr. Diaz was not the father of Angelica Lopez's baby, does it?"

"True. If he was the father, it would have to be proved in some other way."

"We'll take a fifteen-minute recess," the judge announced when Tom Crowder sat down.

Jones and Crowder met up with Sessions in the hallway during the break. "Do we know how the blood sample got contaminated?" Crowder asked.

"It wasn't on our end," Sessions said. "I personally obtained the blood sample and was there when Travis labeled the tube. It had to be on the lab's end."

"How often does that happen?"

"Rarely," Sessions said.

"Let me call the lab," Jones offered. "See what I can find out."

"You do that, Travis," Sessions said. "There should be an incident report in the lab's quality control files that explains how the sample was contaminated."

Schulman showed up beside Crowder as Sessions and Jones headed for the elevator. "Nice job on cross," she said.

"It only temporarily places some distance between Miguel and the Lopez girl's pregnancy and the three murders. The gap will close soon enough when the forensics techs testify."

"You still have the argument that prints weren't found on the only evidence that connects him to the victims."

"But someone had to put the evidence in Diaz's locker. The jury will want to know: If not Diaz, then who? I have no one to give them."

Schulman wanted to change the subject.

So did Crowder.

"I wanted to come over and see you last night but figured you didn't want to be around someone who'd just hit into a triple play with the bases loaded."

Crowder had a flashback of her reverie about them playing like two kids in the bathtub. It made her smile. "The game's not over. You'll get some more at bats."

"You're right. Tomorrow's another day."

"And tonight's another night," Crowder said with an impish grin.

"Detective Crowder, you've just made my day."

"And just maybe your night, counselor."

~

We have what you want. It's on the way over. The text came to Crowder around four in the afternoon from the police academy's training officer who supervised the cadets when they screened the surveillance tapes. A half hour later, a cadet dropped off a computer disc labeled: *Slow mo footage from cameras closest to the locations where the three victims were found.*

A wave of her hand got Steele over to her desk. He pulled a chair closer to her computer screen as they both watched.

The first screenshot showed the date and time of the first tape: Palm Sunday at 4:12 a.m. The film moved slowly as a black Lincoln Aviator moved through the intersection in the direction of St. Stephan's Cathedral, a block away.

She stopped the film when the vehicle was closest to the camera and enhanced the image. The intersection was well lit; so the vehicle was seen clearly. A side shot showed the driver, but only his right hand on the steering wheel. The camera angle didn't allow for the plate number to be seen.

The next screenshot was Thursday at 4:18 a.m.—two blocks from Holy Angels Catholic Church where Beverly Calloway was found. Once again, a black Lincoln Aviator passed slowly through the intersection in the direction of the church. The intersection was not as well-lit as on the first screenshot, but the car was plainly visible. As it left the intersection, the rear of the vehicle came into view. But just as it did, another vehicle crossed the intersection and turned behind the Lincoln blocking a view of the license plate.

"The only other car out at four in the morning, and it blocks our view of the plate," Steele groaned.

The last screenshot was Easter Sunday, two blocks from the archbishop's residence. No footage—just the words: *no Lincoln*

Aviators observed.

Crowder said, "Two for three's not bad. It's more than coincidence that a vehicle meeting the description of Rossi's vehicle is seen a block away from the churches. I need an evidence detection unit ready to go tomorrow at ten, and I want a plainclothesman in an unmarked car on Rossi beginning an hour ago."

"You've got it," Steele said. "What do you make of the vehicle being seen at the intersection going to but not coming from St. Stephan's?"

"Doesn't surprise me. He'd want to pass in front of the church first. Be sure no one was around. He'd turn on a side street and park close to the church. He'd get the shopping cart from the back of his SUV, put the girl in it, cover her with the sheet, and move her to the front of St. Stephan's. Then, he'd take the side streets and work his way home."

"Same for victim number two?

"Makes sense. Remember, the streets in front of both churches are two way. He could have taken the more direct route home, but chose to work his way back on side streets instead. Someone may have driven by, seen him bring the girls to the front of the churches, and stopped to figure things out. By not returning home the same way he came, he left nothing to chance."

Crowder picked up a phone directory. After finding the number, she dialed and connected to a secretary. "Detective Lieutenant Jo Crowder. Will he be in his office tomorrow?"

The secretary provided some information to Crowder who, when she'd finished, said, "Then I'll see him tomorrow morning at nine."

Chapter 36

"Father, what do you know of my birth mother?" Rossi asked, the subject being in the forefront of his mind.

Santini sat across from Rossi in the study of the archbishop's home having late afternoon tea. "Nothing. She left you in a basket in a pew at St. Stephan's with a note she'd written asking that you be taken care of and raised a Catholic."

"Did you save the note?"

"I'm afraid, Thomas, that after so many years, it may be difficult to locate it. Why do you ask?"

"I visited the Reverend Mother this afternoon and she directed me to a letter she'd written. It contained references to my birth."

"If it was written a while back when she was still able to write, it could've been when she was experiencing occasional delusions that preceded the stroke she had."

"The letter described how my mother came to you, and you brought her to the convent where the Reverend Mother and another nun, Sister Margaret Mary, acted as midwives and delivered me."

"This letter, do you have it with you?"

"Yes." Rossi pulled the letter from the inside pocket of his suit jacket and handed it to Santini who put on his eyeglasses and read it to himself.

"I remember Sister Margaret Mary. She was an elderly nun, sickly for years. She may have been deceased by the time of your birth. But I can't be sure; it was so long ago." Looking over his reading glasses, he asked, "Would it make a difference to you, Thomas, if what she wrote was true?"

"I don't know, Father. I can understand deceiving me as a child. But, as an adult, did you not trust my feelings for you enough to share what you knew of my mother with me?"

"Sometimes the past brings back painful memories that are best left forgotten."

"If you mean that I was conceived in sin, I feel no shame for her or for me. God's capacity to forgive … and to love, is boundless. You taught me that, Father."

"I'm afraid that the Reverend Mother was experiencing dementia shortly after you left for Rome six years ago. Not long afterwards, she had her first stroke."

"I remember her being quite coherent when I last saw her. We exchanged letters for a month or two before you informed me of her stroke."

"The onset was rapid. She'd speak to people in her room who were not there. When I spoke of you, she thought you were her deceased husband. Hearing her being called Reverend Mother had her believing for a while that she was Mother Teresa.

"I regretted not being with her after her stroke," Rossi lamented, lowering his head and momentarily staring at the floor.

"I wanted to spare you the stress of the sudden decline in her mental state. The affairs of the Holy Father you were handling were your first priority."

Rossi looked up. "The details in her letter are so precise. Did she just make them up?"

"She probably harbored the belief that your birth mother was a prostitute, which may very well have been true. She just let her imagination fill in some blanks in her story." Santini glanced at the letter as though giving it a quick re-reading. "She says that your mother's death was hidden from the authorities. How is that even possible? She doesn't mention what happened to your mother's body. Did it evaporate into thin air? No, my son, the references to your mother are figments of an elderly woman's unhinged imagination."

"I sensed from my time with her today that she was trying to speak. Her mouth moved, and I thought I caught a word or two."

Santini moved forward in his chair. "She spoke? What words?"

"Two words. 'Forgive us.'"

"Stay for dinner, Thomas."

"No, Father. I should prepare for our trip."

"Then, let's meet for breakfast tomorrow at eight."

Rossi went to the closet for his suit jacket without responding.

"Sleep well, my son," Santini said as Rossi left the study, then he walked to a window facing the front of the house and watched as Rossi drove away.

The phone rang. He returned to his desk to answer the call. It was Sister Agnes.

"Your Grace, the most remarkable thing has happened. The Reverend Mother spoke. Only a few words, but I heard them clearly. She said, '*Perdona i nostri peccati.*'"

"Forgive us our sins," Santini said, translating the Latin phrase aloud. "Did she say anything else?"

"She cried out for the monsignor."

"What, precisely, were her words?"

"Come to me, Thomas. Please come to me."

"I'll be over shortly to visit with the Reverend Mother."

"Should I call the monsignor?"

"No. I'll do that. He's on an assignment for me at present. Let me see if I can comfort her."

Santini hung up and gathered his suit jacket from the closet. He did not call Rossi.

He went to the garage for his car and drove to the convent.

It was time to find out what else the Reverend Mother was prepared to tell Thomas.

~

"Does she continue to speak?" Santini asked Sister Agnes, who sat in a chair beside the bed, holding the Reverend Mother's hand.

"Only to ask for the monsignor. To speak requires so much effort. I dare say she's saving her words for him."

"Sadly, purposefully preserving her remaining strength to speak later means that the end may very well be in sight. Her vital signs. How are they?"

"Stable. She holds on."

"Is she in any pain?"

"It's difficult to say. There was blood in her urine, and she's feverish. I fear she may have a urinary tract infection."

"Yes, which can be very painful. If she's to preserve her strength, perhaps a small amount of morphine will ease her pain. Let me sit beside her, Sister Agnes." The nun ceded her chair to him. "Would you like Sister Agnes to give you something for your pain?" he asked. "Squeeze my hand if you do." The old nun's hand remained rigid. Santini waited a few seconds and then announced: "Good. Then you shall have a small dose to ease your pain and relax you. Prepare it, Sister Agnes."

"Yes, Your Grace," the nun responded obediently. "But just a half dose. A full dose will surely bring on sleep."

Sister Agnes went to the cabinet on the wall beside the bed where the morphine was kept and opened the door. Santini's eyes peered over the nun's shoulder and saw four vials of morphine, three in boxes beside one unboxed, half-full vial. Sister Agnes found a syringe among the medical supplies in the cabinet, removed the sterile packaging and filled the syringe with two cubic centimeters of morphine from the unboxed vial—half the usual dose. She found a vein in the elderly nun's left arm and injected her.

"Now, how's that, Reverend Mother?" Santini asked as the nun disposed of the syringe. "Your pain will soon be gone. Sister Agnes, leave me alone with her. I will pray by her side and wait until the monsignor arrives."

The nun left the room, closing the door behind her.

Santini stood and looked down into the nun's face; her eyes were only slightly opened.

"Thomas," she said in a raspy whisper.

"No, Reverend Mother. It's me, the archbishop. I wanted to speak to you before Thomas arrives." Santini's tone was mellow but firm. "He showed me a letter you wrote him some time ago that he just now read. Are you feeling pangs of guilt? Come now, you must not dwell on the past. Why stain his image of an unblemished past? My plans for him are that he follow in my footsteps, and beyond. As a cardinal, I and my family wield the necessary influence to take us on a blessed pilgrimage—to the Basilica and the Chair of St. Peter. It's time for an American pope, don't you agree, Reverend Mother?"

The nun's mouth opened, and her lips trembled as she spoke.

Santini lowered his head and turned an ear toward her mouth to hear better. "Thomas must know what you did," she murmured, her words barely audible.

"Now, now, we must have none of that," he said, raising his head. "Thomas is convinced that you were delirious when you wrote that letter. Let's not create more melodrama surrounding his birth … and his mother's death."

Santini walked over to the medicine cabinet and opened the door. Sister Agnes had returned the partially filled vial to the cabinet beside the three unopened boxes of morphine. He reached for a pair of latex gloves from a box on a shelf below the drugs, and put them on. He reached next for the morphine— not the opened vial but a boxed one and removed the full vial of morphine from it. He returned the empty box to the cabinet, centering it between the other two, opened the lidded waste can next to the cabinet, and retrieved the syringe that Sister Agnes had used earlier. Sticking the needle of the syringe into the vial, he withdrew all eight cubic centimeters of morphine.

He didn't bother to release the air bubbles that had gathered in the syringe. It didn't matter for what he had planned. He found the small puncture in the nun's paralyzed left arm where the earlier injection had been given and injected her until the syringe was empty. Then he dropped the syringe in the waste can, removed his latex gloves and placed them in one pocket of his suit jacket and the empty vial in the other. He pulled out his cell phone and auto-dialed his most recent call. After four rings, he connected to the person's voicemail and left a message: "Thomas, please come at once. It's the Reverend Mother. She's extremely unwell."

Chapter 37

It was close to eight o'clock when the doorbell rang. This time she knew who was at the door. A quick shower after her workout, a touch of lip gloss, and a spritz of body cologne in the right places was all that was necessary to remind him of their first evening together. Crowder was never much on dressing up, preferring to lounge in her department-issued sweats. But tonight required an upgrade of her ensemble—soft denim Levi's and an blue Old Navy crew neck T-shirt brought just enough of an upgrade.

She was greeted by a man with an easy smile holding up a handled paper bag in one hand and a six pack of beer in the other. "The takeout you ordered, miss. Two po' boys and some Bud to wash them down."

Schulman had dressed casually in corduroy slacks and the shirt he'd worn that day in court, unbuttoned midway to the top, sleeves rolled up, shirt tail hanging out. His casual, comfortable appearance put Crowder instantly at ease.

"Beware of criminal defense lawyers bearing gifts," she quipped.

They settled in on the sofa with beers in hand. The sandwiches were the last thing on Crowder's mind, and she sensed his, too. They took long swigs in silence, just looking at each other, their eyes a roadmap to where they were headed.

Crowder suspected he was as eager as she for an encore performance of their night of lovemaking. Her suspicions were confirmed when he gently brushed his hand on her cheek and said, "I missed you, Jo. I feel like a teenage boy with his first crush on a girl."

Crowder pressed the index finger of her right hand against his lips and said, "Shush!" The time to share how they felt about each other would come afterwards. She placed her hands on his cheeks, leaned into him, and kissed him on the lips—a Schulman kiss—moist, soft and sensual.

Crowder straddled him. Once on his lap, she removed her top. Schulman kissed her neck, gradually working his way down to her breast and nipples, a journey made easier by the absence of a bra. She felt the firmness of his erection as he repositioned himself so he could grip her bottom with both hands while she wrapped her arms around his neck.

He stood.

"The bedroom's on your right," she panted.

"Fred?"

"He's in the spare with a ham bone."

~

They lay back in bed. He held her in his arms; she rested her head on his muscular chest, the beat of his heart still audible, still quick.

So was hers.

She was content to say nothing, do nothing. Just enjoy the moment, and remember the first words he uttered when their lovemaking adventure had concluded. "It's been a long time since I've felt so close to someone," he'd said. "I want you to be part of my life, Jo."

Her words had come just as naturally as his. "And I want you to be part of mine, Drew."

Crowder's feelings for Schulman surprised her. She wasn't looking for love. It had come to her. A deep emotional attachment was forming between them. Whether it would survive the test of time remained to be seen. But, for now at least, she'd ride this train for as far as it would take her and do something she'd not done for a very long time—she'd follow her heart.

When their embers cooled, Crowder sat up in bed, prompting Schulman to do the same. "How did the afternoon go?" she asked.

"Not very well. Gardner testified how your search uncovered the girls' hair on the brush, and the forensics tech boasted about the accuracy of his DNA testing of it. When the tech said the murderer had to have collected the strands by brushing the victims' hair, I could see the women on the jury recoil from the visual he created."

"How did the jury react to the absence of fingerprints?"

"Gardner was ready. He blew it off. He said the murderer was wearing gloves. He wasn't nearly as accommodating as you were at the prelim."

"What did he say when you suggested the evidence was planted?"

"He answered with a question like I knew he would. 'Who would do that?' he said. 'The only people that worked at the clinic were doctors, nurses and a nun, all with airtight alibis.' I had no one to give him."

"Hellman. Did he put the parents on the stand?"

"You bet. They both pointed at Miguel like they were

holding a gun on him. Hellman got Mrs. Lopez all emotional. She cried when asked to identify the only boy their daughter ever went out with. She blurted out, 'We trusted you, Miguel, and you do this to our precious Angel.' Stoney wouldn't recess before my cross examination, so I had to deal with her weeping for the few questions I asked."

"Are you going to put him on the stand?"

"I have no choice. He's the only one who can say who he was with. At least, the appellate court will have a record of how important Tipton's testimony would've been to his defense. But it won't be pretty tomorrow."

Crowder snuggled up to Schulman who put an arm around her. "Drew, I have a suspect."

"Who?" he asked excitedly.

"Rossi."

"The monsignor?"

"I have him in his car at four in the morning a block from the churches where the first two victims were found."

"Have you confronted him about it?"

"He doesn't know what we have … not yet. But when I spoke to him last week, he told me he was home alone when the girls were abducted and in bed when the girls would've been left at the churches."

"It's hard to believe that someone like him would do such horrible things to those girls," Schulman mused aloud.

"No harder to believe than Diaz doing them," Crowder said, with the cynicism that comes with being a homicide detective in a city where the violent crime rate was several times the national average. "We execute the search warrant for his apartment, car and office tomorrow morning. I'll text you if we have enough evidence for an arrest."

"If you do, Stoney will have to grant a postponement, at

least until things get sorted out. Who are you getting to sign off on the warrant?"

"Allen. He's out of the hospital and will be back in his office tomorrow."

"Smart choice. He'll remember what you did in the Sanders case."

Crowder heard her lover sigh. Whether it was a sigh of desperation, or just plain exhaustion, was unclear. What was clearer than crystal was that unless the searches revealed hard evidence that Rossi was a cold-blooded killer, Diaz's fate was sealed.

~

Rossi arrived before Santini returned home. He went to the study to wait for him. He hung his suit jacket in the closet and unsnapped and removed his collar. Both clerics wore the traditional clothing of a priest—black worsted-wool suit, black-silk waistcoat worn over a neckband shirt and a detachable white-linen collar. Being nearly the same height and weight, they often shared their clothing.

When Santini returned and entered the study, Rossi was pouring himself a glass of wine from a mini bar built into one of the walls. "A glass of Chianti, Father?" he asked.

Santini put his suit jacket in the closet and removed his collar, placing it next to Rossi's. "Yes, Thomas. Thank you."

Rossi poured two wine glasses three-quarters full and brought one to him. They sat in chairs facing each other but separated by a coffee table.

Santini took a sip. "My penchant for wine, a good Chianti, in particular, is one habit I brought to this country from Rome when I entered the university here so many years ago."

"And I, as well, when introduced to it growing up with our family in Rome."

"The Reverend Mother's passing, Thomas, while unfortunate, was divine intervention."

Rossi, who had appeared lost in thought, looked up with a surprised expression on his face. "Father, how can you say such a thing?"

"For her to have passed while we were in Rome would have made it impossible for us to have returned to celebrate the Requiem Mass and be present at her interment."

"But, knowing our relationship to her, the Holy Father would surely have allowed us to depart earlier than the others."

"Almost as surely as I would never have allowed you to beseech him. I have the grandest of plans for you and I, Thomas. Never lose the opportunity to consort with members of the College of Cardinals. They alone elect the pontiff. I want us to meet as many of them as possible."

"It's your moment, Father. I would not be so brazen as to intrude upon it."

"And your moment as well, my son. Plans are already underway. Our family will be hosting several events and dinners. Enrico Verducci, the great tenor, will be performing at one. The most important cardinals, and all of the Italians, will be invited. You and I will address them during the affairs and provide them with our vision of the future of the Catholic Church. I've prepared some remarks for you to give."

"Shouldn't I prepare them myself?"

"Certain things are best not left to chance. Your modern-day ideas, while appealing to our congregants here in the states, are anathema to most of the world. Many cardinals, I dare say most, relish the thought of a return to traditional values. The pendulum is swinging back in that direction, and you would be wise to swing with it."

Rossi looked at the archbishop with a surprised look on his face. "I accept our traditional values. The sanctity of life, adherence to the precepts of the church ... but times change ... people change. Surely the Catholic Church has the resilience to change with it."

"A core of cardinals wants to stay the course of change, and they hold the votes necessary to elect the next pope."

"Is the Holy Father unwell?"

"No. He's fine, at least for the present. But there's a plan in place that one day will put me in the line of succession and you to follow me as an American cardinal."

"I know the politics well, Father. Five years at the Vatican taught me that. A bishop is more than a life's worth of accomplishment for any priest. While you are surely qualified to lead the Catholic Church, I'm content to serve this archdiocese."

"Humbly put. But remember that the pope is first and foremost a bishop—the Bishop of Rome. It may very well come to pass that you follow in the footsteps of your father."

"I understand how influential our family is at the Vatican and with the Italian cardinals. I saw it while in the service of the Holy Father. That, and your service to the church, may portend that you lead us."

"That's just it. The Italians are a fifth of the electors in the College of Cardinals, a substantial voting bloc. Yet there hasn't been an Italian pope in almost a half century. The Italian cardinals are restless and will know that their best hope is an Italian with centuries-long family ties to Rome and the Vatican ... who happens to be a North American cardinal. And the American cardinals would certainly support my selection."

Changing the subject, Rossi asked, "Where shall we celebrate the Reverend Mother's Requiem Mass?"

"St. Stephan's, of course. I instructed Sister Ann to notify her closest relatives and to prepare an appropriate obituary for publication tomorrow. The service will be Friday. We fly out Saturday morning. The ceremonial mass for new Cardinals is Sunday morning, and your ordination is in the afternoon." Santini paused a moment, and then said, "Why do you look so sullen, Thomas?"

Rossi's mind was on the Reverend Mother. "I promised the Reverend Mother I would bring back the video in commemoration of our ordinations and watch it with her. I sensed from her eye movements and the strength of her grip on my hand that it would have given her great pleasure. This afternoon, she seemed stronger than I've seen her in months."

"One as disabled as she was could have a downward turn at any moment, as she did today. Thomas, I would like you to do the eulogy."

"I would be honored, Father."

"Then let us have supper and discuss the preparations for our trip."

Rossi followed Santini out of the study, but not before refilling his glass nearly to the top and bringing the bottle of Chianti with him as he left.

Chapter 38

"It wasn't easy, but I got it," Crowder said to Steele when she called him from Judge Allen's chambers. "Where is he?"

"He stayed the night at the archbishop's home and returned to his apartment at nine this morning."

"Good. Have a detection unit search his apartment and car while I search his office at the archbishop's home. Allen cautioned me to limit my search to the four corners of his office. I go anywhere else, he'll want my badge."

Crowder parked her pickup on the street and walked to the front entrance. She overcame the housekeeper's reluctance to allow her to enter by flashing her gold shield in one hand and waving the warrant in the other.

No brush-off this time.

While waiting for Santini to enter the study, Crowder again studied the family photographs on the wall, marveling at how much Rossi looked like Santini. Standing there, her eyes moved back and forth between side-by-side-framed photos of their ordinations as priests. The dates on the bottom of each photo allowed for a nearly same-age comparison—same black wavy hair, high cheekbones, prominent brows, generous lips and penetrating stares.

Santini's voice interrupted her reflections. When she turned, he was standing so close to her that she could smell his after shave. It startled her. Her back stiffened. She muffled a gasp, and wondered how he could have crossed the room with her not having heard him approaching. Though only an arm's length away, she held her ground when he spoke.

"Yes," he said. "The monsignor and I look very much alike, don't you agree?"

He's perceptive as well as intuitive. Crowder figured he must have been standing behind her, watching her in silence for a while. It was beginning to creep her out. "Yes. A striking resemblance," she replied coolly.

"It makes me wonder if his birth parents were, like mine, Italians from Lazio, the region of my family's origins. So how can I be of service to you today, Detective Crowder?"

"I have a warrant to search the monsignor's office," she said, handing him a copy of the warrant.

"And just what do you hope to find in your little scavenger hunt?" he asked, hastily looking over the warrant without bothering to put on his eyeglasses.

"I'll know that when I finish the search," she said, not muffling the edge in her voice.

He led her to a room at the rear of the house, passing by other rooms on the way, including a small chapel. Crowder looked in as she passed by it—eight Italian provincial armchairs with scarlet-red satin upholstered seat cushions and matching kneelers facing a small white-marble altar. A gold-plated crucifix of Jesus Christ hung above it.

"Here it is," Santini said when he came to Rossi's office. He stood at the doorway and waved his hand for Crowder to enter.

"I'll have an inventory of items for the monsignor when I finish so that he knows what's been taken."

"Please do. I wouldn't want him to believe that an intruder ransacked his office and made off with all his earthly possessions. I'll be in the study holding my breath in anticipation of what you might find."

Crowder let the clergyman's sarcasm roll off her back. When Santini was out of view, she put on a pair of latex gloves while giving the room a visual once over. The leather-top desk was neat and organized: cream-colored personalized stationery in a lidless wooden box, a fountain pen lying on top; a half-dozen, sharpened, number-two pencils in a porcelain tumbler; several folders stacked on each side of the desk, and a spiral-bound daily calendar at the top.

She leafed through the documents in the folders— correspondence, mostly from priests and parishioners, addressed to either Santini or Rossi, along with handwritten notes jotted down on pages from a notepad and paper-clipped to some. It was obvious to Crowder that the monsignor served as the archbishop's chief of staff.

The calendar caught her attention. The individual dates were notated with appointments and names. She flipped back to Easter week. There were entries on the days of the victims' abductions. On the first two dates, he'd written *counsel pregnant teen*. On the third, he'd written *Angelica Lopez – 8 p.m. St. Helena's*. A phone number was entered below with the word *cell* in parentheses.

Going through Rossi's desk, drawer by drawer, led her to four small white boxes in one of them. Opening the boxes, she found religious medals in cellophane wrapping. The clear packaging material allowed her to see plainly the St. Mary Magdalene medals inside. In another drawer, she found news clippings about the girl's abductions, Diaz's arrest, the preliminary hearing and the first day of trial.

The treasure trove was complete when she found an envelope in the top-center drawer addressed to *My Beloved Thomas.*

As she read the letter, certain phrases resounded in her mind: *a sin that has blackened my soul ... the young girl was brought to us by your Reverend Father ... couldn't have been more than sixteen years old ... living on the streets ... she cried hysterically for your Reverend Father ... while the Reverend Father was with your mother, she expired ... whose death was hidden from the authorities ... an unholy oath before God.*

Crowder's analytical mind operated at full throttle. Rossi's mother was a street walker who got pregnant—he was conceived in sin. Could that be the motive for killing three pregnant teens, whose babies were also conceived in sin? Farfetched? No more so than learning that Santini had covered up the death of Rossi's mother. Why would he do that?

How was the young girl's body disposed of? If she was buried in a cemetery or cremated, a report would've been made to the authorities. Neurons sparked in Crowder's mind. The striking resemblance of Rossi to Santini when they were both ordained priests in their early twenties—could Santini, the pastor at St Stephan's Cathedral at the time, be Rossi's biological father? Could Santini have gotten the teenage girl pregnant, which is why she came to him for help?

The puzzle pieces all seemed to fit.

She figured Rossi read the nun's letter, put it all together, and flipped out—killing three pregnant teenage girls.

She bagged the letter, calendar, clippings and medals. Nothing else in the room was evidence connecting the monsignor to the three girls. She'd provide an inventory to him later.

And damn the arrogant archbishop—he could get the inventory from Rossi.

Crowder slipped out of the house without telling him.

~

Crowder met up with Steele at district headquarters.

"Anything?" she asked.

"The car was clean. The only thing that showed up in his apartment was this." Steele dangled an evidence bag in his hand in front of him. In it was the same color and style hairbrush found in Diaz's locker.

Crowder looked at the bristles through the clear plastic and saw clusters of strands of hair. "Get it over to the lab right away. If they find a single strand of hair from just one of the victims, we've found the murderer and the person who planted the evidence in Diaz's locker. We need the results as soon as possible."

"I'll deliver it to the lab personally."

Time was of the essence. Crowder needed to tell Schulman that Rossi's arrest was imminent. The prosecution's case would finish that afternoon. The defense was to begin Thursday morning. She wanted to avoid a repeat of the Sanders case— Stoney Jackson would be far less tolerant than Allen if the trial was interrupted by her antics in his courtroom.

Rossi would remain under surveillance.

Crowder's investigation of the Easter Murders was about to conclude, and it all came down to a single piece of evidence.

Rossi's arrest, and Diaz's freedom, would depend on whose hair was found on a brush.

Chapter 39

Rossi parked his Lincoln Aviator in its usual place in the driveway at the front entrance to the archbishop's home. Santini called him as soon as he discovered that Crowder had left the house. Rossi was there to find out what she had taken.

He sat in the chair behind his desk rummaging through the drawers while Santini watched his protégé from a sofa. When Rossi discovered what was missing, he slumped back in his chair. Being a suspect, he should have anticipated that his home, car and office might be searched. In retrospect, leaving the calendar, the medals and news clippings in his desk had been foolhardy. His mind tried to think like Crowder's: the calendar, proof of his connection to the victims; the medals, symbols he'd left around their necks; the news stories, a way to follow his plan to frame Diaz as it unfolded.

"You should not be concerned, my son. What could they possibly find that connects you to the deaths of those girls?"

"My calendar proves that I knew all of them."

"They already know that. So it doesn't matter. Did they take anything from your car or apartment?"

"Nothing from the car that I know of. They took a hairbrush

from my bedroom."

"And what will that tell them … that you have dandruff?"

Rossi didn't answer. Instead, with the top drawer of his desk opened, he sighed. "The letter—the Reverend Mother's letter. The detective read it and probably believes I harbor ill will toward unwed pregnant teenagers—the motive to kill girls who, like my mother, conceived their babies in sin."

"That's preposterous, Thomas."

"Then why would she take it? She doesn't know that the Reverend Mother was delirious when she wrote the letter."

"I'll explain it all to the police if you are arrested, of course, and that you hadn't even known about the letter until after the girls were murdered. The word of a Roman Catholic cardinal must carry some weight, don't you agree?"

"Do you sense that my arrest is imminent?"

"No need to worry. I've already called our lawyer in Baton Rouge. Now, come into the study. Before he arrives, I want you to see the remarks I've prepared for you to give when we entertain the cardinals in Rome."

Rossi was put off by the archbishop's cavalier attitude. He'd suddenly become the target of a police investigation of a triple homicide. The last thing on his mind when he was about to be arrested for murder, and for framing Diaz for crimes he'd supposedly committed, was a speech he hadn't prepared that he was expected to recite like a poem he'd memorized for an English Lit class.

But, as he'd done all his life, Rossi obeyed the archbishop like the dutiful priest he was—and the acquiescent son he'd always been.

Once inside the study, Rossi removed his suit jacket and hung it in the closet next to Santini's. He unsnapped and removed his collar, and then went to the bar to pour two glasses of wine. Just as he began to pour the second glass, Santini said, "Nothing for me, Thomas. I'll be leaving soon to meet with Sister Ann and complete the preparations for the Reverend Mother's funeral service." Santini passed Rossi his notes. "Here, read these. Become acquainted with the direction we believe the church should be going."

Rossi took the folded papers, but just as he began to read them, the doorbell rang. The housekeeper soon appeared at the doorway of the study with a distinguished-looking man in his early sixties with a neatly trimmed mustache. His perfectly tailored blue-pinstripe suit covered a lean, six-feet-tall frame. His gold, diamond-studded Rolex watch matched his cufflinks and gave notice that he was successful and punctual.

"Your Grace," the man said in an inordinately reverential tone as soon as he entered the room.

"We can dispense with the formalities, Silvio," Santini said with a wave of his hand. "We've known each other far too long for that. Tony will do just fine." Shooting a glance at Rossi, he said, "This is Monsignor Rossi, my personal assistant, and the one all the fuss is about."

"Please call me Thomas," Rossi said, standing to shake the lawyer's hand.

The man took a seat beside Rossi. "And please call me Silvio."

Silvio Abessinio was the founding partner of a law firm he'd started twenty-five years ago with another second-generation Italian attorney that had grown to thirty lawyers. The firm had represented the diocese ever since Santini became archbishop.

"Before you speak, Thomas, it's important that we maintain our attorney-client relationship when we discuss this matter. A third person's presence destroys the confidentiality that protects you from having to disclose to others what you tell me."

Santini stood to leave, and said, "Thomas, you are now in

Silvio's very capable hands. Follow his instructions to the letter and this matter will soon be behind you." He went to the closet and took one of the black suit jackets from it. "It's best you stay at your apartment tonight. I'll see you tomorrow for breakfast at eight."

Santini closed the door of the study when he left, then he went to the garage for his car, and drove to the convent of the Sisters of St. Mary.

Abessinio opened his briefcase, took out a small recorder and placed it on the coffee table. After turning it on, he sat back in his chair and said, "Tell me, Thomas. Why does this homicide detective believe you abducted and murdered three pregnant teenagers?"

Rossi summarized as best he could how most of the circumstantial evidence against Diaz also applied to him—his knowledge of the girls' circumstances and their whereabouts on the days they were abducted, accessibility to the clinic and no alibi. He then discussed what the police had seized during their searches. When he finished, he asked the lawyer, "Don't you want to know if I murdered those girls?"

"I never ask that question. All of my clients are innocent unless and until a twelve-person jury unanimously finds them guilty beyond a reasonable doubt and all of their appeals have been exhausted."

When the interview ended, Rossi led Abessinio to the front door. As he left, the lawyer turned and said, "Don't worry. This unpleasantness will all be over for you when Diaz is convicted of these crimes … and I have it on good authority that he will be convicted and most likely sentenced to death."

Rossi sat back in his chair after pouring himself a glass of Chianti. He knew he was drinking more than he should—in fact every night. He had a ready supply of Chianti and bourbon in his apartment. Contrary to the reported statistics, Catholic priests were disproportionately at risk of alcoholism. And it wasn't because of the frequent consumption of sacramental wine in the masses they celebrated.

He'd had his doubts when he'd taken his vows. He had urges—sexual desires. He'd dated in college and those relationships eventually led to the bedroom of his Washington, D.C. apartment. The many private universities that called the District of Columbia home produced an unlimited supply of intelligent, wealthy, attractive females. The D.C. nightlife was robust, rivaling that of any city in the nation, and Rossi had always been a ready and willing participant. His good looks and amiable manner rarely left him companionless. As he remembered it, there was always a young woman around to satisfy his urges and gratify his pleasures. Feeling that he was falling in love was the death knell to any long-term relationship.

Had to be that way.

He couldn't disappoint the man who'd raised him, provided for all of his needs, educated him in the finest schools, whose family had a proud tradition of offering a first-born son to the priesthood. But he also couldn't contain his attraction to women—to hold them, kiss them, touch them, enter them. When he took his vows, he did so knowing that he could not compromise on the vow of obedience; but his vow of chastity would be a matter of negotiation between himself and God.

The affairs he'd had while teaching, and later in Rome on assignment at the Vatican, were often carried out with reckless abandon—and for good reason. There were more than a few priests, and the occasional bishop and cardinal, who'd also felt that strict adherence to the vow of chastity was negotiable.

The Sacrament of Reconciliation was what would save his soul in the end. On more than one occasion, usually after each affair had ended, he'd confessed to a priest his sin of fornication and was absolved of it by a blessing from the priest and his recitation of a simple prayer—the *Act of Contrition*.

His recidivism had tormented him. When he'd returned to New Orleans, he swore to God he'd be chaste. But his dirty thoughts had followed him like shadows—whenever he looked at female parishioners, college girls ... and teenagers. His Grace, what would he say or do if he found out about his son's debauchery, his moral turpitude, his utter disregard for the vow he'd taken when he was ordained?

His father's life, he'd always believed, was a chaste one. Yet, when he read between the lines of the Reverend Mother's letter, he realized that his father, as a young priest, may have felt the same urges he'd personally felt so often in the past, and allowed those urges to overcome reason and lead him astray.

Could he have gotten my mother pregnant?

If Rossi's life was the benchmark, most certainly. As a young priest, he'd often felt those prurient urges when he taught at the university—the young coeds he was attracted to ... flirted with. More than a few had shared his bed.

One he'd gotten pregnant.

He remembered it like it was yesterday. A student at Georgetown University where he'd taught—a senior about to graduate. A beautiful woman, she was a talented violinist in the performing arts program. She'd been awarded a scholarship to attend the Sorbonne in Paris and continue her studies with the finest virtuosos in Europe.

They'd been seeing each other secretly for three months when she learned she was two months pregnant. An Episcopalian, her faith didn't consider a lawful abortion a mortal sin, as he reminded her when she came to him and asked him what she should do. He chose the coward's way out and took her to the neighborhood clinic where her baby—his child—was aborted.

The torment of his shenanigans led to his drinking. Drinking to forget his immoral past. Drinking to dull the pain he'd felt from the hypocritical life he'd led that saw him succeed and advance to become a monsignor and soon a bishop—perhaps one day, a cardinal.

Yet the things he'd done; the sins he'd committed were all known by an omniscient—all-knowing—God. Why would He allow him to pursue such a path, knowing that he was too weak to change? When the pope lay his hands on his head on Sunday afternoon, he'd know that he'd not abandon his secret life. He'd have as much a chance of changing his sinful ways as a leopard would have of changing the color of its spots. His amorality had followed him like a clap of thunder follows a bolt of lightning. No measure of hoping, wanting or praying would safeguard him from the lustful desires he'd felt nearly every day of his adult life.

He tells me the Reverend Mother was delirious when she wrote the letter. But I recall no episodes of delirium or dementia.

She'd been elderly and frail when he'd left for Rome. But her mind was free of delusions, fantasies and hallucinations. He was sure of that. If she was telling the truth in her letter, that would make his father a liar. He'd have deceived him—kept him from knowing about his mother—uncovering her past, a past that might have led him to discover that his Reverend Father was, in fact, *his* father.

If I could have spoken to my Reverend Mother one last time, she would have told me— not just the truth—but the whole truth about my past.

The glass, now empty, he rose to leave. He went to the closet to get his suit jacket and put it on. The sight of his clerical collar on the archbishop's desk was suddenly repugnant to him. He grabbed it and put it in a side pocket of the jacket he wore.

"What's this?" he asked himself, feeling a vial, smaller than the bottle of holy water that was also in the pocket. He pulled it out and studied the label: *Morphine Sulfate. Injection. 40 mg /ml.* He shook the vial. It was empty. In the other pocket of the suit jacket, he found a pair of latex gloves, one folded into the other.

He sat in the archbishop's chair behind his desk and placed a call to Sister Agnes at the clinic. He gave her instructions on what he wanted her to do, and then hung up.

Ten minutes later, she called back.

He had his answer.

He left the empty vial and the gloves on the archbishop's desk for him to find—to know that he knew what he'd done to the Reverend Mother.

He drove home.

A bottle of bourbon waited for him there.

Chapter 40

"Thomas, I want you to come to me," Santini said when Rossi answered his call. His tone was calm, even comforting.

At first, Rossi said nothing, still in shock over discovering what was in the archbishop's jacket pockets—and what it meant. His thumb reached for the cancel button on his cell phone but emotions suddenly roiled within him and he pulled it back. "Will you tell me the truth about my mother?"

An eerie silence followed. Rossi could only hear his own breathing on the phone; he thought the archbishop might have discontinued the call. Then a simple, single word broke the silence.

"Yes."

"And the Reverend Mother?" Rossi demanded.

"Yes, and the Reverend Mother. Now come to me."

Rossi hung up.

He downed what was left of his glass of bourbon.

He wanted answers and he was about to get them.

Santini met Rossi in the hallway of the archbishop's home. "Come. What I have to tell you is best said in the privacy of the chapel."

Rossi followed Santini into the chapel.

"Sit here, my son. I'll sit next to you. What I have to tell you is best said to God through you."

That caught Rossi off guard. "You want me to hear your confession?"

"Yes. I want my sins forgiven by the God we both serve."

Rossi had never heard the archbishop's confession. He'd never known him to have confessed his sins to anyone. Yet he felt he had no other choice—to allow a sinner the chance to atone for his sins and seek God's forgiveness is a fundamental precept of the Catholic Church.

He thought about how paradoxical it was—the parable of the prodigal father was about to unfold. The wayward parent who'd led a life of lies and deceit, and perhaps worse, was about to unburden his soul—just like the Reverend Mother, who could no longer bear the weight of a sin that had blackened her soul.

"Bless me Father for I have sinned," Santini began. "My life was forever changed when I met your mother. She was an orphan who resided at the Catholic orphanage that was closed shortly after your birth. She was one of the older children. No one wanted to adopt her.

"As a young priest, I would minister to the boys and girls there and counsel them about their feelings of loneliness and loss of self-worth. The nuns who ran the orphanage and cared for the children were ill-equipped to handle the consuming responsibilities of parenthood. The children were educated in our parochial schools. The lucky ones were adopted by parishioners; your mother was not among them.

"I took your mother under my wing, and we grew quite fond

of each other. When I rejected her advances, she threatened to take to the streets. I chose to submit to her urges—and to mine. She hid her pregnancy from me and, when she was nearing its end, ran away from the orphanage and took to the streets. She came to me sickly and in labor, revealing to me that I was the father."

"Was the Reverend Mother accurate in the details she provided me in her letter?" Rossi asked.

"For her, painfully so. For me, I now seek forgiveness from you as God's vessel."

"But absolution can only be given to sinners who confess to all of their sins. So I ask you before God, how did my mother die?"

A breathless silence filled the chapel.

Finally, he spoke. "The pain I feel now is the same pain I felt then when I placed the pillow over her face and her last breath was taken. Believe me, Thomas, it was God's will that you be brought to me and that your mother be taken from you."

Acute fatigue overcame Rossi's body—like he was suddenly carrying a great weight in a sack over his shoulder. His father—a murderer. He needed to hear the whole truth. It was Rossi's penance for the hypocrisy of his own amorality. "The Reverend Mother?"

"The fear of her regaining her speech was her undoing, I'm afraid. She violated the oath she'd sworn to me so many years ago."

Rossi couldn't believe that his real father had just confessed to murdering the mother who'd given him life and the mother who'd nurtured him, and he spoke like they had it coming to them. "An unholy oath she was made to swear," countered Rossi remembering the Reverend Mother's words.

"God gives us the free will to select whatever path we choose to follow," Santini said in a cold, emotionless tone.

"Do you not see the evil in your acts, my father?"

"I see that I was an instrument of God's free will. I chose to protect my son from a past that, if revealed, could only have caused him pain."

"I now know the truth of my past … and of yours. What pain could possibly be more grievously inflicted than to have a father confess to his son of murdering the mother he never came to know and the woman who became the only mother he ever knew?" A chill went down Rossi's spine; a dull ache lodged in his stomach. He thought he might vomit.

When the wave of nausea passed, he became reflective, and suddenly clearheaded about why a homicide detective was pursuing him as a serial murderer. But everything that pointed to him as the murderer also pointed to the archbishop—access to the files, to his calendar, to the clinic, to the medals and no alibi on the nights of the murders. He could've simply driven to the clinic when it was closed and planted the evidence in Diaz's locker.

But the one fact that separated the two of them and made it likely that Antonio Ignatius Santini was a coldblooded serial killer was that the man who was about to be ordained a cardinal of the Catholic Church was the same man who had just admitted to him—and to God—that he'd killed two women.

"My father, your soul cannot be cleansed of sin unless you confess to all transgressions. God knows what you have done. If you are to be forgiven and have your only chance of seeing him for all of eternity, confess to all of your sins and be absolved and forgiven."

"You know the truth. When I told you not to worry—that you couldn't have killed those three girls—I knew that because it was I who selected them. It was I who phoned the first two

292

victims and told them you'd meet them in the alley behind the convent and that you had secured places for them in shelters. It was I who contacted the Lopez girl and told her you'd meet her at seven, not eight, that evening.

"It was I who selected the churches and this residence to bring three sinners, whose babies were conceived in sin, and lay them there, naked and childless, for all to know that their sins against God had not gone unpunished. And it was I who brushed the girls' hair with a single brush, and who placed it, a medal and that girl's cell phone in Miguel's locker. So there you have the truth, the whole truth, before God."

His words left Rossi in a state of shock, almost afraid to speak. What he wanted to say was that his father was a monster—a vicious, evil psychopath— whose entire adult life was a lie. Trying to understand the actions of a raving lunatic led him to ask: "But why these girls? Why now?"

"The three girls were a matter of convenience. It could've been only one girl, but the opportunity presented for more. And what better time than Easter week to act as God's instrument?"

"A man we both know stands accused of crimes he didn't commit. A completely innocent man who's about to be convicted and punished for your criminal acts."

"Yes. A martyr whose soul will ascend into heaven as soon as his last breath is taken."

Rossi now knew his father was insane. But could he convince him to do the right thing and make one further confession—to the police? "My father, you ask for forgiveness, but atonement comes with consequences. Your soul can hardly be cleansed if you allow another to die for your transgressions."

"I've confessed to my transgressions."

"Perhaps. But to allow that boy to die for what you've done is to have committed yet another ... murder. Are you not breaking

God's commandment—*thou shalt not kill,* a mortal sin in the eyes of our church?"

"It is the state of Louisiana that will execute him, not me. What shall be my penance, a devout life free of sin? If so, I do solemnly pledge that before God."

Rossi didn't know whether the archbishop was being serious or glib. The man belonged in an insane asylum. Yet he could become the next American cardinal, a leader of the Catholic Church. "My father, forgiveness is given when the penitent is truly remorseful and fully atones for his sins. Your atonement must come at a price commensurate to the sins you've committed. "Give yourself up to the police. Tell them what you've done. Do it freely. Take responsibility for your actions. Accept punishment for your crimes."

"That, my son, I cannot do. I seek only absolution for my sins. If it were God's will that I be caught and brought to justice for my crimes, I would surely accept the punishment I'd be given. Who am I to interfere with His master plan—*Deus vult.*"

An innocent man was about to be convicted and sentenced to death, and he chalked it up to God's will. And what was God's master plan—that he become the leader of the Catholic Church? Pope Antonio I—the *first* Antonio to become a pope … and the *first* serial killer ever to ascend to the Throne of St. Peter.

Rossi made a final plea. "To be absolved, my father, requires that you atone for those you have so grievously harmed. Turn yourself in to the authorities and place your life in the hands of man and your soul in the hands of God." Rossi finished with the usual prayer of absolution: "May the merciful Lord have pity on thee and forgive thee thy faults … I absolve you from your sins in the name of the Father, and of the Son, and of the Holy Spirit."

Santini responded, "Amen."

"Now go, in search of peace, my father." Rossi's voice was faint by then. He rose and walked away, leaving the archbishop alone in the chapel.

Rossi's head spun out of control.

I must think.

I must pray.

I must act.

Chapter 41

The results of the hairbrush analysis were on Crowder's desk when she arrived at district headquarters early Thursday morning. The only strands of hair on it were Rossi's. The searches revealed nothing that Rossi couldn't explain away. Still, it was *his* Lincoln. He must have cleaned it thoroughly, perhaps professionally, after he killed the Lopez girl.

Crowder's mind switched gears.

Schulman. What kind of defense could he put on? All that he could give the jury was his client's bare denials.

While at her desk, she studied the tapes of the Lincoln again, trying to get a better view of the license plate, something that would show that it was Rossi's car. If it was his car, he'd lied to the police—an important piece of incriminating evidence that proved he was near the two churches when the victims' bodies were left there.

But the car wasn't seen near the archbishop's residence where the Lopez girl was found.

Her eyes focused on the driver's side of the Lincoln, specifically on the driver's door window. He'd stopped for a red light a block from St. Stephan's. He had his hand on the wheel—his right hand. She enlarged the frame, concentrating on the hand. And then she saw it. Something she'd seen twice before.

She logged into the Office of Motor Vehicles database and did a search of registered owners. The name matched another 2019 black Lincoln Aviator registered to the archdiocese of New Orleans. She recognized the name of the person who'd signed the registration.

Just then the phone rang. It was O'Malley. "My office, now." He didn't wait for a response and hung up.

Police Superintendent Sullivan was seated in O'Malley's office when she arrived. She chose to stand by the door after closing it, as she did with Hellman, rather than sit in the unoccupied chair next to him.

Sullivan turned his head to face Crowder. "Have you gone off the deep end, detective?" he asked, his words more of a declaration than an inquiry. "Searching the monsignor's apartment, car and his office at the archbishop's home."

"I had reason to believe that Rossi lied about where he'd been on the nights the girls were abducted and murdered. A black Lincoln Aviator of the type registered to him was caught on Homeland Security's surveillance tapes within a couple of blocks of the churches where the first two victims were found."

"Did you have a plate number?"

"No. The cameras didn't capture it."

"Then how do you know it was the monsignor's car?"

"I'd seen his car parked at the archbishop's home when I'd spoken to him there."

"How did you get Allen to sign off on the warrant?"

"He followed the logic of my position—that if the polygraph was valid, Diaz was being framed and the most likely suspect was Rossi, who'd had contact with the three victims and no alibi on the nights they were murdered."

"But the searches turned up nothing implicating the monsignor."

"We still have the hairbrush," O'Malley said supportively. "It's being analyzed for the girls' DNA."

"The tests were negative," Crowder said, realizing that her admission would nail her coffin shut.

Sullivan's exhale was long and deep, like a kid blowing out the candles on his birthday cake. "That ends this investigation once and for all. Am I making myself clear, detective?"

Crowder looked at O'Malley for his reaction before answering. He remained silent, cutting her loose. "I'm prepared to close the book on the monsignor. It looks like I was wrong about him. Is that all, sir?"

"That's all, Crowder," O'Malley said, dismissing her.

When the door was half open, Crowder turned and directed a question to Sullivan. "Did you tell either Rossi or the archbishop that we had a city-wide stakeout of the Catholic churches planned the weekend before Easter?"

"Why is that even remotely important?"

"More important than you can possibly imagine."

"Of course I told the archbishop. He wanted daily briefings."

Now Crowder had the missing piece of the puzzle.

~

When she arrived at the courthouse, Crowder was surprised to see Rossi speaking to Schulman in the hallway outside the courtroom. There were still ten minutes left before the trial would resume. Crowder sat in the back row. Schulman saw her when he entered the courtroom, and they exchanged smiles. He went immediately to his table where a prison guard had just seated his client and removed his handcuffs.

Crowder ripped out a page from her notebook, wrote down two words, folded the slip of paper in half, and wrote Andrew Schulman on the front.

The chair between Hellman and Gardner remained empty, meaning Tom Crowder had not yet arrived and was on his way to the courtroom.

She'd have her courier.

She slipped out of the courtroom and waited for him.

"All rise," the bailiff bellowed as Judge Jackson scurried in from a side door and took his seat behind the bench.

"Bring in the jury," the judge said. When the jury was assembled, he looked at Schulman. "Are you ready to proceed with your opening statement, Mr. Schulman?"

"Yes, Your Honor." He stood and walked to his usual place when he addressed the jury. "Members of the jury, Miguel Diaz sits before you cloaked in the presumption of innocence. He also sits before you falsely accused of crimes—deplorable crimes—he did not commit.

"The person who committed these horrible acts was a monster—someone so deranged and delusional as to think he was God-like with the right to punish three teenage girls whose out-of-wedlock pregnancies were sins in the eyes of the Catholic Church. What better way to show God's wrath than to kill them and their babies and leave the sinners' dead bodies at Catholic churches and the home of its leader, the Archbishop of New Orleans.

"Miguel Diaz isn't a monster. He's not a murderer. The evidence found in his locker was indeed evidence of the crimes committed, put there, not by Miguel—but by the murderer himself. Miguel pleaded not guilty to these crimes because he's innocent. Under the law, he doesn't have to prove his innocence. Under the law, he doesn't have to prove who committed these despicable acts. We will call only one witness. His testimony will leave no doubt in your minds of my client's innocence."

Crowder could see Hellman fidgeting in his chair, as if he was expecting some bad news, but didn't know what.

He'd soon find out.

"Call your witness, Mr. Schulman," the judge said.

Shulman, standing at the lectern, announced, "The defense calls Monsignor Thomas Aquinas Rossi."

The bailiff left the courtroom, returned with Rossi following on his footsteps, and directed him to the witness box.

Hellman stood up as if to object. "One moment, Your Honor."

Crowder watched a back and forth discussion between Hellman and her brother, who was showing Hellman something in a court document. Crowder remembered that Schulman had told her he'd listed Rossi, among others, as a character witness.

"Mr. Hellman, I'd like to proceed," the judge said. "Do you have some objection to this witness testifying?"

More fidgeting.

"Mr. Hellman," the judge barked, an octave higher.

"No objection at this time," Hellman said with obvious reluctance.

Schulman began his questioning. "What position do you hold in the Catholic Church?"

"I am a Jesuit priest, a monsignor. My current assignment is here, in the archdiocese of New Orleans, as the personal secretary and assistant to Archbishop Antonio Santini."

Schulman made sure to explore Rossi's credentials in great

detail—his education, his teaching positions, his publications, his position at the Vatican serving the pope and his imminent ordination and appointment as the next archbishop of New Orleans.

"Do you know Miguel Diaz?"

"Yes. For more than a year. I hired him to work as a nurse at St. Joseph's Clinic here in New Orleans. He came to us with superb credentials. He was to graduate with honors in the nursing program of the university he attended—but then he was arrested."

"Who besides Miguel had access to the key to the clinic and the passcode to the security alarm?"

"The nuns at the Convent of the Sisters of St. Mary, Doctor Latham, myself and, of course, the archbishop."

"Have you ever known Miguel to have taken anything from the clinic—equipment, supplies, drugs—anything that wasn't his?"

"Never."

"Miguel's locker at the clinic; is the room where it's located locked?"

"No."

"Did anyone at the clinic who had a personal locker ever feel the need to put a lock on them?"

"Never."

"So anyone who had access to the clinic could enter the room, open Miguel's locker, and put things in it."

"Yes ... if they had access to the clinic."

"Monsignor Rossi, are you aware of any facts that suggest to you that Miguel Diaz abducted and murdered Amy Stillman, Beverly Calloway or Angelica Lopez?"

"No. What I do know is that Miguel Diaz did not abduct and murder those girls."

Hellman almost knocked his chair over when he rose from his seat to object. "Is the witness stating a fact or giving an opinion?"

The judge looked over his bifocals at Rossi. "Monsignor, are you giving us your personal opinion on the innocence of the defendant, which you must know is irrelevant and improper. You're only permitted to give facts."

"Your Honor, I know for a *fact* that he didn't kill those girls. It was someone else."

The packed courtroom of reporters and spectators was suddenly abuzz with chitchat. The judge banged his gavel and yelled out, "Order in the court."

Crowder saw the jury restless in their seats, looking at one another with expressions of astonishment on their faces, as if a Roman Catholic priest was about to name the serial killer in open court.

But she knew otherwise.

Stoney Jackson had enough drama in his courtroom. He needed to get to the bottom of what was unfolding. "Bailiff, remove the jury."

The jury was led to the room where they'd gathered each morning and would deliberate on a verdict. The witness and lawyers were told to remain in the courtroom. Not a spectator or member of the press left their seats.

When the mumbling in the gallery ebbed, the judge told Schulman to take his seat. It was his turn to ask the questions.

"Monsignor Rossi, to know for a fact that the defendant is innocent means one of three things: you committed these crimes; you were with the defendant when the crimes were committed and can provide him an alibi; or the murderer confided in you that he committed them."

"Yes. I understand that. I had nothing to do with these

302

crimes, and I was not with Miguel when they were committed."

"I see. Well then, who was the person who told you that he abducted and murdered Amy Stillman, Beverly Calloway and Angelica Lopez?"

Those who packed the gallery sat frozen, their eyes fixed on Rossi. Only the barely perceptible hum of the room's new, state-of-the-art ventilation system could be heard above the breathless silence.

Finally, Rossi spoke, mercifully ending the deathlike stillness that blanketed the courtroom. "I cannot tell you the person's name."

"Are you saying that the person revealed himself to you but didn't give you his name?"

"No. I know the person's name."

The judge sighed heavily into his microphone, his exhale audible to all in the courtroom. Stoney Jackson was ready to explode. "Monsignor, this is not a game we're playing here. You come into the courtroom and tell us under oath that Miguel Diaz is innocent, that you know who murdered those girls … and you are refusing to reveal the person's identity?"

"I can only answer your question this way. My vows include a vow of obedience—obedience to the rules priests are required to follow, the rules laid down by the bishops of our dioceses …"

Crowder couldn't contain a smile.

Been there. Done that.

Saw the movie. Knew the ending.

Heard the joke. Knew the punchline.

She felt the urge to stay and watch Hellman and Schulman fight it out over whether the judge should allow Rossi to testify or declare a mistrial. But she knew how it would all turn out. The jury had heard a priest swear under oath that Diaz was innocent … "It was someone else," he'd said. If allowed to give further testimony, Rossi would refuse to identify the murderer because he learned of him during his confession. Everything a penitent confesses to, irrespective of how horrendous the sins, or the crimes, is confidential. No exceptions.

The judge couldn't force Rossi to identify the killer and couldn't hold him in contempt for refusing—so ruled the Louisiana Supreme Court when it upheld the confidentiality of the confessional on religious grounds several years ago.

Crowder felt a pang of guilt. How easily innocent people can be accused, prosecuted, convicted and punished for crimes they didn't commit. First Diaz. Then Rossi. She'd fingered both. Yet each was a victim of circumstances that she'd had a hand in making. She should have suspected that Diaz was being framed from the beginning. It was all too convenient to find such incriminating evidence in his locker.

She should have dug deeper.

Rossi's connections to the victims, while noteworthy, were nothing more than happenstance—no more incriminating than his ownership of a black Lincoln Aviator.

She'd stopped climbing the ladder several rungs too early.

Had she gone to the top, she'd have discovered that the vehicle on the surveillance tapes could have been the archbishop's. Had she studied the hand on the steering wheel more carefully, she'd have seen the gold ring with the amethyst stone on his finger—a bishop's ring, and had known the driver was Santini, not Rossi. She'd have figured out that the reason the murderer didn't leave the Lopez girl's body at a church was that he knew there was a citywide stakeout of all churches. And she'd have known that Angelica Lopez had been taken to the archbishop's home, murdered on the property, and laid to rest under a sheet at the front door by Santini, not Rossi.

Time was running out.

There was no time for warrants or backup.

What she needed to do, she needed to do alone—a face-off between her and Santini.

A man like Santini was as egotistical and arrogant as he was diabolical and deranged. He'd want her to know that he'd killed those girls to prove his perceived moral, God-like superiority— with the right to determine what was right and what was wrong, and who should live and who should die. He'd not confess outright, just brag about what he'd accomplished by nuance and innuendo. But, in the process, he could slip up and drop a solid clue that might lead to evidence that would stick.

Crowder faced a terrible reality: whatever triggered Santini's homicidal crime spree was a time bomb ready to explode at any time. There would be more murders, more sacrifices in the name of a God only Santini believed in. An Old Testament God who carried out mass killings—decimated sinful cities, drowned wicked populations and killed off first-born sons. A God who orchestrated the first murder by having favored Abel over his brother, Cain, who'd then killed Abel in a jealous rage. Crowder wasn't a church-going Christian. The hypocrisy of organized religions was too much for her to accept. But she had a deep moral code that guided her actions as a homicide detective— protect and defend all life, and only take a life to protect the lives of others, and only as a last resort.

Crowder retrieved her weapon from courthouse security on the way out. When she got to her pickup, she opened the glove compartment, reached for her two-shot derringer and strapped it to her right calf.

Her next stop was the private residence of the archbishop of New Orleans to confront a cold-blooded serial killer.

Chapter 42

Crowder parked a block away and approached the residence from the rear. She opened the unlocked side door to the garage and looked inside. The polished skin of the archbishop's black Lincoln Aviator glistened like a polished hearse when the opened door let in a stream of sunlight.

Next, the cottage. The door was locked and, as before, the windows were latched shut. Whatever evidence remained inside would require a warrant to uncover. Anything seized by her without one was inadmissible as the "fruit of the poisonous tree"—a metaphorical legal ruling that evidence obtained illegally by police was inadmissible in court. Many a hardened criminal walked because an overly aggressive cop wanted to take him out without going through the bullshit—but necessary— red tape of getting a warrant first.

Santini could get off scot-free if she didn't play her cards just right.

Backing off, she returned to the street where she'd parked and drove her pickup to the front of the house. When she went to the door and rang the doorbell, it was Santini, not the housekeeper, who answered. "Detective Crowder, back to ransack my study this time?" he quipped.

Santini only needed to close the door and call his $500 an hour lawyer to avoid a showdown. But Crowder knew he couldn't resist a duel of wits. She'd bait him. "I thought you'd want an update on the Diaz trial."

"The nail-biting suspense is just killing me. I can spare you ten minutes. Come to the study."

"I understand you and the monsignor leave for Rome on Friday," she said, sitting in one of the chairs in front of his desk.

"Quite right. I've given the staff the rest of the week off."

She was alone in the house with him.

The room was suddenly smaller; the air in it thinner. She sensed an uptick in her vital signs, but shook off her claustrophobia. The cat-and-mouse game was about to begin. Whether the cat would catch the mouse remained to be seen. Crowder took the first swipe of her paw. "There was a surprise witness at the trial this morning."

"Oh. Let me guess. The monsignor rode into the courtroom on a white stallion to save the day."

"You knew he would."

"I knew he *might*."

"He got on the witness stand, swore an oath to tell the truth, and told the jury Miguel Diaz was an innocent man."

"But—let me see if I can finish your story—he didn't name the guilty party."

"You knew he wouldn't do that if the murderer revealed himself to him during his confession."

"We are quite strict about that. Under pain of excommunication and eternal damnation, a priest cannot disclose the confidences of a penitent."

"It's likely that Diaz's lawyer will ask for a mistrial."

"It's just as likely that the district attorney, a man named

Hellman, will move to disallow the monsignor's testimony and ask the judge to instruct the jury to disregard it."

"It's hard to disregard the sworn testimony of a priest, soon to become a bishop, when he's told the jury that they'd be convicting an innocent man."

"What will a mistrial gain Diaz? He'll just be tried again."

"Time. It will buy time."

"Time to do what?"

"To subpoena Senator Tipton's son who was with Diaz the nights the girls were abducted and murdered. Time for me to find evidence that proves who murdered those girls."

"I would think that someone who was clever enough to do what was done to those girls and not get caught, and have someone else prosecuted for his crimes, would be careful enough to leave not a trace of evidence behind for you to find. Remember, it was your evidence that led to Diaz's arrest, and it will be your evidence that leads to his conviction."

"I can be very persistent," Crowder said. "Wherever the murderer took the last girl and bled her to death and butchered her and her baby, there's a good chance he left trace evidence behind—a single strand of hair in his car, a blood splatter on the floor or a wall."

"Is probable cause still required to search premises and a vehicle?" Santini asked flippantly.

Crowder was inside Santini's head now—thinking his thoughts.

The mouse was playing with her.

He wants me to know he killed those girls.

He wants me to know how clever he's been.

He wants me to know he'll never be caught.

It was time to set the trap.

"You saw how easy it was for me to get a warrant to search

the monsignor's apartment, car, and office," Crowder bluffed. She knew full well that she'd never get Allen, or any other judge, to sign off on a warrant to search the archbishop's home or vehicle. Not after the Rossi debacle. But Santini wouldn't know that.

"Oh! I almost forgot to tell you," she continued. "A vehicle was caught on Department of Homeland Security cameras a block away from the churches where the first two victims were found. The interesting thing is that this vehicle was seen shortly after four in the morning, the time we believe the killer would've left the victims at the churches. So naturally it caught my interest. It was a 2019 black Lincoln Aviator. I thought it was the monsignor's. It turns out it wasn't his."

"So I surmise from your mistake that you have no license plate number."

"No plate number. But there are other ways to identify the owner of the vehicle."

A forced, uneasy smile replaced Santini's chiseled-in-stone expression and penetrating stare. "And I'd love to hear them over a cup of tea. So let me excuse myself and put some on, and when I return we can continue our little chat."

The cat had unnerved the mouse.

Crowder had crawled into the skin of a serial killer, not simply gotten under it. She could almost feel what he was feeling, think what he was thinking.

Santini needed a time-out for a reality check. Crowder was his one true nemesis, a genuine threat to his freedom, and a suspect's worse nightmare—a detective who was relentless, who'd do almost anything to catch a bad guy ... even break the very laws she'd sworn to uphold. He'd remember the news accounts of her daring rescue of Jessica Young, how she'd broken the rules to catch her abductor, how she'd confronted a serial rapist and shot him dead. Dirty Harriet—who was now hot on his trail and who would pursue him until he was caught.

As she waited for him to return, Crowder mulled over her next move.

Stay inside his head—think like him.

It was time to put all of her cards on the table and reveal the ace up her sleeve—a bishop's ring on the right hand of the driver of the Lincoln, and undeniable proof that the vehicle was his and he was driving it.

A look at her cell phone revealed a text from Schulman: *Adjourned for the day. Mistrial motion to be ruled on tomorrow. Where are you?*

She began to respond to his text but before she could type her first word, she felt the pinch of a syringe in her neck and the icy feel of a drug being injected into her carotid artery. She slumped back in her chair and went limp.

For Crowder, day became night.

The smell of cleaning solvent and bleach acted like smelling salts, and Crowder awoke to find herself lying face down on a table in a room she didn't recognize.

Her hands were cuffed behind her.

Her cuffs.

Her feet were bound with duct tape.

His duct tape.

How in the hell did she let this happen?

A piece of duct tape across her mouth assured her captor she'd be silent.

She felt groggy, disoriented and was seeing double. The coverless overhead fluorescent light was headache-inducing bright. When things finally came into focus, she raised her head off the table to survey her surroundings. The room was an open space that served as a kitchen and living area. Its pedestrian décor suggested to Crowder that she was in the cottage. The proximity of the sink to the table made the draining of blood and its disposal easily achievable. A scalpel was unnecessary, the cutlery undoubtedly included knives sharp enough to cut into the stomach of a pregnant teenager.

The workshop of a madman.

He murdered Angelica Lopez here.

His plan was to murder her, too.

Here in his workshop.

The propofol was wearing off, but it was best to feign being sedated when he returned. Surprise was her only weapon.

He'd removed her jacket and holstered gun. It was nowhere to be seen. But she could feel the holster of her derringer still strapped to her calf. If she could just free her hands and put them in front of her, she could reach for her backup pistol. It had saved her once. It would be needed again.

Where was he? He'd know the drug would soon wear off.

The sound of a garage door opening broke the quiet. Was he driving away in his Lincoln or just now returning in it from an errand?

Think like him—like a murderer about to murder again.

He'd need to get rid of her pickup. He'd find the key in her jacket and drive it to a place no one would know to look.

The knocking sound the engine made was a sure sign her pickup was overdue for a tune-up, and that it was about to be driven into the archbishop's garage until it could be disposed of later. The bayou was the perfect burial ground for her pickup … and her dead body.

She didn't tell anyone she was heading over to speak to the

archbishop. Normally, she'd tell her partner what she planned to do, but she didn't want Steele complicit in her decision to pay Santini a surprise visit. She had to face the consequences of boldly defying Sullivan's directive to close the investigation—alone.

Having let down her guard with Santini could very well prove fatal. The die was cast when he injected her with propofol. He had no choice now but to kill her. A bold but necessary move on his part, and she should've seen it coming.

Suddenly, it all made sense. Again inside his head, she thought like him. By baiting him the way she did, he'd know that the cat would pursue the mouse until caught. Someone, like her, willing to confront a serial killer alone was a formidable adversary. And he'd know from his daily contacts with the police superintendent that the investigation was closed and that she was there acting on her own.

Nobody knew she was there.

Santini's plan was now as obvious to Crowder as it was to him. He'd dress in street clothes and drive her pickup to some swamp in the bayou. His only passenger would be a dead homicide detective. He'd dump the body first. The gators would do the rest. The pickup would be next—pushed into a swamp a mile away. After a long walk, he'd call an Uber that would drop him off a quarter mile from his home. Then, after a short walk and a thorough cleaning of the cottage, he'd shower and finalize his plans to travel to Rome and become a member of the College of Cardinals.

Crowder left the mind of a murderer and re-entered the mind of a homicide detective. Escape was not a realistic option—not while she was bound and gagged. Time was running out. Being able to reach for her derringer was her only option. But first she needed to get her hands in front of her. She wiggled until she was close to the edge of the table and then rocked back and forth until her momentum allowed her to roll over on her back without falling off the table.

The next step was more difficult, but she'd trained for it. She lifted her backside up and wiggled her butt through her hands in a Houdini-like move; then, with her knees bent tight, lifted her cuffed hands under her feet and legs.

She heard noise outside near the garage, and then Rossi's voice, "Father, what have you done to her?"

"It's best you leave things to me," Santini said, his tone calm but firm.

Crowder ripped the duct tape from her mouth and yelled, "Rossi, I'm in the cottage. He has my gun."

Crowder heard a scuffle and Rossi yell, "Give me the gun, Father."

A shot rang out. Footsteps approached the door. When it opened, Rossi entered with her Smith & Wesson in his hand. He put the gun on the kitchen counter and started to walk toward her—she being about fifteen feet away. Two steps later, and just as she screamed "Don't give up the gun," Santini appeared behind him with Crowder's gun once again in his hand.

"I wouldn't release her, Thomas," he said, the cool, calmness of his voice the eerie trademark of a psychopath. "She knows too much about the skeletons in our closets."

Rossi turned to see the gun pointed at him. Behind him Crowder sat on the table, her legs hanging over the side still duct taped together, her cuffed hands now in front of her.

"Father, the killings must end. Now, give me the gun." Rossi reached out a hand for it.

"Don't think for a moment I won't shoot you, Thomas. One of us could've been shot when you wrestled me for the gun. This time you'll not get close enough to me for a rematch. God's plan is for me to one day ascend to the papacy. I'm afraid our detective friend has other plans for me."

"You need not worry, Father. I'll see that you get the help you need. I'll stand by you."

"I'm not the least bit worried. Now move away from her. Sit in that chair while I explain your options." He pointed the gun in the direction of a chair and Rossi moved to it. Crowder took the moment of distraction to raise her right leg and reach for the derringer in the holster strapped to her calf.

Her hands came up empty.

"You didn't really believe I'd not frisk you, detective. My, my—do you have so little respect for my talents." Santini reached into a pocket of his trousers for Crowder's two-shot derringer and put it on the counter. Crowder dropped her leg and sat up on the table. It was then she noticed that Santini was wearing latex gloves.

"Now, Thomas, I've loved you like a son and you've returned my love. But your love for me must be unconditional. I'd like your help in disposing of the detective and her vehicle. I had planned to do it alone, but you've forced me into a partnership with you. I need you to be a part of this so that you have as much to lose as I."

"And the alternative, my father, what might that be?" Rossi asked, speaking like a battered man with little, if any, hope.

Crowder understood the alternative all too well.

"You see, Thomas. Things aren't always as they appear to be. When your dead bodies are found here in the cottage—a bullet in the detective from her gun in your hand with your prints on it, and a bullet or two in you from her derringer in her hand with only her prints on it—the rest is just a matter of staging the scene and my testimony that I heard a scuffle from the house and then a scream, a woman's scream, and then the shots, which brought me to the cottage where I found the two of you dead.

"You are already a prime suspect in the murders of those girls. The detective made sure of that. I've become quite good at planting evidence. I'll hide locks of the girls' hair and an item of their clothing in your bedroom here at the house, the only place the police haven't yet searched, but soon will. I'll place the syringe with remnants of the propofol you injected in the detective on the floor by your dead body. I will, of course, express my shock that you could commit such diabolical acts."

Rossi looked at Crowder. She returned his stare, knowing that her life was now in his hands. It was as if he, not Santini, was holding the gun and pointing it at her.

But Rossi had bravely showed up at the trial to save the life of an innocent man. He could never be complicit in her murder. Rossi looked back at Santini and spoke softly as if in a whisper. "Deus vult," he said. "If it's God's will that I, too, must die, then it shall be so."

Rossi jumped from his chair and lunged at Santini—he got no closer than halfway when a shot rang out from Crowder's gun. The bullet entered Rossi's chest nearly dead center and he collapsed to his knees. Blood gushed from the hole in his clothing. He used one hand to cover the entry wound and reached out with his other hand and stuttered, "F-father, my father," as he fell on his side and curled up in a fetal position.

Rossi lay motionless on the floor.

Crowder didn't hesitate. She jumped from the table and hopped, as if she were on a pogo stick, thrusting her body towards Santini. Her outstretched hands struck him on his right side, pushing him hard. He stumbled backwards against the kitchen counter, his gun hand striking the counter's edge.

The gun slipped out of Santini's hand and ended up on the floor by his feet.

315

Crowder used the confusion of the moment to slither her way to it, but her legs were like dead weights slowing her movement. Just as she reached for her gun, Santini kicked it away.

The gun came to rest by Rossi, and the commotion awoke the man thought dead. Rossi took the gun in his hand and pointed it at Santini who was still standing with his back to the kitchen counter.

"My son. Forgive the sins of a father," Santini said as he reached his hand behind him and felt for Crowder's derringer.

Crowder lay frozen on the floor, her eyes moving back and forth between father and son while Rossi, his hand trembling, kept the gun aimed at his father. If she could see the gun shaking in his hand, so could Santini. He'd figure that Rossi was near death and reluctant to shoot.

The hesitation on Rossi's part gave Santini the time to grip the derringer in his hand.

"He's got my derringer," Crowder yelled. Further indecision by Rossi would be fatal. "Shoot him. Shoot him," she screamed.

Santini's hand darted forward; the derringer aimed directly at Rossi.

Shots rang out.

Simultaneous blasts.

A shot from a derringer was often off target even at close range. Did the bullet miss its mark, passing by Rossi without striking him? She couldn't tell. But when she looked at him, he was limp on the floor, her pistol loose in his hand.

When her line of sight shifted to Santini, she saw him doubled over from a bullet in the stomach. His knees buckled. Spittle oozed from his mouth. One hand went to his wound; the other held the derringer still pointed at Rossi—one shot left. Acting on raw instincts, Crowder rolled over her right-shoulder, coming out of it with her bound legs fully extended; the soles of her shoes struck Santini's hand as he fired the last shot. The gun flew from his hand, and he fell forward.

The startled, dead-eyed expression on his face telegraphed to Crowder that Santini was a goner. He hit the floor face first. Gunshots to the stomach bleed profusely, and Santini's was no exception. Within seconds blood puddled on each side of his body.

But what of Rossi? Did the last shot hit its mark?

He wasn't moving.

She removed the duct tape from her ankles and dashed to him. Kneeling at his side, she felt for a pulse. It was faint, but there was one.

She sprinted to the garage. This time the side door was locked. Two kicks to the door later and she broke through. She found her jacket folded on the front seat of her pickup. Her cell phone was in a pocket. She dialed 911 and requested two ambulances and police backup.

A quickly composed text alerted Steele and O'Malley: *the archbishop's home—now.*

She found the key to her cuffs, still in an inside pocket of her jacket, and freed herself from them; then she returned to the cottage, knelt beside Rossi, and waited.

The faint sound of distant sirens grew louder until they soon screamed outside. Several EMTs entered the cottage through the door that Crowder had left open. One stopped to confirm that Santini's vital signs were "absent."

"Here," she said to another. "This one's still alive. Single shot—.38 caliber into the sternum. No exit wound."

A few minutes later, Steele and O'Malley entered the cottage, followed by several CSI investigators. Rossi was still on the floor, Crowder's gun still in his hand.

O'Malley stopped by Santini's body and looked down at

him. "How?"

"Gut shot. Bled out in minutes," Crowder replied.

Steele stood beside his partner, his eyes fixed on Rossi. "You were right about the Lincoln being driven by the murderer," he said matter of factly.

Thinking out loud, O'Malley said, "Who'd have thought that Rossi was a cold-blooded murderer. The archbishop finds out he killed those girls and Rossi kills him."

"Right about the Lincoln, wrong about the driver and the murderer," Crowder said.

"What do you mean?" O'Malley asked, eyebrows raised.

"When we couldn't get a plate number, I reviewed the first tape again that showed the driver stopped at an intersection, his right hand grasping the steering wheel." Crowder diverted her gaze to Santini's outstretched right hand. "The ring of a Catholic bishop. The DMV records proved his ownership of the car."

"Did he kill the girls here?" Steele asked.

"The first two were killed at the clinic. He lured them there. It was convenient. The girls wouldn't have been overly suspicious."

"And the last?"

"Sullivan tipped off Santini about the citywide stakeout. He needed another location. The cottage was perfect. No one but Santini was home. He probably met the Lopez girl at her church earlier than Rossi had arranged it. He would've seen the meeting scheduled on Rossi's calendar and contacted her to change either the time or the place."

"How do you fit into all this?" O'Malley asked.

"My bloodwork will show evidence of the propofol Santini injected into me."

"How come you're not DOA?"

"I would've been if not for Rossi putting a slug in the archbishop."

Just then, Travis Jones showed up.

How strangely ironic, Crowder thought. Like his three victims, Santini's last moments of life were spent bleeding to death. And, like his three victims, Santini's last ride on the last day of his life would be in a body bag in the back of the meat wagon.

Epilogue

Rossi survived to give his account of what happened, corroborating Crowder's testimony to internal affairs. The fact that her guns, with her prints on them, had been used to kill an archbishop and nearly fatally wound a monsignor gave rise to the inquiry. But when all facts were revealed, Crowder's badge and weapons were returned to her with a commendation from the police superintendent.

Judge Jackson granted Schulman's motion for a mistrial and dismissed all charges against Miguel Diaz. Hellman and Gardner would be delivered more bad news when Jones discovered that the lab where Angelica Lopez's fetal blood was analyzed had a report on file from an untainted specimen unequivocally establishing that Diaz was not the father.

Internal affairs launched an investigation of Gardner who ratted out Hellman. Gardner was fired for concealing, and then fabricating, evidence; Hellman was held in contempt of court for his role in the subterfuge and cover-up. Judge Allen personally presided at his hearing and fined Hellman $10,000 as reparations to Miguel Diaz for his deliberate withholding of exculpatory evidence the defense was entitled to receive. A referral to the bar association's disciplinary counsel was tacked on as well, with him recommending to the Louisiana Supreme Court that Hellman be suspended for six months. The Supreme Court disagreed, making the suspension one year instead, effectively ending Hellman's tenure as Orleans Parish's district attorney—and his political aspirations.

Diaz was exonerated by the district attorney's office at a news conference handled by Tom Crowder, the acting district attorney in Hellman's absence. His first order of business was to rehire Hellman's opponent who'd been fired after Hellman won the election for district attorney, and appoint him chief prosecutor. His second was initiating reforms that required prosecutors to provide sworn affidavits prior to trial that all potentially exculpatory evidence had been disclosed to defense counsel.

George Attwell was given a sentence of twenty-five years for aggravated rape of a juvenile, the fetal blood testing conclusively proving he fathered Amy Stillman's baby. Amy's mother divorced Attwell and returned to her former married name. Amy was buried in All Saints Cemetery in New Orleans next to her father.

Beverly Calloway's body was claimed by her aunt who arranged and paid for her funeral and interment.

Miguel Diaz completed his nursing requirements, finishing second in his class. His parents were joined by Angelica Lopez's parents at Diaz's commencement ceremony, where Miguel gave the valedictory address, the top student ceding the honor to him after reading about his ordeal. He spoke just as eloquently at Angelica's memorial service, thanking God, for having sent an "angel" to be his kid sister.

Diaz returned to St. Joseph's Clinic to work full time alongside Dr. Latham and Sister Agnes, both of whom wrote stellar letters of recommendation for his application to medical school.

Bryce Tipton overdosed on his antidepressant medicine on the third day of Diaz's trial when the national news reported the likelihood of Diaz being convicted—a death sentence almost surely to follow. He recovered but lost interest in academics and sports, and dropped out of school.

Senator Tipton could not come to terms with his son's sexuality. The senator's wife could not come to terms with her husband's stupidity. They legally separated.

The police investigation of the *Easter Murders* officially concluded with a finding that Antonio Ignatius Santini was criminally responsible for the deaths of Amy Stillman, Beverly Calloway and Angelica Lopez.

Santini's other murders remained buried with his victims.

Santini's body was claimed by his family and transported to Rome. The funeral service was private. Rossi's hospitalization following his injury prevented him from attending.

Rossi fully recovered from his injury after a week-long hospitalization and another week in rehab. He returned to Rome a month later, was ordained a bishop by the pope, and appointed the archbishop of New Orleans.

Archbishop Rossi maintained his relationship with the Santini family in Rome, who funded a foundation to provide food, clothing, shelter and healthcare services to the urban poor at the sites of the St. Joseph's Clinic and the Convent of the Sisters of St. Mary. Plans called for the clinic to be torn down and replaced by an urgent care center with physician and nursing services provided 24/7, and the convent to be renovated and serve as a professionally staffed temporary shelter for homeless women. Sister Ann was named its first director of services.

The archbishop's residence was sold at Rossi's direction. The proceeds were used to acquire more humble accommodations, with the balance going to charitable causes.

Crowder had visited Rossi in the hospital following the shootings. So had Miguel Diaz. Rossi had saved their lives and perhaps in the process had saved his soul.

When Rossi returned from Rome, he called Crowder and asked her to meet him at the convent. It was early summer on a clear day under a late-morning sun with comfortably cool breezes. He led her to the walled garden of the convent where they stood in front of the flower bed that surrounded the statue of the Madonna holding baby Jesus.

Crowder stood by his side and listened as Rossi recited a simple prayer—a prayer a child might say: "Holy Father in Heaven, bless all mothers who give us life, who take care of us, and who love us every day of our lives."

After Rossi finished the prayer, he spoke: "My Reverend Mother, who raised me until I went to live with the Santini family in Rome, brought me here nearly every day to say that prayer." He paused a moment as if he was reflecting on a pleasant memory. "You read the letter she wrote me when your search of my office uncovered it."

"I regret prying into your past," Crowder said apologetically.

"I have no regrets. It was an important step in your investigation. Suspecting me led you to eventually suspect my father." Rossi bent over to snap off several blooms which he placed at the foot of the statue. "I asked you here, Detective Crowder, to confess to you something that I now know to be true."

Crowder reviewed the nun's letter in her mind, this time to discern its importance to where Rossi had brought her—to a statue of a mother holding her baby. What the Reverend Mother had written came to mind. How Santini was the last person to be with the girl before she lay dead in her bed. How the nuns had been instructed to hide the girl's death from the authorities. What better way to have concealed the body of a girl who'd been murdered than to have buried her within the walled garden of a convent? What better way to have commemorated her gravesite than to have placed a statue of the Madonna as a headstone? What better way to have remembered her than to have brought her child to the site of her interment to say a prayer?

"There's no need for a son to confess the sins of a father," Crowder said. "I'll leave now, so you can be alone with her."

As she walked away, Crowder heard Rossi speak softly in Latin—no doubt the prayers of a son for two mothers: one, who had given him life; one, who had taken care of him; and both, who had loved him every day of their lives.

~

He sat at the bar of the Bayou Club nursing a scotch and soda. His flight jacket hung over the back of the stool next to him; a glass of Chardonnay sat on the bar in front of it.

"You're late," he said when she appeared at his side.

"You're early," she said.

He removed his jacket from the chair, and she sat down. "Then so are you."

"Eager, I guess."

"So was I." He leaned into Crowder—she could smell the fresh, bold scent of his cologne. "Tomorrow, let's take the plane and fly somewhere?"

"Where?"

"Anywhere."

"Can't."

"Why not?"

"Tomorrow morning, I'm paying a surprise visit on Nathan

Helmsley."

"As in Helmsley and Harris, the real estate developers?"

"One and the same. Stan Harris's Mercedes was pulled out of the Manchac Swamp yesterday afternoon."

"And Harris?"

"It's looking like the gators got him."

"Do you suspect foul play?"

"I can think of millions of reasons to suspect foul play."

"Oh."

"Helmsley and Harris took out a $10,000,000 life insurance policy on each other a year ago to protect the business if one of them died."

"So you suspect Helmsley?"

"Among others."

"Oh?"

"Harris's second wife, a former Las Vegas showgirl and twenty years younger, also took out a $5,000,000 policy on his life around the same time."

"So you suspect her as well?"

"People kill people for lots of reasons, and for no reason at all. But when lots of money's involved, murder is almost always premeditated."

"'No body, no case,' we defense lawyers like to say. He could have been inattentive, inebriated, or trying to avoid hitting a white-tailed deer when he accidentally ran off the side of the road into the swamp. He drowned after he got out of the car and was fodder for the gators afterwards."

"I don't believe he was in the car when it went off the road and submerged."

"Were any windows open?"

"Driver's side window and the sunroof were both open."

"Two escape routes."

"Made to look that way. I looked on the internet for recent photos of Harris. A short guy. His driver's license lists his weight as 315 pounds ten years ago. No way that sixty-five-year-old heavyweight squeezes *that* body through *that* window or sunroof—a geometric fact."

"Helmsley and Harris are wealthy. They own a bunch of malls and office buildings. Why kill Harris?"

"Two reasons. Since the recession hit Louisiana, there's been a glut of available office space and retail leases are down by half at the malls they own."

Crowder paused just long enough to prompt Schulman to speak. "And the second?"

"Both policies had double indemnity provisions. Thirty-million dollars is a lot of money—even for rich people."

"And a lot of motive."

Crowder had enough shop talk.

So had Schulman.

Each finished off their drinks in one swallow.

The bartender appeared. "Refills?" he asked.

Schulman looked at Crowder.

Crowder saw a familiar gleam in Schulman's eyes.

"No," he told the bartender, tossing a twenty and a five on the bar. "We have to be somewhere else." As the bartender walked away, Schulman asked: "Your place or mine?"

"Mine. Fred's in the spare bedroom looking forward to a ham bone."

A Note From the Author

Did you enjoy my book?

If so, I would be very grateful if you would write a review and publish it at your point of purchase. Your review, even a brief one, will help other readers to decide whether or not they'll enjoy my work.

And I invite you to read my other Jo Crowder books, *Identical Misfortune* (AIA Publishing, September 9, 2020), available in hardback and paperback at richardzappa.com, and *Double Indemnity* to be released early in 2022.

An excerpt from *Double Indemnity* follows the preview of *Identical Misfortune*.

About Identical Misfortune

When Veronica, a heartless sociopath, learns that her good-hearted identical twin, Ann, has married into a wealthy family, she very cleverly manipulates family members and the police into believing she's Ann, then stages Ann's suicide and makes off with millions. In a duel of wits between a cold- blooded killer and a cop, each brilliant in her own way, Detective Jo Crowder pursues Veronica while she schemes, lies and murders her way in and out of families on both sides of the Atlantic. But can Crowder stop the killing without turning her back on the law she's sworn to uphold?

Here's what the reviewers said about *Identical Misfortune.*

"A grim and engrossing procedural with a stellar cast." — Kirkus Reviews

"A winding roller-coaster ride of betrayal and intrigue ... as harrowing as the journey is, it's worth the effort." — Charles Ray, Awesome Indies Book Assessor

"Utterly spellbinding crime drama/thriller ... a well-imagined and outstanding work of fiction. — Online Book Club

"Suspenseful battle of wits ... that balances cerebral puzzle solving with vigorous action." — Indie Reader

Do you want to be notified of new releases?

If so, please <u>sign up to the AIA Publishing email list.</u> You'll find the sign-up button on the right-hand side under the photo at <u>www.aiapublishing.com</u>. Of course, your information will never be shared, and the publisher won't inundate you with emails, just let you know of new releases.

Double Indemnity

Prologue

The face of a scruffy old coot stared back at him from the mirror. He'd given up shaving three years ago, the day after he buried Alma, his wife of fifty-two years, just as his father had done when his mother passed. The only difference, a big one, was that his mother had died unexpectedly from a heart attack in her sleep. Alma, on the other hand, took her time dying and fought through two years of radiation, chemotherapy, and a couple of experimental treatments first.

Through veiny eyes, he watched himself brush chipped, yellow-stained nubs. The water he cupped in his hand to rinse his mouth did little to blunt the taste of the whiskey he'd drunk. Above thick, untamable eyebrows, the furrows across his forehead cut deep. He splashed water on his face and squeezed his beard to drain the moisture rather than dry it with a towel. His skin, tough as cowhide, was as weathered as the pair of old leather boots he'd be stepping into when he awoke in the morning.

Standing there in his pajamas, Cletus Moss saw the face of his father.

The life of a sugarcane grower was hard, but he'd lived it every day for as long as he could remember, as did his daddy and his granddaddy before him. Three generations of cane produced by the Moss family had made Sugarland Plantation into the one of the top growers in Louisiana. Had his son survived his deployment to Iraq, instead of stepping on a land mine on some unnamed road to some godforsaken village in the desert, Clete Jr. would have taken up the mantle for sure. He'd loved working the farm with his father—a sense of civic duty, though, had lured him into military service. After all, weapons of mass destruction were in the hands of a madman—so the president claimed—when the country went to war a second time against the Butcher of Baghdad. Now, all that remained of Clete Jr. were the memories of a lonely old man. The boy's medal and sympathy letters from his commanding officer and George II remained hidden away beneath a stack of documents in the safe.

~

A large sign reading "Sugarland Plantation, Est. 1887" glistened in the illumination of a harvest moon. They'd arrived at their destination. At three in the morning, there was no need for headlights—the ambient light was more than enough for Hawk to see down the asphalt driveway that snaked its way to the main house a quarter of a mile ahead.

The sugarcane stood tall and thick in the fields that covered nearly a thousand acres. Hawk knew it would—it being harvesting season. The file they'd been given inked out the long history of the farm. Homesteaded by Clayton Moss in the 1850s, he supplied cane to both the Union and the Confederacy. Clarence followed in his father's boots through the Great Depression and two world wars. Cletus, the grandson, picked up from there.

Until recently, Sugarland Plantation had been luckier than most cane growers, turning a profit more often than not. To do

331

that took all the skill of an experienced farmer and some luck. Natural predators abounded: red rot, spider mites, borers, white grubs, wireworms and weevils could eat into the stalks, as well as the profits, of even the most experienced grower. Too little rain. Too much rain. Unexpected heat waves and cold spells. Climate was a grower's fair-weather friend. Global market conditions played its part too. A five-year-straight decline in yield per acre, and foreign competition, had brought Sugarland Plantation to the brink of bankruptcy.

It was all there in the file they'd been given—along with aerial photos mapping out the geography and buildings. The farmhouse sat just beyond two large wood-frame, tin-roof barns that housed the tractors, cultivator, sett cutter, stubble shaver, and the all-important combine harvester. In the distance, three large cabins served as barracks for the seasonal farmhands who lived there rent-free while earning minimum wage during planting and harvesting seasons.

"The old fool told me he didn't need the security alarm system I wanted to sell him because his loaded twelve-gauge, double-barrel shotgun by his bed was all the protection he needed," Hawk said. "The migrants won't be arriving for another week. Satellite images show no human activity other than the target on the property."

Wolf, sitting next to him, put on tight-fitting black leather gloves, then pulled out a Glock 17 and loaded a ten-round clip.

Hawk drove their rental with the stolen out-of-state plates around the back of the barn closest to the house and parked it there. He shot a quick glance at his Casio G-shock watch—the kind used by Navy Seals. "I want to be in and out in under twenty minutes."

The earthy smell of uncut crops hung heavy in the humid air. Only the distant hum of the tree cricket's chirp and the great horned owl's hoot disturbed the quiet stillness of a pre-dawn Louisiana morn.

Dressed entirely in black with matching ski masks, the duo appeared like ninjas at a door in the rear of the house. Hawk activated the timer on his watch and nodded to Wolf, who picked at the door lock until it released.

Wolf entered first, gun drawn. Hawk followed in his partner's steps through the pantry, scented with the sweet smell of spices, and into the kitchen where unwashed dishes lay in the sink and an empty uncapped bottle of Jim Beam sat on the counter. They made their way to the staircase and slowly ascended the steps. Their rubber-soled shoes absorbed the creaking of the risers like sponges soaking up spilt milk.

With no one else living in the house, Hawk knew that the bedroom door of the target would be open. Predictably, the doors of the three other bedrooms were closed.

Hawk, six-feet-two-inches tall, stood behind Wolf, a half foot shorter, giving both an unobstructed view into the room. A man lay on his back on one side of a four-poster bed, a white sheet pulled up to his chin. A straggly, salt-and-pepper beard stretched almost to the folded hands that rested upon his chest. The uneven sound of his snoring telegraphed his restlessness—he could be easily awakened.

Wolf walked to the foot of the bed, the Glock pointed at the target's midsection. Hawk went bedside, pausing only long enough to reach for the beaded chain of a lamp that sat on a nightstand beside a King James Bible, a pair of wire-rimmed spectacles, and an empty glass.

The moonlight beamed through a window just enough to allow Hawk to see the old man's shotgun leaning against the wall next to the bed and easily within arm's reach. He picked it up with a gloved hand as the light came on.

Moss instinctively reached for his gun, but soon saw its two barrels pointed at his face.

"Easy, old man," Hawk warned. "Cooperate and we'll be out of your life very, very soon."

"What, what do you want from me?" Moss stuttered, the wide-eyed, open-mouth look of terror on his face a familiar one to the intruders.

Hawk cocked a hammer on the shotgun. "Speak only to answer my questions; move only when I tell you to move. Where's the safe?"

Moss's gaze darted from one trespasser to the other before replying, "In my office on the first floor."

"Now listen carefully," Hawk said. "I want you to walk slowly, very slowly, to your office and open the safe."

Hawk liked giving orders and making demands, telling people what to do and watching them twitch, sweat, even pee themselves and loosen their bowels, when he told them to do something they knew was wrong, like betray a comrade or their country, or breach a moral code they believed was inviolate. The price of refusal could be dangerous—even fatal. Like having to spin the barrel of a revolver loaded with a single bullet, put it to one's head, or the head of someone else, and pull the trigger … and then, if someone's brains weren't splattered on the ground, to do it again. Or be made to walk blindfolded through a minefield. Or play a water sport that required a cloth hood and a hose. Or, forget the gamesmanship, and either give in or take a bullet in the head—their choice. He'd done those things and worse—in Afghanistan, Syria, and Somalia—in search of a cache of weapons, an enemy's hideouts and positions, and information about planned terrorist attacks and assassinations. Hawk took his special skill set with him when he left government service to become a privately-retained independent contractor.

So did Wolf.

The man rose slowly from the bed and stood beside it. "I have nearly twenty thousand in cash. Take it and get out."

"And your wife's jewelry?"

"What little I have is in the safe. I gave most of it to my daughter when my wife passed away. Her wedding band was on her finger when I buried her." The old man sighed as he spoke. "What's left has only sentimental value."

Wolf left the room first and descended the staircase, keeping the Glock pointed at Moss as he came down the steps. After uncocking the hammer of the shotgun and returning it to its place against the wall, Hawk followed.

The floorboards of the corridor squeaked under the bare, sweaty feet of a slump-shouldered old man as he led them to the safe. Hawk found a table lamp on the desk when they entered the office and turned it on. Flanked by his captors, Moss, his hands shaking, removed the reproduction of Whistler's Mother that hung on a wall and placed it on the floor. He dialed in the combination to the safe behind it, slowly rotating the dial from right to left and right again until a click was heard. The man was perspiring so much his pajama top stuck to his back.

"Move away," Hawk said. "I'll open it." He suspected that Moss may have been cautious enough to put a loaded handgun in the safe as added protection if the need ever arose.

The need arose … but not the opportunity.

Hawk opened the safe and found a pistol resting on the top shelf. On the shelf just below sat several piles of cash bundled in rubber bands and an open box of jewelry. He pulled a cloth bag from a jacket pocket and put the money and jewelry in it. The bundles of documents that lay beside the cash were neatly bound—undoubtedly deeds, wills and other important papers. Hawk removed the rubber bands around them and, with a passing glance at the documents, threw them on the floor. A medal and the two letters followed next.

"You got what you came for … now get out and leave me alone," Moss pleaded. Beads of perspiration dotted his forehead.

Hawk moved away from the safe and stood beside Wolf. "A last request and we'll be finished with you; I promise. I want you to reach inside the safe and bring me your pistol."

A look of surprise on Moss's face was replaced by the pallor of a corpse. He showed a reluctance to move away from his desk, taking the time to wipe his runny nose and drool from his mouth with a sleeve. Wolf pointed the barrel of the gun in the direction of the safe to coax him on. Moss lumbered over, reached in the safe for the gun, and turned around to face his intruders.

Two shots rang out.

Both from the same gun.

A couple of 9mm slugs.

One entered Moss's chest slightly left of center.

Another blasted a hole in his forehead.

The old man, his face frozen in terror, collapsed to his knees with a thud, then tumbled forward to the floor. Blood quickly puddled on the floor next to his head.

Wolf holstered the weapon used to shoot Moss. Hawk went to the dead man, who still had the gun gripped in his hand, and knelt beside him. Manipulating Moss's hand, he raised the old man's gun and fired a shot into the wall in the direction Wolf had been standing when Moss was shot. Their work completed, the intruders left the room, walked to the kitchen and left through the door they'd entered, locking it on the way out.

Wolf moved quickly to their vehicle, staying on the pavement and asphalt road so as not to leave footprints in the soil.

Hawk found a first-floor window, punched out the pane closest to the lock, unlatched it, and opened the window. He pinched off several blades of nearby grass and some mulch from a flower bed and sprinkled the particles on the floor inside the house below the window. He then retraced his footsteps by backing away from the window until he found the paved walkway Wolf had taken.

Hawk drove to the entrance to the farm and stopped just long enough to deactivate the timer on his watch before pulling onto the road. As he did, he turned to Wolf and said, "Nineteen minutes, thirty-two seconds."

A half hour later, Hawk stopped the car on Highway 90 midway across the Vintage Bridge. Wolf took the bag with the loot that lay on the seat between them, got out of the car, and dumped the cash and jewelry into the muddied waters of the East Pearl River.

Chapter 1

The call came over the police radio while Crowder and Steele were on their way to the coroner's office. The chief medical examiner had the results of his autopsy of a badly decomposed body discovered by several Boy Scouts who'd wandered away from their campsite during a weekend outing.

The call came from O'Malley.

Frank O'Malley was head of the Violent Crime and Homicide Division of the New Orleans Police Department—the position had come with his promotion to captain more than a decade ago. A tough job in a tough-to-live-in city of a million and a quarter people of diverse religious, ethnic and cultural backgrounds—a city famously known as much for Mardi Gras, music, and merriment as it was for muggings, mayhem, and murder.

"Crowder, I want you and Steele over to 2712 Landsdale for a domestic dispute in progress," he said in his usual no-nonsense manner.

Detective Lieutenant Jo Crowder, a deceptively-toned, five-feet-five, one hundred-twenty-five pound, thirty-six-year-old woman with raven-black hair and intensely inquisitive honey-hazel eyes, was O'Malley's diamond in the rough. Fourteen years on the force, she had degrees in criminal justice and criminal forensics, was well trained in weapons, martial arts and crime scene investigations—and she was the best damn homicide detective on the force. She was tenacious, could be impetuous and impudent, and occasionally insubordinate. But, in the end, she was O'Malley's go-to detective in the most difficult homicide cases.

"What's homicide doing responding to a domestic?" Crowder asked, knowing O'Malley had a good reason for overriding the police dispatcher and contacting his detectives directly.

"Someone at probation and parole fucked up, and the wrong Michael Hopkins was released. The one they let out was only three years into his life sentence for murdering the guy the former Mrs. Hopkins was screwing."

"Let me pick up on the narrative," Crowder interrupted. "The first thing he did was to make a beeline to his ex's house to finish what he'd started."

"He's holed up in the house, threatening to kill her and the kids."

"Kids?"

"Four. All under twelve. With him in the house."

"The ex-wife?"

"Rope-tied to a tree on the front lawn."

"Who's responded?"

"A couple of black and whites. State police. They have the house surrounded."

"Crisis negotiator?"

"Samuels is on his way … Crowder?"

"What?"

"It could get real ugly out there today if Samuels can't sweet talk Hopkins into ending this without bloodshed."

Several blocks from their destination, Crowder told Steele to cut the siren.

Detective Sargent Sid Steele, early thirties, was Crowder's physical opposite—six-feet-three, lanky, shoulder-length, densely curly, mocha-brown hair pulled back in a ponytail. He'd been her partner the last three years—ever since Crowder's previous partner had taken two bullets in the chest in a shootout. He'd have taken more had Crowder not put two slugs between the eyes of the shooter. She saved her first partner's life that day, but couldn't save the lung he'd lost or his career as a homicide detective.

Crowder had never forgotten that day.

She'd relived it every time she attached her gold shield to her belt.

A day filled with regret.

Regret in not insisting that she approach the suspected meth lab from the front and that he provide the cover. But being the more experienced and senior officer, her partner always insisted on being the one most in harm's way, like an overly protective big brother.

Crowder felt the same way about Steele. She'd trained the former undercover cop when he came over from vice, just as her previous partner had trained her. She was now the experienced, senior detective and the one expected to call the shots—just as her previous partner had done. And as he'd done, she'd do whatever was necessary to shield Steele from harm.

She had never allowed Steele to be the first one in.

And she never would.

"Pete's on a losing streak," Steele said, referring to Pete Samuels, the department's crisis negotiator—the third in five years. "A jumper he couldn't talk down, and that disgruntled hardware store employee who shot the bullhorn out of his hand

and two of his coworkers before turning the gun on himself."

Crowder understood the roller coaster ride it was to be a crisis negotiator. She'd gotten drunk with a few of them after they'd worked a scene together—for better and for worse. Euphoria came with saving a guy who'd lost everything in the stock market or at the casinos and avowed to do a swan dive off the roof of a high-rise, or appealing to an abductor's inherent goodness and persuading him to release a hostage unharmed. But when the guy jumped or a bullet sent a hostage to the afterlife, a profound sense of failure, dissatisfaction and regret punched you in the gut and took your breath away.

The bipolar world of crisis negotiators required that they have thick skin, cold blood and titanium nerves. Few did. Burnout was an occupational hazard.

"Let's hope his luck changes," Steele continued, interrupting Crowder's reflections.

"I have a bad feeling about this one, Sid"

"Why so?"

"A guy who's already serving a life sentence for murder has little to lose. If he kills someone today and lives through his ordeal, he'll have a lethal injection to look forward to." She paused a moment, assessing the situation further. "Another thing—he's a very angry man. He was angry enough to kill his wife's lover instead of opting for a simple divorce. He could have used his get-out-of-jail-free card to go into hiding and plan a new life. Instead, he returns home to exact revenge on his ex-wife in a public display that guarantees he'll be caught. He has no intention of giving up and returning to his cell to sleep on the same lumpy mattress and eat the same shitty food for the rest of his life."

"I see what you mean. Samuels has nothing to offer him, to bargain with."

"Precisely. Hopkins is putting on a show. He wants the ex-wife to suffer. Not just physically, but mentally and emotionally, like he's suffered the past three years. So he ties her to a tree for all the neighbors to see her terror, feel her humiliation, and witness her execution."

"Cap's right." Steele sighed. Cap was what most of the detectives in the homicide division called O'Malley. "It could get real ugly out there today."

About the Author

Richard Zappa is a trial lawyer turned novelist. A graduate of the American University Washington College of Law in Washington, D.C., he was an editor of the American University Law Review and Dean's Fellow to Arthur Goldberg, former Associate Justice of the U.S. Supreme Court and Adjunct Professor of Law. During the course of a distinguished career as a top personal injury and medical malpractice lawyer, Zappa has litigated and tried numerous cases in state and federal courts, many of which resulted in multimillion-dollar recoveries for his clients. He retired in 2018 to write novels full time. A black-belt martial artist and self-taught pianist, he writes from his homes in Wilmington and Rehoboth Beach, Delaware, and St. Thomas, Virgin Islands.